EARTHWRECK

"We've been monitoring the background from below," Farrington said. "Our computer model says it's already ten times the A.E.C. maximum and still rising."
"Still rising?"
"The bastards are still shooting at each other," Farrington said.
"But that means — "
"I'm well aware of what it means," Farrington said. "It may mean the end of everything."

The end of the world, Longo thought. The words had no meaning. He felt cold and distant, unable to apprehend the enormity of what the colonel had said.
"Holy Mother of God," Piaseki's voice breathed in his ear.

Earthwreck

Thomas N. Scortia

CORONET BOOKS
Hodder Fawcett Limited, London

Printed and bound in Great Britain for
Coronet Books, Hodder Fawcett Limited,
St. Paul's House, Warwick Lane,
London, EC4P 4AH
By C. Nicholls & Company Ltd,
The Philips Park Press, Manchester

ISBN 0 340 19888 5

For my big brother Arthur
and his special satellite, Dorothy.

Post-historic Man's starvation of life should reach its culminating point in inter-planetary travel. . . . Under such conditions, life would again narrow to the physiological functions of breathing, eating and excretion. . . . By comparison the Egyptian cult of the dead was overflowing with vitality; from a mummy in his tomb one can still gather more of the attributes of a full human being than from a spaceman. . . . No one can pre-tend . . . that existence on a space satellite or on the barren face of the moon can bear any resemblance to human life.

LEWIS MUMFORD,
The Transformation of Man

On the other hand, if there were no other choice . . .

It was an hour before sundown. The refugee camp sprawled under the long shadows, its ragtag collection of tents and lean-tos drab and faded from the sunlight of years. The settlement had originally been temporary, while the displaced peoples found new homes in Lebanon or neighboring Syria, but the perverse ways of human politics being what they were, the temporary settlement had become more and more permanent, though certainly no more well established, until forty years had seen the accumulation of human effluvium, the debris of lost and abandoned lives. The shattered no-roots population now called it "our village."

That was the way of it in the Middle East. If one settled for a year or even a month, the place became "our village." Yet they still hoped for a home. It was not that they ever expected to return to Israel, or even to find homes in the disputed areas. They were discards, Allah's stepchildren who watered at a common hole and fed on the leavings and slept in sand-spattered beds or hammocks while their children were born, grew up, and shared the same restlessness and bitterness to which the parents had been born.

In the drab lean-to of Fuad Kasimir, the two strangers appeared, recently returned from the marshaling camps in Syria. They squatted in stoic positions on the dirt floor, buttocks tucked precisely around upended heels.

"I fear," Giro Nakamura said, "that any plan we might develop may surely mean our death."

Fuad shrugged fatalistically. "It is the way of the world," he said. "We have a common cause and if it means death, then there are surely millions who will benefit from it."

"A comforting thought, an inspired thought," Kazumoto Tanaka murmured, his broad spatulate face impassive, his bright black eyes veiled by heavy lids that emphasized his Mongoloid fold. His companion Nakamura had very Western eyes that bespoke an early operation to remove the fold. It had been done by his parents when he was quite young and their pathetic desire to ape a Western culture they admired had caused him much pain and had finally alienated him from them completely.

"There is only one way that we can finally achieve the true Marxist world for which we all yearn," Fugita declared fiercely. "My brothers in Nihon join with you, my brothers of the West, in the ultimate adventure."

"Dare we? Dare we?" breathed Fuad.

"Are you afraid?" Tanaka challenged him. "We in Japan have dared for years. Remember, I lost brothers in Tel Aviv, New York, Osaka, Manila."

"And I in Munich and Paris," Fuad reminded him. "The temper of the world has not responded to us as we wished. The outrage we expected has not come."

"So we turn our minds to more immediate and pressing provocations," said Fugita. "Do we dare? Of course we dare."

"My other brothers will be with us shortly," said Fuad. "Your plan is daring and most dangerous. You know how deeply entrenched are the sponsors from the People's Republic."

"The Chinese," Fugita sneered. "They are babes in world politics. They have always been; otherwise they would not have been so long hapless vassels of the West. Even now, they play games with the West in the vain hope that this will avert the inevitable confrontation between them and the Soviet revisionists."

"But this is far more than a mere bombing, far more than an armed assault against a few pitiful athletes," Fuad protested.

"Let your brothers decide," Tanaka said. "They are, I am told, more fierce than you, more daring."

"That is true," said Fuad.

"But you will support the final decision," Fugita challenged.

"Of course," Fuad said tiredly. "I have sworn so."

"Besides," said Tanaka, his voice faintly contemptuous, "you value your life."

"No," Fuad said, "not as much as all that. Besides, if we adopt your plan, I shall surely lose my life. It is only a matter of days. Whether it be at the hands of my fellows or at other, more bitter hands, it will be the same. I would prefer it be in the service of a good cause. To shed the blood of one's brother is an unclean thing."

"You are most sensible, Fuad-san," Fugita said, and fumbled in his Western suit coat for a package of cigarettes. "Most sensible, most sensible," he intoned.

One

Captain Quintus Longo, wrapped in the silver cocoon of his spacesuit and breathing the mechanical smell of his portable air-conditioning unit, leaned forward in the service lorry to get a better view of Pad Five. They were approaching it rapidly on the left as the driver casually tooled his vehicle first port, then starboard, following the confusing complex of macadam roads that served the forty launch pads of Kennedy Space Center. They still called it Kennedy Space Center, although the Cape itself had reverted to its original name of Cape Canaveral in 1973.

Beside Longo, Lieutenant Steinbrunner, who was the official pilot for this launch, seemed completely bored with the proceedings. This did not particularly surprise Longo, since Steinbrunner was one of the regular ferry pilots and made as many as two launches a month in the days when the station was first being assembled. To him the job was little more exciting than driving a bus or piloting a transcontinental jetliner. He was quite at home in the white suit and continued to read his morning newspaper, canting his head to the side to avoid reflections off the faceplate.

Amazing, Longo thought, *that we have come so far that there are no spectators, no newsmen to watch the launch, and the pilot is so bored he's spending his last minutes on earth reading the sports page.*

He grimaced as he caught the black headlines on the front section of the paper: MIDDLE EAST CRISIS DEEPENS. He wondered when that situation would finally be resolved. The Arab nations and Israel had glared across their armed frontiers for seventeen years since the U.N. Cease Fire, and the Suez Canal had become so heavily insilted that it was unlikely that it would ever be a major economic factor in world trade again. There had been rumors before the latest coup in Cairo that the U.A.R. might finally make peace. Certainly the Libyans wanted peace so that they could continue to exploit their oil reserves without the constant Israeli raids, but the Syrians and the Egyptians remained completely intractable.

They were drawing abreast of Pad Five now, historic Pad Five that still served the cargo launches. Longo sighed, thinking of the three months to come. They had talked about it last night, he and Martha, after he had roughhoused with the two boys, popped them in the shower, and hustled them off to bed. In the warm darkness, with the heavy moist Atlantic breezes blowing in from the Cape, he and his wife had lain warm and close, with only a light sheet covering their nudity.

Longo loved that hour before sleep when the kids were snoring in their room; he could lie with her, savoring a leisurely cigarette, its warm fire glow lighting the rounded contours of her body as he drew each slow puff. She had gained weight since they were married so that now her figure was full with the jungle lushness of the bayous of her native Louisiana. Her hair had been jet black when they met but by the time she was thirty it was already threaded with strands of an almost iridescent white, giving her a full all-mother look that pleased and excited him. She was not a beautiful woman, not even a particularly pretty woman, but her compassion and quiet sense of dignity in the midst of the small and large emergencies of life filled him with wonder and respect. As the lorry came to a halt, he savored the low banked feeling of love, realizing how completely she filled his spiritual and physical life. Their love-making, like last night, was a constant adventure, and suffusing all of the bright, building pattern of lust was the deep sense of loving and being loved.

As he dismounted, dragging the air-conditioning unit behind him, and made clumsily for the elevator at the foot of the gantry, he reflected that she had truly given him everything he wanted: stability, a warm sense of being a part of home and all that implied, two marvelously vigorous strong sons . . . something he'd always wanted, since those days of growing up with his own intensely loving, intensely masculine father. The next three months would be a constant pain, but the thought of returning and what that would mean more than made up for it.

The four men of the personnel crew in white suits mounted the elevator with them. He nodded distractedly to them, not even bothering to identify them. One, he thought, had been here on his last launch, but the old intimacy and sense of adventure was gone. The launches were too routine; one scarcely remembered the faces of the white crew, without bothering to find out their names.

At the top of the gantry, they left the elevator, Steinbrunner sidling along the catwalk as though he were on his morning constitutional. The four men of the white crew fussed with the decontamination lock, checking the precipitron plates and air-cycling devices. They still went through this drill even though the crew compartment of the Orbiter II was entirely separate from the sensitive sections where dust might cause a problem. They had not abandoned their early concepts of depending on human reactions although, so it was rumored, the Russians had persisted in their emphasis on automated controls. Longo preferred the American approach. When he piloted, he liked the idea of personal control, of flying the great clustered birds by the seat of his pants. The boost stage was always pretty well automated, of course, but after that the human pilot was the important mechanism in the guidance cycle.

Just for an instant he looked down before they entered the vehicle. The mass of the bird stretched out far below him: a cluster of seven 156-inch solid boosters, above them a core of three 156-inch and the liquid stage in which they rode. The original shuttle configuration had used only two strap-on boosters, but with new payload requirements and the larger capacity of Orbiter II, the configuration was once again three stages. The present mission was a cargo mission; his and Steinbrunner's roles were secondary. He wasn't even sure what the cargo was, although he supposed that the supplies in the capsule below must be inert. Had they been ferrying something sensitive, such as tanks of liquid fluorine-oxygen mixture (known as FLOX) to top off the orbiting reservoir, the launch discipline would have been much more rigorous.

Inside the Orbiter cabin, they strapped themselves in acceleration couches, Steinbrunner taking the command position. Behind them the white crew closed the hatch and dogged the door, sealing them in their own self-contained oxygen-nitrogen atmosphere. Longo sounded out the appropriate checks as Steinbrunner went through his abbreviated countdown in a voice that seemed completely bored. They both looked up momentarily as a steady vibration filled their compartment. It was the primary gantry moving away. Now only the top-off umbilical and the launch pad retainers held them to the earth they were about to leave on a pillar of flame.

Good-bye, good-bye, he thought inanely, thinking of Martha lying naked on the morning bed, looking out the window for the heavy rising trace of aluminum oxide smoke that would mark his departure for a quarter of a year. The—what number was it?—departure. God, he'd lost complete track of the number of times he had left her shivering in the morning air while he mounted one of these birds and shook off the fragile gravity ties of earth.

Steinbrunner, his countdown sheet clipped to the bulkhead before him, was finishing his drill, speaking laconically into his throat mike. It was almost completely a one-man operation. Longo had little to do except check auxiliary controls and voice an occasional "check" as Steinbrunner's countdown included his auxiliary instrumentation. A milk run, Longo thought. He was primarily a passenger, going up for a three-month tour of duty on the station as engineering officer. They'd evacuated his counterpart, Merklin, two days before, after he suffered a concussion in freefall. Colonel Farrington himself had called Longo to apologize for cutting his earthside leave short. Farrington, Longo thought, was the sort of officer he'd always admired, a true product of the Academy with the kind of rigid service morality that enabled you to know exactly what he required. Not at all like his second, Lieutenant Colonel Rothgate, who was a reservist turned professional and often given to moodiness and arbitrariness. He heard that he had been much different before he lost his wife while on attaché duty in the East. Longo had never been able to ascertain the whole of that story, except that there had been a local Communist-backed rebellion, crushed quickly, during which the American legation had been bombed.

At the count of three, Steinbrunner keyed ignition. Far below in the combustion chambers of the great solid boosters, seven pyrogens ignited. Small rockets with consumable cases, they spewed out a jet of flame that touched the rubber-aluminum-ammonium perchlorate of the primary propellant while building the internal pressure of the booster to five hundred psi. Where the pyrogen flame touched, the primary flame front built rapidly, reaching a steady-state combustion in seconds. The whole bird trembled against the retainers, building to maximum thrust. The aft view on the pilot's pickup showed rolling clouds of intense opaque white that roared up about the bird and finally obscured all sight. The clouds were masses of colloidal aluminum oxide mixed with the steam from the cooling waters that poured like a deluge over the launch pad.

"Lift-off," Steinbrunner shouted above the roar and vibration, and in the next instant Longo felt the first gentle acceleration. From the outside, the bird seemed to poise on its boiling white cloud and then rise slowly. Take-off acceleration was only two Gs, one of which was lost in simply canceling out the earth's gravitation. Nitric oxide thrust vectoring stabilized their flight at this point. The resulting acceleration was slightly over 33 feet/second squared, but even at this modest acceleration the bird gained velocity quickly. Acceleration mounted as the bird lightened from expended propellant, while the thrust of the motors stabilized at a steady twelve and a half million pounds.

Longo felt his body pressing down deeper and deeper into the couch as the acceleration built up. There was a lateral force acting now, the centrifugal force of turning as the bird canted under programming and sought the ideal synergistic curve that balanced minimum drag losses of a vertical ascent against minimum gravitational losses of a tangential ascent.

When booster separation came, the sound of the explosive bolts separating the stages sounded like a firing squad. Before the second stage cluster ignited, Longo felt the briefest sense of coasting, followed by a sudden spurt in acceleration. The pilot's pickup showed masses of clouds below, the towering tail of oxide piercing them, and the cluster falling slowly away. As he watched, hidden pyrotechnic gas generators pressurized the deflated paraglider and the mammoth lifting surface sprang free. It caught the air as its retaining cables halted the relentless acceleration of the empty booster cases. He knew that closures were now sliding over the still hot nozzles, sealing them so that the boosters would be watertight. The paraglider would spiral the cases down into the Pacific Ocean, where they would sink below the surface, then rise, bobbing like giant buoys until the hydrofoil salvage vessels raced out to recover them. Without the watertight closures on the nozzle, there was about a 50 percent chance that the cases would still float, since their center of gravity was far forward. Eventually the maraging steel cases would be broken to their modular segments, sandblasted, refurbished, and refilled with solid propellant. The segments would be reassembled and fitted with nozzles, and take their place again in a boost cluster. Their expected life span had in recent years been extended to ten missions. The recovery statistics on the second-stage booster cluster were unfortunately poorer, but it generally averaged four to five flights.

The three-cluster second stage ignited now, pushing him back further into the couch. He watched yellow-pointed digits flicker across the pilot screen, giving thrust, pressure, and other data. For seconds, while Steinbrunner keyed other sensors throughout the ship, the screen generated random numbers. Then a new series of readouts occupied his attention. When second-stage burnout came, Longo watched the cluster of three modular units fall away as their paraglider inflated. The cluster tugged at the restraining cable; in a second one cable parted and the cluster began to tumble.

"That's one cluster they won't recover," Longo said and Steinbrunner grunted as the three Analine-IRFNA motors of the Orbiter II ignited. Analine and inhibited red fuming nitric acid were hypergolic. The two liquids ignited instantly on contact. For the coming minutes the ship would be throttled initially by internal programming and then manually by Steinbrunner as they approached MOS, the Manned Orbital Station. Two smaller motors provided orbiting thrust for maneuvering. The present propellant combination was less energetic than the liquid-hydrogen/liquid-oxygen motors of the earlier Orbiter I, but the present system could hold for days or even weeks on a pad without "topping off" or fear of cryogenic damage to delicate components.

Steinbrunner was busily matching velocity with the station so that Longo had long moments in which he could use the auxiliary pickup to scan surrounding space. The MOS, an angular double-tubed structure that rotated slowly around its central hub, was some five hundred miles away at this point. Its hub was a modified skylab vehicle, orbited years before. The hub itself was shielded by a ball of lead some thirty feet from its cap. During periods of solar flares, station personnel retired to the central lab, whose cap always pointed sunward, and lived within the gamma-shield shadow of the lead sphere. It presented a workable optical solution to the problem of reducing weight while still providing for protection against solar-flare gamma radiation. The outer ring of the station was lashed to the spinning hub by cables, and several personnel chutes of mesh-reinforced silvered Mylar formed the spokes of a rough wheel. The station was not perfectly circular—its rim was composed of empty 156-inch rocket cases of maraging steel. There were two layers of such cases for each segment, and the segments were joined by expanding accordion joints of the same mesh-reinforced Mylar. The motor cases had been the obvious solution to a construction problem in space, since only four strap-in 120-inch motors of four segments were needed to orbit the second-stage cluster that would normally have fallen back to Earth. A few peroxide EVA space bugs to maneuver them into place, a careful impression of spin, and the whole structure was complete. It was remarkably fragile, however, and slight variations in spin loss on the rim might have torn it apart except for the accordion joints, which tended to transmit velocity throughout the rim and compensate for the stresses of centrifugal force.

Orbiting at perhaps twenty-five miles were the girders and fuel tanks of the moonship, now nearly half-completed. This was quite a different beast, designed as a massive freighter to land the personnel and equipment necessary to set up a retaliatory launch station on the moon. Its masses and capacity had been carefully worked out at the SALT talks ten years earlier, and Longo knew that, for all of their different design approach, the Russian ship had similar characteristics.

He wondered as the view in the scanner changed if he could see the Russians' MOS at this distance. It occupied a slightly higher and more eccentric orbit than the American station and was generally about a hundred miles away, a very carefully calculated distance that allowed each station to keep close watch on the other. He scanned the screen hopefully, but no pickup was oriented properly to pick it out. It was quite distinctive, Longo knew: a wheel arrangement of Salyut IV capsules linked to a central hub by nylon ropes and joined both radially and circumferentially by the same sort of mesh-Mylar personnel tunnels that the American station used.

They were matching orbital velocity with the station now, using the maneuvering motors and the thrusters on the wings of the Orbiter. Longo saw that they were approaching the ungainly spider structure of the unfinished moonship. Steinbrunner said, "We're carrying two F-2C motors for cargo. We'll orbit near the ship and take EVA bugs over to the station." Then he lapsed into silence and a posture of concentration.

Longo shrugged to himself. Steinbrunner was known for being taciturn. He avoided all close contact with other members of the launch crews. He was not unfriendly, but he always acted on his guard against knowing anyone too well. He was a big man, with heavily thewed arms. Longo knew that he worked out regularly at the Cape Officers' Club, and played a silent and aggressive game of handball; he seemed always to be pushing himself physically. He was one of the few of the pilot complement who had any kind of private transportation, and seemed to expend all of his affection on the modified Norton that he tinkered with every Saturday. The motorcycle was an expensive luxury, not only because of the price of the machine, but because of the inordinate smog-tax on it. Longo imagined that he must spend a full 10 percent of his salary on the upkeep of the machine, but there was hardly a duty-free period when one could not see him in front of the BOQ, smeared with grease and muttering to the machine, or resplendent in black leather pants and jacket with oversize goggles, roaring through the residential streets and out onto the highways, heading north. Longo had heard that he picked up the hobby where he grew up in East Germany. One story ran that he had actually escaped from Berlin by literally jumping the Wall with a cycle when he was barely twenty. Somehow, it seemed almost believable.

Steinbrunner was using the wing and tail vernier thrusters, slowly approaching the orbiting moonship. Far above the ship another object orbited in the viewer, a great metal-banded silver sausage that looked for all the world like an ancient dirigible. A faint drifting haze expanded from one end. The sausage was the Teflon-lined storage tank for liquid FLOX. It was only three quarters full at the moment, but periodic launches brought new material to increase its bulk. The liquid fluorine-oxygen would be the oxidizer for the moonship when completed. It would be transferred to the great oxidizer spheres now being positioned within the framework of the ship. Liquid fluorine was a fantastically dangerous material: Longo shuddered at the thought of what this much FLOX would do if the storage tank should collapse. The fluorine in the mixture would unite violently with almost any organic material.

Even human flesh would burst into flame in such an atmosphere.

They were drifting silently near the moonship now, and several suited figures with hand packs drifted out toward them with nylon cables. In minutes they were anchored to the frame of the ship. Steinbrunner cut the main propulsion power, then placed the life-support systems on standby and began to unstrap. Longo followed suit, noticing the strange lightness of his body and the way his internal organs drifted in disturbing fashion against the retaining mesenteries. After all this time, the sensation was still strange and exhilarating.

He followed the silent Steinbrunner down through the lock in the floor of the cabin and waited while the lower lock cycled. From the wall they procured EVA packs and strapped them on their backs. Steinbrunner checked Longo's pack and Longo did the same for him. Finally, the cycling complete, Steinbrunner keyed the switch that rotated the pressure door away. He stepped out into the blackness, holding to a nylon cord, and Longo followed.

Longo touched the visor of his helmet and lowered the Polaroid shield. The reflection of sunlight from the frame of the moonship and further "below" the station was blinding. He watched as Steinbrunner cast off and activated the peroxide back pack. He followed the brilliant half-lighted figure as they both maneuvered past the ship complement, who were finishing the mooring of the third stage. They would open the Orbiter II's clam-shell hatch and unload the cargo compartment later in the working day, checking out the motors before towing them across to the moonship frame. In the meantime, Longo wanted more than anything to get to the station and feel some sensation of weight, however small, on his feet again.

He touched the buttons on his chest, releasing tiny vents from the back pack as the concentrated hydrogen peroxide in the pack decayed over its permanganate catalyst bed and turned to steam and oxygen. Small jets to the right and left vectored him and Steinbrunner toward the station hub. At the last moment they decelerated, and touched the entry port lightly. Steinbrunner bounced against the curved surface and held out his hand for Longo, while his other grasped a welded handhold on a protruding spar. They stood in an awkward ballet for seconds, and as his helmet drifted close to Steinbrunner's he looked directly into the silent man's eyes, which were nearly black with widened pupils and long, almost feminine lashes. The eyes were suddenly the softening influence that gave his craggy face humanity. They were eyes, not of an arrogant man, as Longo had thought, or even of a man withdrawn and disdainful of the world. They were eyes mirroring pain and much compassion. The sudden intimate insight shook him and he backed away, feeling embarrassed.

Steinbrunner touched his shoulder and in an almost comradely manner gestured to their rear and down. Longo turned and saw the misted blue-green globe of their home world drifting in the deep black far below. It took over 80 percent of his field of vision at this point. He could see the Mediterranean quite clearly. The cloud cover here was sparse, and he saw the Red Sea extending down into the Indian Ocean. This was heavily overlain with clouds, but his mind's eye automatically provided the obscured details of coastlines and peninsulas.

It was at this moment, just at the tip of a finger of cloud that stretched from the Red Sea toward the Mediterranean, that the three small points of light bloomed almost simultaneously. Over the intercom, Longo heard Steinbrunner gasp.

"My God!" Longo said. "What's that?"

Steinbrunner seemed to spit out the words. "Low yield nuclears. Maybe ten, fifteen KT."

"Who?"

"Who else?" Steinbrunner snapped irritably. "The Arabs probably. They have ground-to-air missiles from the Chinese with about that yield."

"That's idiotic! Suicidal," Longo said with a sinking feeling.

Two

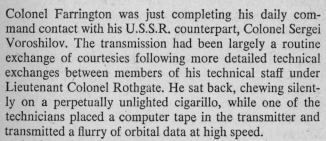

Colonel Farrington was just completing his daily command contact with his U.S.S.R. counterpart, Colonel Sergei Voroshilov. The transmission had been largely a routine exchange of courtesies following more detailed technical exchanges between members of his technical staff under Lieutenant Colonel Rothgate. He sat back, chewing silently on a perpetually unlighted cigarillo, while one of the technicians placed a computer tape in the transmitter and transmitted a flurry of orbital data at high speed.

At forty-five, Farrington had the lean scarred athleticism of a gray tomcat that had eaten well and fought hard, emerging from endless fights with an erect carriage and an alert wary eye. He was married and had two sons on Earth, one of them teaching macrochemistry at Purdue University and the other, the younger, finishing his senior year at the Academy in Colorado Springs. He and his wife were inordinately proud of these two, thinking that his own special strength had sired two men of strong and capable personalities, tempered by her genteel San Francisco upbringing. He did not talk much of them, preferring to sit as he did now in quiet contemplation of those two sons and what they must be doing back on Earth while he in his glamorous roost in the sky was grinding through a daily routine as boring to himself as it must be to Sergei.

He smiled to himself and looked at the unlighted tip of the cigarillo, wishing they could spare the oxygen and the strain on the air purifiers so that he could smoke as much as he wanted. Rank, of course, had its privileges, and he allowed himself one cigarillo or three cigarettes in his quarters at night before bedtime, feeling somewhat guilty all the while that only Lieutenant Colonel Rothgate and the engineering officer who was third in command could enjoy similar privileges.

The thought of the engineering officer brought a frown to his face. Damn that clumsy Merklin for being so eager outside on ES activity. Two days ago during some EVA on the orbiting moonship, he'd kicked off too enthusiastically from a stanchion on the frame and managed to crack his skull against one of the fuel tanks. That meant the disruption of shipping him back earthside, and cutting Captain Longo's leave short to replace him. He'd called Longo and apologized, and the big swarthy Italian had taken it in his stride. A good man, Longo, with a great deal of creative engineering talent, though a bit emotional in typical Italian old-world fashion, and a marvel at juryrigging quick solutions to pressing engineering problems. The sort of man who was indispensible in an assignment like the EOS and the half-constructed moonship. Sergei's Major Bucholtz was in his own way as sound, but much more formalistic, less inventive in his approach.

The thought of Sergei returned him to the communications bridge where he sat as the final technical transmission of the day was coming to an end. The agreements that had come from two decades of SALT conferences, and their successors, the MilLimS, the Military Limitations in Space, called for the most scrupulous contact between the two rival space stations to assure each of the other's careful adherence to the basic agreements. A peculiar kind of camaraderie had grown up from this odd arrangement. It was not that each exactly helped the other on their essentially military assignments, but there was a special bonhommie between the U.S. and the U.S.S.R. technicians as each applauded some special technique of the others, or simply offered a sort of grudging admiration.

Airman Second Class Sugiyama, his olive face impassive, his black eyes glittering, rose from his seat before the transmission console and came to Farrington. "Sir," he said, "except for some of Dr. Svoboda's data, that's the end of the business transmissions. Their commander would like a final word with you."

Farrington nodded and walked toward the console, thinking that he would have to speak with Longo when he arrived about the life-sustain system. The air was pure enough, but the rather musty mechanical smell, resembling that of an overheated tractor, was getting more prominent. Morale was good enough, but he'd heard complaints from several of the juniors about the air. God knows, they lived on a thin enough margin up here without this pervading odor in the air system beginning to develop. Perhaps some of Dr. Svoboda's accelerated chlorella might be useful here, but he hesitated to bring that up. She resented any intrusion from the military, even though she existed here on their sufferance. He sighed. So many diverse personalities, military and civilian, to keep in harmony. The military, at first glance, seemed more tractable, with the overlarding of discipline, but humans were humans and one had to make allowances for a hundred and fifty men (and one woman, he amended) living a kind of hothouse existence so far from home, with the menace of violent death a few millimeters of steel or mesh-reinforced plastic away.

He seated himself and signaled Sugiyama who cut in the vision transmission. The match between the Russian scanning system and the American was relatively good, but as he watched the forming image of Sergei Voroshilov of the People's Space Force, he was irrationally annoyed at the heavy bands of white drifting across the screen. "Clean this up, damn it," he snapped at Sugiyama, then caught himself. No use letting a minor irritation show. He prided himself on maintaining a carefully self-disciplined exterior. He'd rather his people think of him as a cold, rule-bound military machine than as the person he knew himself to be. He had always carefully disguised the tension and the constant nagging responsibility that he felt for all these lives.

A moment later Colonel Voroshilov's image flickered on the screen and then cleared as the electronic lock completed the scanning match. Voroshilov, squat with a broad beefy face that seemed vaguely Oriental, smiled out of the wafer iconoscope. "It seems, my dear Comrade, that we missed a golden opportunity in our MilLimS talks, as you call them; we should have agreed on a mutually compatible scanning pattern."

"It would have simplified things, Sergei," Farrington agreed. "It's the sort of trivial detail no one thinks of and that we must painfully live with afterwards."

Sergei shrugged. "It is, I suppose, the history of our lives, this failure to anticipate where accommodation is necessary."

"Even here," Farrington said, "it takes only the patience of two men of good will."

Sergei nodded, his image flickering slightly. "My grandmother, who was a Kurd, had a remarkable saying about that. I must tell you sometime, but more to business now, eh?"

"The data from your last Mars probe has been causing quite a stir among our technical staff here and Earthside," Farrington said. "May I congratulate you. It's the sort of job you people have been uniquely clever in doing."

"Thank you," said Sergei. "We're about to launch our second probe—in two days to be exact. I shall, of course, contact you with complete orbital and escape elements so that we should not seem"—he smiled ironically—"to be doing anything untoward."

"Of course," Farrington replied. "I believe our astronomy people have just completed transmitting the tape on the elements of Toro's orbit as we now understand them."

"Is it so?" said Sergei. "Do you feel you have it well established now?"

"They tell me so. I haven't the knowledge to judge myself. We're still having some trouble with the two lesser companions, however."

Sergei frowned. "What marvels are coming to us, my friend," he said. "To find that we will shortly visit the ancient moon and build a place to live upon it."

"A military encampment, I'm sorry to say," Farrington corrected him.

"No matter, we will live and work on the ancient moon, and now we have extended our sights to find the small moon predicted in the midseventies, and two still smaller companions with it."

"Rather hard to call it a real moon," Farrington said. "At first they called it a pseudomoon, thinking it was a part of the total Earth-moon system, but that would call for a general solution of the three-body problem and only special solutions are possible. Still, with its high eccentricity, it looks very odd for a moon."

"A marvelous name," Sergei observed, "with romantic overtones of the Moment of Truth."

"I didn't know you were interested in bull fighting."

"I was once an attaché in Brazilia, and later in Seville. It is an odd blood sport that seemed at first degenerate but develops a special hold on military men. We who are trained, as your American author Marquand said, to be heroes. Heroism is something to be admired in a matador and in a bull as well."

"Is there anything further we should discuss?" asked Farrington, seeing the chronometer above the microphone approaching the time for his Senior Staff Meeting.

"We shall, of course, speak further tomorrow," Sergei said. "My good wishes to you and your staff. In a few months we may well walk across solid ground on the moon to clasp each other in person."

"I'll look forward to that," Farrington said, and signalled to Sugiyama who took over to cut transmission with his Soviet counterpart.

He sat for a moment, thinking, *funny, this is the face of the enemy.* Well, not really *enemy* any more so much as global and now space antagonist. The rivalry between the two powers and the People's Republic of China was as fierce as ever, but it had grown more subtle with the years as each realized the overwhelming power of the others. You couldn't eliminate the constant jockeying for political and commercial ascendancy in the world, but, pray God, they were learning how to live with each other in a civilized and rational manner. It was such contacts as this wary friendship building between him and Sergei Voroshilov that might eventually be the salvation of the battered world far below.

He turned in his swiveling plastic chair and felt a small glow of pleasure. Damn it, he was beginning to like and admire that somewhat stiff-necked Kurd orbiting a hundred miles away. They had met in person three times,

once at the final Soviet-U.S. briefing and twice when each
had exchanged courtesy visits to the other's stations. The
Russian extrastation-activity equipment was somewhat
limited, and Farrington had provided vehicles for both exchanges. The Soviet colonel had been embarrassed, of
course, and had been formally courteous for the first part
of the visit. After the initial amenities were over, however,
he had relaxed somewhat, and before the end of the visit
Farrington saw with some pleasure that there was a real
chance of developing rapport.

Farrington rose and walked slowly through the commo
deck, past the two technicians in their sling chairs now
developing photographic printouts of the data received
earlier from the Soviet station. His eyes noted the bright
colors of their brief coveralls, the rich earth colors of the
walls and surrounding panels, and the crisp, comfortable
modernity of the rest of the room. When the station was
built, the Air Force had wisely hired a team of top designers from the American Institute of Interior Designers,
knowing that the stark utilitarianism of previous space vehicles would be a bad morale factor for men confined to
space for extended periods. The A.I.I.D. designers had
met the challenge in a number of remarkable ways, including the use of recessed skylights above the working areas,
colorful folding tables that disappeared into walls, bright
coveralls and tunics, light carpeting with an intricate pleas-
ing design on all the surfaces.

When Farrington had first come aboard the station, he
thought he was entering some well-decorated modern
house trailer rather than a space station. There was a no-
ticeable lack of blues and purples, except where they were
combined dramatically with reds and yellows. The whole
effect throughout the station was one of brightness and
cheeriness that did much to lift the spirits of the men confined to this small world. It was a pity, he thought, that the
Russians hadn't taken a similar approach. On his one visit
their station had impressed him with its drabness, and he
had left feeling vaguely depressed.

He passed through the connecting passage, just wide
enough for two people, and made his way to the briefing

room. His body had by now adjusted to the one-fourth gravity of the station, but he still overcompensated occasionally. He did this now in reaching for the button that keyed the sliding hatch. His hand slipped and for a moment he stumbled. His outstretched left hand sank into the soft plastic of the wall for an instant, and then he had righted himself. He touched the door plate again, and the hatch slid silently open.

They were ranked about the table, waiting for him. Someone had opened the partition that led to the galley and he could smell the rich smell of coffee. The briefing room also served as a dining area and the briefing materials, when not in use, slid into the wall and were hidden by rollers of plastic film on magnesium railings. Hardly a secure arrangement, but security had been sacrificed to convenience and weight in this case. For materials requiring special measures, there was a magno-aluminum-stressed safe in his administrative quarters.

Colonel Rothgate rose and greeted him. "Here, Will, the coffee's just brewed."

"Call this slop coffee?" asked Dr. Janice Svoboda, looking severe and unapproachable.

Farrington accepted a cup and addressed Rothgate. "You'll be getting orbital components on the next U.S.S.R. Mars probe tomorrow, Jeb. Better get the printouts immediately and set up your observation team."

"Be just like those people to try something special," Rothgate said, frowning into his coffee.

"Nothing of the sort," Farrington said, "and you know it."

"Do I?" asked Rothgate. "You may be too trusting, Will."

"Gentlemen," Dr. Svoboda said coldly. "You may have all the time in the world to indulge your private military fantasies, but I and Dr. Lieberman and I'm sure Colonel Rothgate have more important things to do. Besides, your engineering officer should be on board in an hour and I'm sure you'll want to get him briefed immediately."

"To be sure," Farrington said, coloring. Damn the woman, he thought. She was only thirty-five but she managed to look fifty. No, that really wasn't fair. She was a fairly presentable woman, though not physically attractive. It was her distant way of handling him and the other military, her complete withdrawal from any softer human contact. It might be a pose, he thought, since she was the only woman aboard and certainly wouldn't want to invite any intimacies. Still, he wished she weren't so damnably arrogant when they were alone. It made for a difficult problem in communication.

He took his seat at the head of the briefing table and opened the portfolio Rothgate had laid before him. He found a stylus positioned precisely in the small niche built for it in the portfolio.

"Before we begin the technical briefing," he said, "I'd like Colonel Rothgate to fill us in on the developing political situation Earthside."

Rothgate frowned and fussed with the papers before him. "The latest intelligence reports," he began, "indicate an increasing tension in the Middle East and on the Sino-Russian border. The Middle East situation is complicated by the activities of the Black September branch of the Fatah, who have teamed up with several extremist Japanese groups who have recently come into Egypt and Lebanon. Intelligence estimates are that these groups are planning major sorties against the Israelis in the near future. Without atomic weapons, however, it is unlikely that the worsening political situation in this area will affect our basic mission."

Janice Svoboda sniffed. "What are the Japanese doing in this?" she demanded. "This is something that simply makes no sense."

"Well," Farrington pointed out, "Japanese terrorists have been increasingly active in the Middle East since the fatal shoot-out at the Tel Aviv Airport in seventy-two. The Japanese government is concerned, of course, but they can do little with their citizens abroad. Their system is simply not set up to handle a surveillance in detail of all the people wanting exit visas. Now, if this were in the period of the Tojo imperialism, that would be another story."

"The Sino-Soviet tensions are of more concern to us," Rothgate said, interrupting. "Intelligence briefing points out that if there should be an eruption on this border, now that the Russians have occupied Outer Mongolia, one side or the other might construe us as potential enemies and launch an attack against the station."

Major Lieberman, the station's space surgeon, had to this moment been silent. Now he spoke up. "Gentlemen, gentlemen, I have sat patiently for some weeks as we heard these intelligence briefings at each meeting. Surely, they do not concern us with our special mission to establish a moon launching station. It seems to me that the Russians and the Chinese are in a complete quandary as to whether we represent enemies or friends, a tribute, I think, to the cleverness of the President's foreign policy. Both want to be friends and each comes crying to us about the injustices of the other. Why should one or the other attack us?"

"Because," said Rothgate fiercely, "both are Communist governments with a kind of built-in paranoia that can turn against you in a moment."

"That is an oversimplification, I think," Farrington said. "In any event, station regulations set up by DOD require that the briefing sessions open with a resumé of the political situation Earthside. We have at least paid lip service to that directive. I suggest that we now get down to the immediate business that occupies us."

"The voice of sanity," sighed Janice Svoboda.

"Thank you," Farrington said. "Sarcastic or not, I appreciate the comment."

The intercom beside him chirped and Farrington turned it on. Sugiyama's agitated face appeared on the postage-stamp-sized screen. Farrington had given strict orders that the briefing session was not to be interrupted except in case of emergency. He knew that Sugiyama would not have broken in unless it was important.

"Colonel, you'd better come to the bridge."

"What's wrong?" Farrington demanded.

"All hell's broken loose below. We've recorded four nuclear signatures in the Middle East and Colorado Springs has just transmitted a Code Four."

Farrington felt his scalp tighten. Of course, it was only Code Four, a natural precaution but—

"Will you kindly tell us what is happening, Colonel?" said Svoboda.

"Yes," Lieberman insisted. "What is Code Four?"

Farrington cut the connection and faced the group. "Code Four is for yellow alert," he replied.

"Oh," Svoboda said disdainfully. "The military are playing their games."

"This is not a game," Farrington said, holding his temper. "We have a full-scale nuclear war developing Earthside."

In the U.S.S.R. station, Sergei Voroshilov cut the transmission and leaned back thoughtfully in his chair. He rubbed his chin and frowned, realizing that he had not shaved as thoroughly this morning as usual. He would have to return to his wardroom as soon as possible and correct the deficiency. Certainly, if the commander's appearance began to decline, one might expect a similar decline among the other personnel. This would be intolerable, since the Station Committee had prescribed very precise rules for personal neatness and cleanliness aboard the station.

His engineering officer, Major Nikolai Bucholtz, came over and rested a hand on his shoulder. "You look tired, Sergei," Bucholtz remarked. "You should get more sleep; you drive yourself too hard."

Voroshilov shook his massive head. "No more than the other comrades. It is necessary. What do you think of our American counterparts and their Toro data?"

"It's very pretty, of course," Bucholtz replied with a shrug, "but hardly of great moment. A second moon of perhaps two kilometers in length by one and a half in diameter. Granted, a rather high mass from their density figures of 8.21—probably mostly iron with some heavier metals—but we have known for some time there were other satellites. Hardly surprising. Quite unlike the significance of our own probe program."

"A strange insight into a dead planet," said Voroshilov.

"Hardly a dead planet," Bucholtz pointed out. "There are primitive plants and the atmospheric pressure is certainly much higher than we anticipated. The first American radar deflection measurements from their fly-by showed pressures measured in the tenths of a millimeter of mercury. Now, of course, we know that it is nearly three orders of magnitude higher. The dust storms of the seventies should have told us that."

"Still, what must it have been like in the eons before?" Voroshilov said dreamily. "Our last four probes have each taken the same sort of borings. If we believe them, the planet is covered with an almost continuous bed of primordial peat at depths of scarcely ten meters—a strange situation."

"Ah, yes," Bucholtz said, catching something of Voroshilov's mood. "It must have been a lush planet a billion years ago."

"Who knows, perhaps even with great lumbering beasts like our own dinosaurs."

"This we will discover in the next decade if the explorations continue," Bucholtz declared.

"It is something to look forward to," said Voroshilov. He consulted his chronometer. "I will go to my quarters for a short while. In thirty minutes ask Comrade Sonya to report to me. I would like to discuss the final orbitals for tomorrow's probe launch."

"I have already checked them thoroughly, as have my people," Bucholtz told him.

Voroshilov rose. "Indulge me, my old friend," he said. "I have a sense of the romantic and I enjoy seeing these details. It is not a command weakness, believe me."

"Of course not." Bucholtz said, smiling reassuringly.

Voroshilov left the commo bridge, wedging his heavy body past one of the commo technicians whom he knew only as Comrade Nadya. The soft pneumatic feel of the girl's body as he passed her roused him momentarily, and then he forced the thoughts from his mind. It was hard enough to be away from Katrin and the two children, but to be constantly exposed to the younger female members of the station's complement was sometimes too disturbing. He supposed that lesser members of the staff were finding their special accommodation with each other, but in his position of authority this would never be allowed to him. Party and service regulations prescribed the most rigid kind of moral conduct in isolated assignments like the station, but everyone knew that the regulations ignored basic human behavior, so those in authority chose to ignore all but the most flagrant violations.

The floor of the connecting passage through which he walked was light perforated aluminum and the plastic walls looked insubstantial and fragile. Actually the wall could be punctured only with a sharp instrument, and then with the greatest difficulty. Still, the feeling of being separated from the cold death of space by the most tenuous of membranes persisted. He would, he was sure, never quite dispel that faint flicker of unease.

In the quarters section he went to his wardroom, which served as quarters and staff room, and seated himself before a small desk that he unfolded from the wall. He frowned when he noticed a trace of food from the morning meal. Egg stains, he decided, and thought to caution his orderly. This was his one indulgence to his rank. While the rest of the station breakfasted on a variety of preserved meats or thick wheat cakes with herring, he allowed himself two eggs with large red specks giving them the faint blood taste that he had learned to love as a child. Even in a classless society, he reminded himself, those who contributed heavily to the common effort deserved some small special advantage. This was his.

When Comrade Sonya knocked discreetly on his door, he called to her to enter. She was young, certainly not more than twenty-five, with dusky blond hair drawn severely back over her ears. Her figure was lush, with great breasts meant for a platoon of children. He found the faint disturbance stirring in his loins again.

"These are the final orbital components, Comrade Colonel," she said, laying a fiber portfolio on his desk. "They have been checked here on our on-board computers and verified by those in Tyuratam. Major Bucholtz said that, nevertheless, you would like to add your final approval."

"That is correct, Comrade," he said, conscious of her clean natural odor as she leaned over the desk.

Sergei, he told himself, it is not enough that you are commander. There must be more. Restraint, restraint, this is the whole key.

Sonya had not noticed his trepidation. She continued to spread the sheets across his desk, speaking of orbital calculations and the need for verification of certain components. He watched her young hands caressing the papers as if they were the heavy muscles of a young lover and he thought and remembered.

Another Sonya.

He had been scarcely sixteen then, and the terrible war had raged over the motherland until they began to drive the hated invaders back. Was it forty-five? He was fairly sure it was. He had killed his first man in forty-four, when he was only fifteen, but his shyness and his feeling of being less than a man had kept him from the excesses of his older fellows. Until that day on the Polish border when they had mounted a major cavalry attack and he, clinging to the mane of his horse, had come into the town with his fellows. He was still small for his age and the other men called him "Sergeiovitch," which he bitterly resented. At the edge of the city, they came upon a farm, stripped of crops, the livestock slaughtered. The men dismounted for water and rest. In the distance the shelling of the city continued, black spirals of cordite smoke filling the skies.

The mother and daughter came out to meet them. The mother, graying and tired, with worn liver-splotched hands, threw her arms around the lieutenant and cried, "Comrade, Comrade, how good it is to see you! Our prayers are answered."

Krapotkin pushed her away and snapped, "I am not here to answer your prayers, woman. Only to get food and drink for my men."

"God has sent you," she persisted.

"There is no God," Krapotkin snapped. "Only food for our bellies, and you can see to that."

The woman shook her head sadly, then brightened. "I have some porridge, and a few pieces of salt pork."

"A feast!" one of the men yelled.

"And some black beans," she added. "With maybe a bit of cabbage. It is old, but it is cabbage."

They dismounted and watered their horses while the old woman scurried around in the kitchen of her house, the only part that remained undamaged. Soon the smell of good pork and boiled cabbage filled the outside air, and the men grew restive with the odor. The daughter came among them with a heavy loaf of black bread and a knife, cutting off great pieces to assuage their hunger until the food would be ready.

She stopped before Sergei who stood awkward and shy and said, "Would you like some bread, little one?"

"Little one," guffawed a neighboring horseman. "Our little Sergei."

He blushed, then drew himself up in great dignity and said, "I am no little one. I am a soldier of our valiant socialist state."

"Of course," she said.

"I have killed many men," he lied.

"I can see that you are a strong man," she said, this time without mockery, and he subsided. He took her piece of bread and watched as she moved among the troops, doling out the remainder. He felt a certain pride when he realized that she had given him a very large piece.

Later the old woman brought them a cabbage soup, thick with pieces of salt pork swimming in a deep floury broth, and beside it a plate of thick black beans and more bread. They ate and bragged and drank from the brandy they had found in the town before and soon they were all sprawled about, some of them snoring, others cleaning their weapons. Near Sergei the sergeant named Vanya eyed the girl and rubbed his crotch.

"I have another hunger," he told Sergei, and Sergei colored.

The girl must have heard, for she looked up from filling a canteen cup with water and flushed, her eyes suddenly fearful. Sergei found himself suddenly on his feet and walking toward her. He touched her arm and said, "While I am here, you have nothing to fear."

She nodded her head silently and continued her work. He watched her as she completed her tasks and withdrew to the shattered cottage.

Sergeant Vanya snorted into his canteen cup. "You are a fool, Sergeiovitch," he snorted. "Can't you see she wants you?"

"I don't believe you," he stammered, embarrassed.

"Oh, go take her, little Tovarisch," the man said. "I'm too tired and too full."

"She will not have me," he said.

The man laughed. "What difference does that make?" He turned to the soldier near him. "Hear that, Alexei? She won't have him."

Alexei's brutal battered face opened in the beginning of a guffaw. "Poor little Sergeiovitch," he laughed. "She won't have you. Are you such a fool? Take her."

He paused, undecided, while the laughter spread through the ranks. "You are a man, aren't you?" Sergeant Vanya taunted, and the others took up the chant.

Quite without realizing how it happened, he found himself suddenly on his feet, squaring his shoulders in an exaggerated gesture and walking toward the house. "Good, good, good, little father," Vanya chanted behind him as he pushed open the shattered door. He stood, letting his eyes adjust to the light before he saw her, cowering on a straw-filled mattress at the far end of the common room. Carefully, deliberately, with what he hoped was manliness, he walked over to her.

She sat feeding jagged pieces of charcoal into a crude clay brazier. When she looked up at him with fearful eyes he realized that his earlier assessment had been wrong—

she was scarcely older than he. The full skirts and the dis-
arrayed hair that peeked out from the faded babushka had
deceived him. The girl couldn't have been more than fifteen or sixteen, and in spite of her brave demeanor she
was very much afraid.

"What do you wish?" she asked, staring at the feather-
ing white ash in the brazier.

"I—" He drew himself up, thinking that he must preserve face. "I wish to speak with you."

"I heard what they said outside," she murmured.

"Oh," he said. "Are you afraid?"

She turned large black eyes up to him. Her lips were
white and there was a faint tremor about them. "Of you?
Yes, I suppose I am." Then she paused. "No," she said,
"not that you should not be feared, but I am not afraid."

He sank down beside her and looked into her eyes. The
black depths seemed to swallow him. "Don't be," he said
earnestly. "They are rough men but they are good men,
and they think that life is very . . ." He spread his hands.

"Simplified?" she said. "It's true, you know. Life is very
simple now."

"I would not hurt you," he said. "God knows, I would
not."

"God," she said. "You do not believe in God."

"It is not something that one says easily," he admitted.

She reached out and touched his hand. "Is it so hard to
be a man among all those?"

He drew himself up fiercely. "I *am* a man," he snapped.
Then his voice softened. "Surely, you can see that."

She nodded. "Yes, I can see that. You are very much a
man." She paused. "Have you ever had a woman?"

"Many times," he boasted.

"Have you?" she persisted.

"I could have if I had wished," he said.

"Yes," she said. "It is as I thought. Would you like
me?"

"I am supposed to take you," he said. "Have you had a
man?"

"Once," she said, shuddering. "A German soldier. He
took me and that was all there was. He was quite as young

as you and very handsome, but he insisted on taking. It's not like that, you know. You do not take. You give."

"I'm sorry," he said, suddenly rising. "I did not want it to be that way." He started to turn. "Don't worry, I will protect you from the others."

"Would you like me?" she asked again.

He paused, looked deeply at her and finally in the smallest of voices said, "Yes."

She spread her arms to him and in an instant he was close to her, savoring her warmth and the smell of hay on her clothing and he touched her and she touched him in the most delicate gentle way he had felt since his mother died.

Later, after the soldiers mounted and left the farm, Vanya nudged him in the ribs and demanded, "How was it, our Sergeiovitch?"

"Marvelous," he said with a wild joy.

"Tell us about it," another insisted. He invented the details of how he had mastered her and taken her against her will, and how she had finally fallen into his arms and begged for more. They loved it, and as he watched their eyes he saw they did not believe it. Any more than they believed their own tales. Vanya clapped him on the shoulder nearly unseating him.

"Our Sergeiovitch," he announced to the troop. "He is a man. No more Sergeiovitch. He is now our Sergei."

Sergei felt his chest swell with pride.

"Our Sergei," Vanya repeated with faint mockery. "Our Sergei, Master of Love."

"Comrade Colonel, is something wrong?" Sonya asked, her face mirroring concern. Voroshilov realized that he had lost track of her explanations in his woolgathering and that she thought the faint smile playing across his features was one of criticism.

"No, no," he assured her. "Something amusing just occurred to me. This is fine work, Comrade, as fine as the work your group has done on the previous probes. You have an enviable talent."

She flushed under the praise, then visibly brought herself under control. She was a delightful-looking woman, Voroshilov thought. Very much like his Katrin when she was younger and—he sighed—very much like the Polish girl, who had disappeared into the morass of time and war and perhaps now lived only in his idealized memory.

At this moment, Bucholtz opened the wardroom hatch without knocking. Behind him one of the commo technicians followed, his eyes wide with fright. Bucholtz was visibly disturbed. "Comrade Sonya, please leave us," he commanded.

Sonya looked at Voroshilov, who nodded. She gathered up her portfolio, saluted, and departed, while Bucholtz fidgeted anxiously. He reached out and closed the hatch on the anxious technician.

"Sergei," he said breathlessly, "I brought this the moment it was decoded."

Voroshilov read the message flimsy quickly, his heart sinking as he read. The message was brief, placing the station on stand-by alert.

"How could it happen?" he demanded.

"You know the *Fedayeen*," answered Bucholtz. "I was with our training mission in the early seventies before we left. They are madmen, without even a primitive understanding of the Western mind. When they had formed common cause with the Japanese extremists, they seemed to feed each other's paranoia."

"But surely the sponsors from the C.P.R.——"

"The Chinese?" Bucholtz sneered. "You know how the Chinese are, always devious, never willing to believe that anyone else would act quickly and violently in a situation they believe they control."

"They're fools, incompetent fools," Voroshilov said angrily, crumbling the flimsy. "To let a group of terrorists capture their own ground-to-air missiles."

"We saw the signatures from the observation deck," Bucholtz said. "About twenty to twenty-five kiloton yields, but all three were on Tel Aviv."

"Don't they realize that the Israelis have an immediate answer with their Monitor Missiles?"

"That answer has been delivered, I'm afraid," Bucholtz said. "We saw the signature just before I came here. It was clearly in the megaton range."

Voroshilov swore. "This is monstrous! Where will it end?"

"I fear to think of that," Bucholtz said somberly.

Colonel Farrington was annoyed, mostly at Janice Svoboda, who had conducted herself with typical arrogance during the meeting. She seemed to consider the major military mission of the station quite incidental to her own operations. More than that, she had the gall to say so in so many words, completely alienating Rothgate, who was himself a humorless man. It had taken the better part of fifteen minutes for Farrington to cool tempers and bring the morning briefing to a reasonable, if not a successful conclusion.

She failed to recognize that a military operation is essentially a holding operation. She had become so obsessed with space missions as operations for establishing permanent enclaves of the human species, that she could not understand that the moon operation was dictated by purely political motives, and as such, would be significant for perhaps five years before the situation changed. Her whole pattern of research had been directed to building a permanent home for man among the planets, and the limited amount of work she had been allowed on the station had been directed to this end.

Farrington was, of course, impressed with the quality and the depth of her work. Her primary assignment had been the transplanting of a new strain of accelerated chlorella to the moon station to provide the oxygen needed. This marvelous plant had been bred in Earth laboratories by careful microbiological manipulation of the chlorella genes. The techniques for such manipulation were now well advanced, especially with direct microstage techniques that allowed the removal of individual chromosomes of a cell, their modification by subtle chemical techniques, and their return to the living organism. One could almost retailor a complete species in this manner, whereas in the past only varietal changes had been possible.

Svoboda's chlorella was a product of this sophisticated technique, a plant of heightened metabolism that approached that of a mammalian organism in rate. He had seen strains of the plant *in vitro* absorb carbon dioxide at a fantastic speed, releasing oxygen in the process, in the laboratory. She had assembled the sample culture and hooked it to a Warburg apparatus so that one could watch the steady, almost racing change in the mercury column that spoke of the conversion.

"It isn't only chlorella that we can change in this manner," she once told Farrington. "We understand so much now about plant metabolism that we could—and will—develop strains of wheat and corn that will grow and ripen in a month or less."

"This is remarkable," he had responded, half in appreciation, half in an attempt to salve her ego.

"No more remarkable than sharpening a pencil," she sniffed. "This is the problem you military men have. You are so far behind the technology. You talk knowingly about the "state of the art" and you're still in the dark ages of the sixties. Every schoolboy and girl knows about this. I suspect that a good ten percent of the school children growing up now could do it if they had to."

"And what are we to do with accelerated harvests," he challenged her, "when we have surpluses in the United States that are throwing the whole economy out of joint?" It was true. Ever since the massive Chinese and Russian wheat purchases in the midseventies, American grain production had accelerated to the point where wheat and corn were a glut on the world market. American farmers would be starving if it were not for extensive federal supports.

"Yet throughout the world men are starving," she retorted. "Famines in India and now in the Philippines. North Africa existing at a bare subsistence level. Does it ever strike you, my dear Colonel, that the villain of this whole tragedy is man and his political systems?"

Farrington had to agree that there was merit in her stand, but he wouldn't let her get away with that. "Technology is something akin to a God to you, Dr. Svoboda," he said. "You think technology can solve all of man's problems."

"It can," she insisted.

"Look at the world today," he said, "can you deny that the accelerating state of the world's technology is largely responsible for all of our troubles?"

"I *can* deny it," she said fiercely. "I *do* deny it. The problem we're facing is not the burgeoning technology, which should have ushered in a new golden age for all men, all nations. It's the stupid politicians and their right arm, the military, that have corrupted that technology and made it subservient to political aims. Political aims, Colonel, if I must remind you, that are so transient that we can speak of establishing a moon station for five years and then abandoning it as the political alignment on the Earth changes."

It was an open-ended argument. He knew that and he realized that he was a fool for being sucked into it. Men were men and the system was the system, and while one might, with good will, make modifications in the system, it remained huge, imponderable, with a massive inertia far greater than the ideas that had once sustained it.

"Thank you for the demonstration," he said finally, somewhat stiffly.

"I can see that it has impressed you," she said resignedly.

He retired from her laboratory, thinking that he had acted unlike himself, that he had indeed confirmed all that she felt about the military. Well, how do you deal with prejudice? he asked himself. She was determined that the eagle on his collar branded him as a certain type of personality, and that there was only one way for her to deal with him. It was too bad, he thought. She was still young, with a mind he much admired. Her barriers had been erected early in government research and there was little he could do to penetrate them. From that early confrontation two months ago, their relationship has evolved to a formal one, not a declaration exactly of a state of war, but certainly of a state of siege.

That attitude had manifested itself particularly badly today in the briefing session. He was annoyed that she had chosen to attack Rothgate rather than himself. He could handle her, knowing the source of her bitterness and something of her background. Rothgate was particularly vulnerable to her, however. He was a stiff and formalistic man who had suffered much in his personal life, and had withdrawn into a well-structured shell through which he communicated with the outside world. Farrington wished that he might have been assigned another second officer; Rothgate worried him, with his icy outer demeanor that periodically dissolved into tense, controlled rages. His hatred for the Russians was another factor, although Farrington could understand that hate intellectually. Still, why bait him as Janice Svoboda did? She seemed to relish his attitude that whoever was not committed to the major project was suspect.

As the briefing broke up, Farrington motioned to Rothgate, who followed him from the room. On the commo bridge, he asked Sugiyama, "Anything further developed?"

"We're getting a mixed transmission now," Sugiyama said. "I can give you the clear transmission immediately." He offered a message flimsy. Farrington read it, frowning.

"Did you see the later signatures?" he asked Sugiyama.

"There was one, at least a megaton, from the fireball. About ten minutes after the Tel Aviv attack."

"Damn fools," Rothgate muttered. "The Israelis have had nuclear capability since the late sixties."

"It was a Monitor launch," Farrington said, showing Rothgate the message. "Just where you would expect it—right on the Aswan Dam."

"Good God!" Rothgate exclaimed. "Twenty million cubic feet of water!"

"And all radioactive by now," Farrington said. "It will inundate most of the Nile Valley and make it uninhabitable for years. Pray God the Israelis stop with that one."

Rothgate's eyes were wide and excited. "God damn them," he said fiercely. "They asked for it. They're getting what they deserve."

For a second Farrington could only look at his second's flushed face in wonder. Is this all that's left for us? he wondered. To kill senselessly and then to kill again?

"Let's get to the commo bridge," he said tiredly. It was going to be a long watch ahead.

Three

Longo found Colonel Farrington on the commo bridge, talking with Colonel Rothgate. Longo stood waiting while Rothgate, obviously in the throes of a poorly controlled anger, erupted, "Damn it, Will, I think we should take some action to consolidate the defense of the station."

"We've had yellow alerts before," said Farrington. "Besides, any offensive capability would have to be jury-rigged."

"I know that," Rothgate said impatiently. "I just don't want to be floating here like a sitting duck if our Commie friends decide that all bets are off."

"All right," Farrington said tiredly. "Suppose you draw up a defense plan with appropriate alternates. We've never felt the need for them, but you may well be right. Longo can give you help in some of the technical areas."

"Defense plan?" Longo broke in startled. "Do you think the situation is that bad?"

"I do," Rothgate said.

"Very well, Jeb," said Farrington. "I suggest you get to it while Longo and I work out some other details."

As soon as Rothgate had left, Farrington said, "He may be right, Quint. I just don't know. You know how monomaniacal Jeb can be about the Communist menace."

"I suppose he has some reason," Longo said, "after what happened to his wife and children in Karachi."

"I suppose so. Yet, you know, it was just one of those fluke things. The local zealots were the ones who decided to bomb the American attaché offices. I doubt if they were put up to it by whichever power happened to be backing them."

"What's happened below?" asked Longo.

"It's sickening," Farrington said, turning in his chair to look at the screen that showed the calm cloud-shrouded planet below. "Almost all of Cairo was carried away and what isn't has been poisoned. For practical purposes the whole Nile basin has been sterilized for ten years or more."

"My God!" Longo exclaimed. "That's a terrible thing."

"No worse than what happened at Tel Aviv and the military encampments to the south. Three million casualties at last report. There's a U.N. emergency session scheduled in an hour but things aren't waiting that long. The Russians have been vying with us as sponsors of Israel in the last five years, and they've taken the involvement of the Chinese as a direct challenge to their operations. They have fifty divisions marshalled on the Chinese border and reports are coming in of border clashes."

"Well, that's been going on for fifteen years," Longo said.

"It may be different this time. It appears the Russians may be launching a preemptive strike into Sinkiang. Some reports already of tactical nucs being used, five to ten kiloton, that sort of thing. The Chinese are retaliating by moving north through the Arab states to seize the Russian Mediterranean sea bases."

"That's insane! And where do we stand now?"

"That's the beauty," Farrington sighed. "After courting both powers for a decade, we find ourselves right in the middle—no one's friend, no one's enemy—officially."

"What can the U.N. do?"

"Truthfully, I don't know. Probably very little," replied Farrington. "Actually, Rothgate is probably right. We should start to consider placing the station on a ready basis."

"In a yellow alert?"

"Colorado Springs radioed me to anticipate a red alert if the situation doesn't improve."

"What does Colonel Voroshilov say?"

"I've been trying to contact him but he seems unavailable," Farrington replied drily. "I can appreciate his situation. Without a clear set of instructions from his superiors below, he can't afford to undertake anything on his own initiative."

"So much for the state of sanity of mankind," Longo said bitterly.

"Well, perhaps we can keep our fingers out of this pie. Perhaps, if they must fight, they will do so in their part of the globe and we'll pay a minimal price for their folly."

"The minimal price being what level of radiation?" Longo asked.

"That," Farrington admitted, "is the single thing that worries me and the people below. Even if we aren't in it, who knows what our casualties will be?"

Sugiyama approached with a message flimsy. "This just came through the automatic decoder," he said.

Farrington read it and his lips tightened. "It appears that our Chinese friends had more firepower throughout the Arab Republic than we realized. They just launched preemptive strikes against the three major Soviet bases on the Mediterranean. From all accounts they caught a good portion of the Soviet Mediterranean fleet at anchor."

He crumbled the flimsy and sailed it into a waste chute in the wall. "This will mean some pretty massive retaliation on the border, I'm afraid."

"I wonder if the subs got away?" said Longo.

"Let us hope not."

Longo raised an eyebrow.

"There's just too much firepower being mobilized below as it is," Farrington explained. "With a hundred or so Mendelyev class nuclear submarines loose, God knows what additional provocation can come."

"At this point," said Longo sadly, "it seems as if we've passed the point where we can talk about mere provocation. This looks like the making of a full-scale nuclear war."

"I'm afraid you're right," Farrington said, and turned to stare moodily at the screen. He seemed to withdraw, ignoring Longo completely. Longo understood the mood and moved away. He stopped Sugiyama and asked him if he would page Lieutenant Georgeoff, the second engineering officer, to meet him at the station engineering bridge. Longo decided he'd better bring himself abreast quickly of the state of work on the moon ship and the present engineering state of readiness of the station.

The watch wore on with little fresh news from below. Farrington moved restlessly through the station, a vague sense of foreboding oppressing him. Surely, he thought, this can't be happening after decades of armed truce—after decades of discussions of what a final nuclear confrontation could mean. So far the responses from both the Russians and the Chinese had been fairly limited, albeit devastating in their own right. If the confrontation should escalate, it would mean the involvement of other powers. The U.S.S.R. definitely had multiple independently targeted reentry vehicles, and from all estimates the Chinese People's Republic had been equally successful in the last five years in developing such devices. The thought of all of that massive firepower on the planet below brought a new wave of dread.

He returned to the hushed business of the commo bridge. In the screen the clouded planet far below seemed to turn at an alarming rate. Their present orbit carried them around the mother planet once every ninety-four minutes, with a polar inclination of 63 degrees. Thus they were able to scan a major part of the globe in twelve hours. The high-resolution tapes were spinning ceaselessly, recording what had gone on below. He didn't need to replay the tapes. Their image was imprinted violently in his mind's eye. He saw again the tiny flashes of light, diffusing through the cloud covers, turning their soft white into a fantastic brilliant glare that faded to an evil red.

"Colonel, we're picking up a North American broadcast from the U.N.," said Alec Gerbert, Sugiyama's second. His young face was unnaturally flushed, his blue eyes excited.

"Put it on the command console screen," Farrington ordered.

The screen flickered and then cleared to show the interior of the General Assembly. He recognized the U.S.S.R. delegate Vorinski. The seat for the Chinese delegate was empty. Mr. Byingham, the U.S. representative, was speaking.

Farrington listened, wondering at the precise phrases the man was speaking. For a moment he did not understand the true import, but the meaning slowly became clear. Byingham was calling for sanctions against both belligerents, warning of the inevitable disaster that would come from a major confrontation. The issue, Byingham said, was too important to entrust to the Security Council. It must be resolved by all the nations in the Assembly. Pending their debate and vote, the United States was taking upon itself unilaterally to enforce a cease-fire.

My God, Farrington thought, does the man know what he is saying?

The United States, Byingham was continuing, called upon the U.S.S.R. and the Chinese People's Republic to cease all military action against each other. To fail to do so would be considered a grave breach of the peace that the United States hereby pledged itself to keep.

Lieberman had come onto the bridge and positioned himself behind Farrington. He leaned forward at this. "Colonel, what is the man saying?"

"Very simple, Doctor," answered Farrington. "Throw down your guns. I've got the drop on you."

"But will they, will they? This is tantamount to——"

"To an ultimatum," Farrington said. "Wait——"

He had seen the first movement to the right of the U.S. Delegation. The chief U.S.S.R. delegate rose, glared at Byingham and stalked up the aisle, followed by his assistants and secretary.

"They're walking out!" Lieberman exclaimed. "What does it mean?"

"I hope it's only a gesture," said Farrington. "The next few hours will tell us."

"I can't believe they will do anything."

"Doctor," Farrington said, turning in his chair, "I admire your faith in the ultimate good sense of your species. History, however, does not bear you out."

As soon as Longo had reported aboard the MOS, Far-

rington assigned him to assume Captain Merklin's duties.
Merklin had been evacuated twenty hours before, and
during the intervening period several pressing problems
with the air renewal system had developed. Longo conferred with Lieutenant Gamblin, who was in charge of the
life support system, and between them they located the
trouble in short order. Longo had previous experience with
the catalytic beds that decomposed the reabsorbed carbon
dioxide, and knew how easily the microsphere catalysts
became poisoned. After three hours they had regenerated
the catalysts, and the acrid odor that spoke of a side reaction leading to formaldehyde disappeared from the effluent air.

By this time he was dead tired and his whole body felt
sticky. He had been quartered with Steinbrunner perforce,
since Farrington had ordered the pilot to stay aboard rather than return to Earth with the Orbiter II. During the developing emergency below, Farrington felt, they should
not be launching any vehicle that might be picked up by
one of the warring powers. Since the present glide path of
the Orbiter to the Cape was nearly eleven hundred miles,
even that flat reentry trace might be misinterpreted before
Orbiter's jet engines fired to power the craft to its final
touch down. The resolution of most modern radar was
sufficient to distinguish the shape of the distinctive delta-
wing craft, but one did not take needless chances at a time
like this.

When Longo entered the small cabin with the spare
bunk pulled from the wall for Steinbrunner, he found the
man gathering up toilet articles from his musette bag.

"Just going for a shower," Steinbrunner said. "Join me?"

Longo paused for an instant. "Sure, be right with you."
He felt mildly surprised at the invitation because Steinbrunner did not normally invite friendships or show any
special disposition to seek out company.

As soon as he had secured his razor and hand towel,
they left the cabin and walked down the corridor, their
feet touching the surface with unaccustomed lightness.
Steinbrunner walked easily under the reduced pseudogravity, his big muscular frame moving with an unexpected

grace. The community shower was empty at this hour, for which Longo breathed silent thanks. Steinbrunner held to a stanchion in the small anteroom and began to strip off his work coveralls, his eyes opaque and unfathomable. Longo removed his own coveralls.

He'd never been comfortable in the buff around other men. His shyness probably due as much as anything to his extreme hairiness, a product of his southern Italian ancestry, and the many times he'd been kidded about it. Steinbrunner was a dusky blond with the hairiness of the northern German blonds, and Longo felt less self-conscious. The constant exercise and physical conditioning that Steinbrunner subjected his body to showed in the tight muscularity of his flesh. He showed little if any excess fat, although his skin was the thicker skin of the mid-thirties athlete, with its light underlayering of subcutaneous fat. He had done a marvelous job of keeping his body in good condition, Longo thought. Longo envied him for that, although he really didn't have too much to complain about himself. Nature had treated him kindly, with a high metabolism that kept the fat from his belly and buttocks without too much work. He worked out three times a week on Earth—weights, running, calisthenics, handball—certainly not the almost Spartan regime that Steinbrunner followed but effective enough.

In the shower he found a magnaluminum head and adjusted it to a needle spray. Bars of space soap, a detergent that could be easily precipitated from the effluent water by a chemical treatment, were ranged around the small room. Even with only two men in a space designed for four, the quarters were cramped, and several times as he soaped down he felt Steinbrunner's detergent-slick body touch his. The man seemed unusually warm, with a high body temperature. By habit, Longo faced away until he was rinsing. Then he noted that Steinbrunner had been standing all the while, a faint quizzical smile on his face, watching Longo wash.

Longo felt himself flushing slightly. He didn't like the intimacy of the shower, and Steinbrunner's peculiar look disturbed him.

"You take good care of yourself," Steinbrunner remarked laconically.

"Not as good as you," replied Longo, not knowing how else to respond.

"Still, you're in good shape, not like most of these lardasses around here. I admire that in a man."

Longo felt embarrassed. Could . . . ? No, of course not. That was quite silly. It was just the offhand compliment of one athlete to another, the sort of thing traded constantly in locker rooms. Steinbrunner's eyes became veiled again, cutting off the exchange.

Afterwards as they dried in the hot-air blast, he tried to start the conversation again, but Steinbrunner had returned to his old taciturnity. Funny guy, Longo thought. Except for this brief exchange about keeping in shape, he'd never had any real contact with the man, and he supposed no one else had. He wondered what went on in the secret recesses of the man's mind behind those carefully shielded eyes. The man seemed always to be in hiding from his fellows.

They were just walking back to their cabin when the intercom in the passage crackled and Farrington's voice said, "Attention, all personnel, this is the commanding officer. The station is now on red alert. I repeat, red alert. Report to your stations immediately. Lieutenant Longo report to me on the commo bridge."

"Christ," Steinbrunner said. "What does that mean?"

Longo zipped up the front of his coveralls and set out in as best a sprint as he could manage. The passageways to the commo bridge were filled with scurrying figures. He saw face after face, some cold, some excited, a few betraying the first signs of fear.

Colonel Farrington stood glaring at the monitoring screen, his face tense and white. "Longo," he said without preamble, "I want a report on our life-sustain capability within three hours. Reserve oxygen supplies, food, recycling capability, the works."

"Yes, sir," Longo said. "Is it that serious?"

"God damn it man, if it weren't that serious, I wouldn't be asking you. You heard the red alert." The colonel seemed to stiffen for a second, then added, "I'm sorry, Quint. We just got the red alert ten minutes ago. Hardtack has intercepted three warheads aimed at Caspar Wyoming ICBM complex."

"Only three?" asked Longo. "They wouldn't launch only three."

"Who knows," Farrington said. "Maybe someone got trigger happy. How can you explain the insanity going on down there?"

"Colonel," Sugiyama called. "We've lost the New York beam signal."

"Colorado Springs voice transmission in the clear," one of Sugiyama's technicians called out.

"Switch it here," Farrington commanded.

The wafer speaker on the console crackled and a voice said, ". . . extensive launches. Powered MIRV warheads. We've had one near miss so far. All stations, this is not a drill. The condition is red. I repeat red. All stations——"

After that there was nothing.

"Colonel," Sugiyama said, "Brussels NATO is off the air."

"Oh, God," Longo groaned, looking over the Colonel's shoulder into the screen. Eastern Europe far below glowed in a dozen places, bright eruptions that pierced the night with incredible brilliance. "The stupid bastards," he said, half hysterical. "The incredibly stupid bastards."

"It must be like that at home," Farrington said, his voice cold and distant as he stared at the screen.

The long-scan radar operator said, "I have a bogie. ETA forty minutes."

"Sugiyama, what is it?" demanded Farrington.

Sugiyama moved to the radar console. The NCO in charge traced the blip for him. Sugiyama turned, his eyes wide.

"It's a warhead, Colonel. Unpowered. Maybe a MIRV warhead off course."

"How close?" Farrington demanded.

"Collision course," Sugiyama said. "Thirty-eight minutes."

Four

"It's pretty definitely a MIRV warhead," Longo said, examining the orbitals.

"Some damned Commie deliberately took a pot shot at us," Rothgate exclaimed fiercely. "Damn them, we're not a military target."

"No matter. If that thing comes within a thousand feet of us, we'll trigger its radar fuse," said Farrington.

"Give me three men and four EVA bugs," said Longo. "Maybe we can intercept it."

"And detonate the thing?" Rothgate asked. "That's a small help."

"No," Longo replied. "If we get to it soon enough, we can apply thrust with the bugs and jockey it to a higher or lower orbit."

"I'll go with you," said Steinbrunner. "I've had plenty of experience on EVA. You'd better choose two other men who've logged at least twenty hours on extravehicular activity."

"Very well," Farrington said. "Take Bruce and Piaseki. They've both been working outdoors for several weeks."

Sugiyama keyed the intercom and sent out the call for the men to report at the hub. Longo led the way, Steinbrunner following. "We'll keep tracking the bogie," Farrington called after him. "I'll let you know when you've goosed it enough."

"*If* we've goosed it enough," Longo heard Steinbrunner mutter behind him, but ignored him.

They transversed the rim of the wheel to the nearest lateral passage and entered. The Mylar-and-metal passage bore handholds along its passage, which became necessary as they approached the hub and lost the last of the impressed centrifugal pseudogravity. The two other men were waiting for them in the hub.

"Bruce, go with Steinbrunner," Longo ordered. "Piaseki, you're with me. Do you know which bugs have been refueled recently?"

"Numbers five, three, and one are fresh," Bruce said. "Number two has been out for about half an hour. All of the others are low."

"All right, one, three, and five it is," Longo said, activating the hatch. They donned white suits, entered the small air lock, and waited as the door closed and the airlock cycled. Interminable seconds later, the outer hatch slid aside. The dark blackness of space outside was cut by the brilliance of sunlight, reflecting from the wheel and from the distant moonship. They moved out, holding to the stanchions cemented to the hub. There were six EVA bugs moored near the spoke that entered the hub at this point. Their numbers were stenciled in large red letters on their sides. Longo made a slow motion with his arm. Steinbrunner and Bruce cast off, using their back packs to propel themselves to the bugs marked 1 and 2.

Longo touched the stud on his chest and felt the soft pressure of a peroxide jet push him toward number 5. He turned once to watch the heavy figure of Piaseki following him with a dreamlike slowness. He drifted himself into the pilot's seat of the EVA bug, and waited as Piaseki settled into the seat of number 3 near him.

He touched the communication button on his chest and was rewarded with the sound of breathing. "All right," he said. "We'll have to cancel some of our orbital velocity. That will cause us to decay until the bogie catches up with us. Then we'll have to goose these buggies fast to match velocity with the thing. Under no circumstances is anyone to get in front of the bird. We don't know how sensitive the radar fuses are, although they should be relatively insensitive to anything as small as us."

"Right," Steinbrunner replied laconically.

"Let's go; keep it tight," Longo said. He grasped the tiller of the bug and eased open the peroxide throttle. Deep in the vitals of the bug, 90 percent hydrogen peroxide vented into a chamber, hitting a bed of catalyst that instantly decomposed the peroxide to oxygen, water, and large quantities of heat. The water appeared as superheated steam and the resulting hot mixture vented through an expansion nozzle, emerging as a faint, rapidly dissipating cloud. The end result was thrust. The motor could be throttled as few liquid motors can, but this time Longo summoned full thrust. The resulting acceleration was nearly a full g, 32 ft/sec/sec. His velocity built rapidly. Rather, he reminded himself, his velocity decayed rapidly, since the thrust served to cancel some of his orbital velocity while altering the orientation of his orbit. The MIRV warhead was in an orbit that intersected the station orbit at a 20-degree angle. From his viewpoint he was approaching the still unseen warhead rapidly; actually, he was slowing down and allowing the warhead to overtake him. Their relative closing rate built rapidly in less than half a minute to five hundred miles an hour. He did not dare go faster, since he would have to regain the velocity he had lost to match with the warhead. In the meantime, in losing the velocity, his orbit was decaying so that he was dropping inside the orbit of the warhead.

He looked around and saw that the other three bugs were matching his maneuver. All but number 2 within twenty feet of him and 2 was trailing by perhaps another ten feet. He could make out Steinbrunner's massive figure, but the reflections from his faceplate obscured his features. He keyed the transceiver in his suit again and said, "MOS, have you locked on us?"

"We're reading you," came Sugiyama's voice tensely. "Your closing rate is four hundred and eighty mph. Orbital displacement is now approximately three hundred fifty feet. Estimated planar intercept in ten minutes."

"That's not soon enough," Longo said. "We'll increase closing to six hundred mph."

"Your maneuvering g loading will be too great," Sugiyama protested.

"We'll have to chance it."

"You should be in sight of the bird," Sugiyama said. "It's now about one hundred eighty miles from the station."

"There it is!" Piaseki's voice cut into the transmission.

Longo looked up and ahead. He saw the glint of dull metal and a second later made out the massive warhead. He muttered a silent prayer and signaled for reverse thrust. The bugs simultaneously activated their side thrusters and slowly, as in some mechanical ballet, turned one hundred eighty degrees.

"Okay," Longo said. "Match as quickly as you can."

It was a half-blind maneuver, since he couldn't keep glancing back to watch as the warhead inexorably overtook them. They were pushing heavy acceleration now, regaining their lost velocity as quickly as possible.

"Speed of closing now fifty mph," Sugiyama said. Then: "Forty . . . thirty-five. . . ."

Longo stole a quick look behind him. The bird was drifting toward them now, their relative velocities down to a mere thirty miles an hour. In the meantime, the increased velocity of the bugs had raised their orbits. Now they were in danger of being run down. Longo applied some lateral thrust and waited fearfully as the warhead drifted abreast of his bug. The others surrounded it, matching velocity with vernier thrusters.

"All right," Longo ordered. "We'll have to give it a quick push."

"Why not guide it into a lower orbit?" asked Bruce.

"Because the orbit will eventually decay and that damned thing will land on somebody's real estate below. There's enough of that going on now."

The four bugs were maneuvering now, closing on the rear of the warhead. As they had surmised, it was a powered reentry body, Longo saw as they approached the squat conical nozzle of the reentry solid motor. He thought, pray God something doesn't trigger the motor while we're maneuvering. The intense flame from the rocket would char them in a second.

They lined up around the coupling skirt of the warhead, positioning the heads of the bugs against the stanchions welded to the skirt. Longo saw that the warhead had the typical boilerplate look of a Soviet device, and he saw stenciled Cyrillic inscriptions on one side of the skirt. He wondered what they meant. From somewhere the idiot thought came that they could well mean "This end up."

The bugs were all positioned now, and at Longo's command they opened their throttles. Longo called out thrust figures from his accelerometer as the others tried to build their thrust in unison. At first the bird yawed slightly from Piaseki's side, but the man quickly corrected.

"Give me close tracking, Sugiyama," Longo called.

"Your delta V is fifteen feet per second . . . twenty . . . thirty . . ." Sugiyama chanted.

Barely twenty miles per hour, Longo thought, signaling for more thrust. His bug chronometer told him they had barely ten minutes left. They'd have to use full throttle. He signaled, then shouted a warning as the bird started to yaw again.

"Delta V one-fifty feet per second," Sugiyama said. "One-eighty," he said a minute later. Longo wondered if it would be enough. He looked at his peroxide gauge and saw that his fuel level was dropping dangerously.

"Two hundred," Sugiyama called.

He looked ahead and saw the silhouetted wheel of the MOS with the spiderweb moonship near it. He was looking down at an angle now and he realized that they had been steadily increasing their orbital altitude with the acceleration.

"Watch it!" Steinbrunner yelled.

Number 2 fell away, its fuel tanks exhausted. With the unbalanced thrust, the warhead began to tumble, its massive nose rotating toward Longo. He hit his forward verniers and prayed. The other bugs were falling back as well. He heard a metallic rubbing noise. The leading edge of the warhead scraped alarmingly across the front of his bug. For an instant he held his breath, wondering if the impact or the radar shadow of the bug would be sufficient to detonate the warhead. Nothing happened.

He signaled the other men and they rotated their bugs, using the last of their thrust to cancel their forward velocity. As his motors sputtered out, Longo looked back and saw the bright point of the warhead move up and past the station. It was a good twenty-mile miss, he saw with relief. The bugs were rapidly overtaking the station. They would pass above and in front of it.

"You'd better send a tow truck," he told Sugiyama.

"I've dispatched two cargo handlers we've been fueling," Farrington's voice came through. "A good job."

"That's as close to a near miss as I want," Longo said.

"I'm not sure it makes much difference," Farrington's voice said tiredly.

"What do you mean?" asked Longo.

"We've been monitoring the background from below," Farrington said. "Our computer model says it's already ten times the A.E.C. maximum and still rising."

"Still rising?"

"The bastards are still shooting at each other," Farrington said.

"But that means——"

"I'm well aware of what it means," Farrington said. "It may mean the end of everything."

The end of the world, Longo thought. The words had no meaning. He felt cold and distant, unable to apprehend the enormity of what the colonel had said.

"Holy Mother of God," Piaseki's voice breathed in his ear.

Five

They were back aboard the station in a little over an hour. The cargo handlers carried peroxide charges for their bugs and they were able to return on their own power. Steinbrunner, who had fallen behind the group, was the last to be refueled and return to the hub. Longo waited for him, his mind filled with a dull sense of futility.

He could not believe that all that had meant being a part of humanity was about to be lost. Surely they must have made some mistake. Surely there would be survivors. If not that, there were the personnel of the space station—after the madness below had abated they could return and people the Earth afresh. Only everything that made that old life worthwhile would be gone. He thought of Martha and the boys and suddenly it came home to him—along with the loss of the world, they too would be lost. The sudden realization was like a black cloak settling over his thoughts.

Steinbrunner followed him into the hub. The air lock cycled for what seemed an endless time, the distant vibration of the pumps transmitting itself through Longo's boots. As soon as pressure had reestablished itself, the lock door swung open easily and they entered the hub proper. The other two men had taken a different lock and were in all probability returning to their stations now. Longo removed his helmet and watched Steinbrunner rotate his slowly and methodically, freeing the pressure seal. The man's face was utterly impassive, but his eyes seemed wide and staring. Is this the only reaction? Longo thought sickly. The only reaction to the end of the world?

For a second Steinbrunner placed his gloved hand on Longo's shoulder. Longo realized that his own shock must be all too obvious. He shook his head, trying to dispel the clouds of oppressive thought. His whole body felt distant

—divorced from him. He sensed the dead weight, crouching in his vitals. It was too soon for sorrow, too soon for agony, but he knew that it would come and that he would have to fight to overwhelm it.

"We'd better report," he said mechanically.

Steinbrunner grunted and divested himself of the suit. As soon as they were in coveralls, Longo motioned and they made their way down the spoke toward the station rim. The returning pull of pseudogravity was like an impossible weight.

Caution, he told himself. Caution. Take each step as it comes. There's nothing you can do.

They made their way along the corridors, strangely empty now as though all of the pulsing life of the station were stilled. On the commo bridge, silent technicians ignored them. Sugiyama was nowhere to be seen, but one of the non coms, Gerbert, turned as they entered and said, "The Colonel is waiting for you in the briefing room, Captain Longo."

"I'll stick here," Steinbrunner said. "There isn't much I can do otherwise."

Longo nodded and left the commo bridge. At the entrance to the briefing room, he stopped, squared his shoulders, and forced his face into the semblance of a mask. Then he keyed the hatch and entered.

Rothgate was saying, "Damn it, we've jury-rigged five probes with charges of Comp. B. They'll take the Ruski station out in minutes."

"Don't you think they're doing the same thing?" Farrington demanded. "One overt move and we'll be shooting at each other up here."

"I'd say the overt move had been made. If Longo hadn't intercepted the warhead, we'd be so much vapor and debris, floating in orbit."

"We don't know that the warhead was aimed at us," Farrington pointed out patiently.

"I don't believe in coincidence," said Rothgate, "especially in ballistics and a sure-intercept path."

"They haven't made any overt move on the station," Janice Svoboda observed. "Surely they must recognize the probable situation as well as we do. Colonel Voroshilov is not a fool. Indeed, he has always impressed me as a very civilized man."

"A civilized man from a civilized nation that just may have wiped out the major part of human society in the last hour," Rothgate said contemptuously.

"We did our share," Janice Svoboda pointed out wearily.

"This is getting us nowhere," said Farrington. "Longo, take a seat and we'll get on with the main purpose of this conference."

Longo found a seat dully and sat, watching the mechanical faces about him. He felt himself completely divorced from the situation of the moment. What's happening? he thought. Surely they must feel as I do, but they're all so controlled, so self-contained.

"First," Farrington said, "we must know what the situation is below. We have only our remote instrumentation and that's subject to some misinterpretation."

"Do you honestly believe anyone can survive below?" asked Lieberman. "Is there any doubt of the outcome?"

"Yes, there's doubt," replied Farrington. "We know nothing of the local levels of contamination. What we are monitoring is a statistical world. There are still radio stations on the air, although we haven't been able to communicate with anyone for an hour. We must know the degree of destruction, the level of contamination, and the probable half-life of that contamination."

"The most logical approach to that is to equip a reentry probe with an ionization chamber and monitor the background in the upper atmosphere," said Longo. "We can bring it in to a hard landing and monitor it on the way down."

"That tells us true background," said Lieberman, "but it doesn't give us any feel for the probable half-lives."

"We might be able to get that information from Earth contact if we can reestablish it," Sugiyama suggested.

"I wouldn't count on that," said Longo, marveling at how calm and competent his voice seemed. "We must have an atmospheric sample to analyze, to determine the distribution of hot elements and the probable half-life of the Earthside contamination."

"That presents its own difficulties," pointed out Lieberman. "We don't have a mass spectrograph aboard the station, and simple chemical analysis will tell us nothing."

"The Russians have one," Janice Svoboda said slowly.

"Impossible. Do you think they would help us?" Rothgate interjected.

"Jeb, it's not a question of us helping them or them helping us. Don't you see, we're all in the same boat together?" said Farrington.

"And if the level isn't deadly, or will decay within a reasonable time, don't you think they would want to take special advantage of that?" Rothgate protested. "Damn it, Colonel, they're responsible for this disaster. They'll try to reap every political advantage they can from it."

"As will we," Lieberman observed wryly.

Farrington heaved a deep sigh. His body seemed to shrink physically for a moment before he recovered and visibly straightened. "There is," he said, "one terrible possibility that we all recognize but that we seem to be avoiding. It is the possibility that the Earth below may become totally uninhabitable in the near future."

"There is that distinct possibility," Lieberman said slowly. "It is the ultimate tragedy of our time, but it is a reality we must face."

"I think it more likely that the planet's surface will be denied to us for a relatively short time," said Svoboda.

"And in that period, the race of men as we know it will have ceased to exist," Longo said sorrowfully. The reality was pressing in on him again and he fought back the mood of black depression. Martha and the boys. . . It was too much to consider. Better pretend that it didn't exist.

"We may well then be the sole remnants of the human race," said Farrington.

"We here . . . and the Russians," Lieberman added.

"This is a lot of errant nonsense," Rothgate errupted. "Let's first find out just what the situation is below. I am not in favor of cooperating with the Russians in this venture. They are and they remain our enemies. They are the ones that have attacked us and may indeed have destroyed us. I'll be damned if I'll sit down to supper with Jack Ketch."

"You're out of order, Jeb," Farrington said. "If the situation is as bad as we are speculating, then we need the personnel of the Russian station very badly."

"Need them? For what purpose?" Rothgate sneered.

"Because . . ." Janice Svoboda said slowly, "because they have all the women."

"I fail to see——" Rothgate began.

"If all life disappears below," Lieberman said, "that is, if all human life disappears, we have a responsibility to renew the race as soon as we can. Our station complement, except for Dr. Svoboda, is entirely male. The Russian complement is about evenly divided."

"Use those bastards for breeding stock?" exclaimed Rothgate.

"It comes down to that, I'm afraid," said Lieberman. "Only they would never consent to that statement of purpose. If indeed we are forced in this direction, it must be on equal terms."

"That's treasonous!" Rothgate half shouted. "To make common cause with the enemy!"

Janice Svoboda had been relatively silent during this exchange. Now she suddenly erupted. "Don't be a fool, Colonel," she said hotly. "Don't you realize that, if this is true, there is no such thing as an enemy? Only humankind."

Farrington interrupted them. "I think we can dispense with any further outbursts. The military is in command of both stations and we must find out just what the situation is. Longo, I want you to get together with your people and see about launching probes."

"Is there a chance that we can get an atmospheric sample back?" asked Lieberman.

"If we had the Russian Mars probe at our disposal, we could land and sample at ground level. As it is, we'll have to depend on a shallow penetration probe and upper atmosphere sampling, say at the most a hundred and fifty thousand feet."

"Is that satisfactory?" asked Farrington.

"I think we can get some indication of the contamination," Lieberman replied.

"We may not need the mass spec of the Russians," said Janice Svoboda. "We can run the sample through our chromatograph and check the radioactivity level of the fractions. If we can identify the element, we will generally have the choice of isotopes reduced. If Cobalt sixty is a major contaminant, we should be able to identify it by a process of elimination."

"Cobalt sixty," Longo repeated. "Surely no one would have been using that kind of bomb."

"The Chinese are said to have built a number for use against the Russian heartland."

"Let us devoutly hope that they did not," Lieberman breathed.

The rest of the meeting was concerned with the details of the probe. Farrington gave directions to Sugiyama to renew his attempts to contact any remaining installation. Sugiyama reported that they were getting transmissions from Georgia and Caspar, Wyoming, where one of the major Minuteman complexes had suffered a near miss.

"We need as much information on the military situation at present as you can get," Farrington told him.

"I'll keep a twenty-four-hour watch on the transmitter," Sugiyama promised. Then he smiled wistfully. "Do you think it will be any use?" he asked after a moment.

"Men don't die easily," Farrington said. "There are installations throughout the world buried under concrete with their own life-support systems. There'll be survivors —that we can be sure of. Your job is to contact them."

As the meeting broke up, Lieberman took Farrington aside.

"Is something bothering you, Doctor?" asked Farrington.

"A mild understatement," Lieberman replied. "I'm concerned with the overall psychological health of the station crew. We are facing a period of great tension and I'm not sure how all of the men will react."

"These men were hand picked," Farrington objected. "They are the best of their kind and eminently stable."

"Under ordinary circumstances, I would agree with you," the space surgeon said. "However, we are faced with the most unusual of challenges, the realization that we may indeed be the survivors of our race. Men are accustomed to think of themselves as a part of a mass, a greater whole. We don't state it in so many words to ourselves, but we are Americans. We are Space Service men. We are human."

"Yes, of course," Farrington agreed.

"Don't you feel it at all, Colonel? Surely, I am not alone."

"This sense of suddenly having no identification, of being a part of nothing?" asked Farrington. "God, it's all I can do to put it out of my mind. We both know what we're going to find."

"Yes, we do know, and the ultimate test of our humanity will be how we perform with that knowledge. For some of us with emotional ties too close to Earth, the reaction will be acute. We must watch these men, keep them busy, and above all not allow them to be overwhelmed with their sorrow."

"Sorrow? An inadequate word under these conditions."

"Is there a better word for this sense of fear, of loss—of regret and—face it, Colonel—guilt?"

"I suppose not," Farrington said. "It's something we will all have to face in our own minds eventually."

"I'm particularly concerned about one of your men."

"Who's that?"

"Captain Longo."

"I can't go along with that," Farrington objected. "Longo is one of the hardheads. He's tough and capable —certainly not the sort to crack up under a situation. He's fairly emotional, of course, like most men raised in old-world Italian families, but that's purely a superficial volatility."

"I was watching him during the meeting," said Lieberman. "He's in a state of shock far more profound than most of the others. We all have our emotional ties below, and the potential loss of them can be pretty devastating. Longo is one of those rare men, a completely happy married man with his whole emotional being invested in his wife and children. They're the sum total of his world, far more so than any personal drive or any identification with larger aspects of the world. They are his life and the children are his personal commitment to the race. That's much too intense and personal a loss. He may not survive it without some care on our part."

Farrington shook his head. "That seems unlikely. His reactions today under the stress of the warhead and his behavior during the meeting showed all of the calm good sense I've depended on. I think you're mistaken."

"Perhaps," said Lieberman. "I don't hold myself to be as astute in these matters as perhaps I should be, but I would watch the captain closely. When the initial shock wears off, we may have a problem on our hands."

"What about the others?" Farrington asked.

"Rothgate is probably capable of coping with the problem. His special hatred of the Russians may be his best defense. I think his commitment to military discipline will prevent any untoward reaction motivated by that hate. Svoboda . . . Well, Janice is something of an enigma. I've been working with her on her projects in my spare time, of course, but I find it hard to get close to her. She seems to have sealed herself away from any too intimate a human contact, a not unusual reaction among professional women. It may stem from a variety of sources—a disappointing love affair, a general low involvement with people. Still, I would think she'd be one of your rocks in a storm. Sugiyama, Longo's man Georgeoff, the rest of the crew will bear watching, of course. As time goes on, assuming that the worst we expect is indeed what has happened, there will be mounting tensions and a general feeling of either hysteria or profound apathy. We'll deal with these as they arise. For the moment, I think we should prescribe a mild sedative for the members of the crew. No orders to take it; just make it available by individual issue and let each man cope with his problems as he can."

"That seems like a cavalier way to handle any potential problem, Doctor," said Farrington.

Lieberman smiled ironically. "What would you have me do, Colonel? Interview each man? Put each one on the couch or under narcolepsy? We're faced with a real and pressing disaster affecting over a hundred men. There isn't time for individual attention. We must wait out the coming twenty-four hours, hope that the disaster is not as complete as we fear, and—"

"And if it is?"

"Then we must quickly devise some plan, any plan that will occupy the men. Make work if necessary. Anything to give the illusion that all is not lost, that there is still something constructive to be done."

Farrington sighed. "That's a weight of responsibility that I'm not sure I can bear."

"You'll bear it," Lieberman said. "In the meantime, I want you to take the sedative. You need your rest."

"Doctor—" Farrington said.

"Yes?"

"You too. That prescription goes as well for you."

Longo had summoned Lieutenant Georgeoff to the probe bridge to discuss the modifications needed for the sampling mission. With Georgeoff came his chief propulsion technician A/2C Kurman, a short wiry man of thirty-eight with prematurely gray hair and a distracting habit of chewing his lower lip while he talked.

"We have four probes that can be modified," Georgeoff said. "I can't vouch for our complete control once inside the atmosphere. They were intended for purely orbital missions."

"Can the transmitters be modified for high-speed, high-resolution transmission?" asked Longo.

"Well, we have six channels to play with on the Mark V and fourteen channels on the Mark VIII," Kurman reported, chewing at his lip.

"Can you rig the ionization chamber into the system?"

"The problem is to get a meaningful sample," Kurman said. "It's rather like high-speed atmospheric sampling.

You want to read the airstream but ram air can give you a false reading by a concentration effect that is purely an artifact of your probe velocity."

"Why sample the airstream?" Longo inquired. "Why not read through the skin?"

"You have much the same problem either way," Georgeoff pointed out. "Local skin boundary layer concentration effects will throw you off. You have to sample aft of the airfoils in the stagnant area and hope this is representative."

"All right," said Longo. "We'll assume this is representative. God knows anything will be better than what we're getting now from our station instruments."

"As for the fly-bys," Georgeoff went on, "that's another matter. We can penetrate from about a hundred and fifty thousand feet to perhaps as low as a hundred thousand with reasonable assurance of recovery. The problem of getting a representative atmospheric sample and knowing what we've got is another thing."

"Let's rig an intake on the leading edge of the ogive," Longo suggested. "We'll use a silver felt screen to filter out the particulate matter. That's good for particles down to about a tenth of a micron. Then trap a stagnant sample to determine overall concentration of gaseous and particulate matter and we can extrapolate from the filter analysis."

"Which assumes that we're dealing with particulate matter above one tenth micron and that anything below that, including gases, is not important to the contamination problem," said Kurman.

"I know," Longo said tiredly, "but I don't see any other quick way to solve the problem. Any results we get will be suspect without weeks of preparation and an analysis of the problem." He paused and shook his head, feeling the black mood again threatening to descend over him. "If the contamination is at the level we think it is, this will be close enough."

Kurman shrugged and said, "Okay, Captain. It just isn't going to be neat at all, nothing that I'd put my reputation on."

"Damn it," Longo snapped, "unless you've got a better

way—" He halted. He saw the cold anger in the man's face, and the carefully controlled effort to suppress it. There was no point to his outburst, Longo knew. They were both doing the best they could. Nothing was to be gained by letting his irritation gain the upper hand.

"I'm sorry," he said, rubbing his forehead. "The strain, I guess."

"It's all right," Georgeoff said, his black eyes cold and disapproving. "We're all feeling the strain."

Longo nodded and left them to their work. He thought of going to the commo bridge to see if Sugiyama was having any luck in contacting the remaining transmitters Earthside, but he knew that he would only be in the way. The fatigue of the last few hours weighed heavily on his limbs. He decided to get some sleep until the probe modification was finished. There was little he could accomplish by hovering around Kurman and his technicians.

On his way to his quarters he passed the briefing room. It was open now and the galley section was lighted, while the odor of fresh coffee drifted into the passage. Janice Svoboda was sitting silent, staring into a cup of coffee and drawing rings in the wet marks on the plastic table. She looked up as he passed and said, "There's more coffee."

He shook his head. "I'm going to catch a nap while I can."

"That's a good idea," she said. "Lieberman's tech, Mulhill, left a sedative in your room. One for you and one for Steinbrunner. The Colonel says take them."

Longo shook his head. "Two hours at the most is all I can afford. I'm afraid of sedatives."

"They're only mild tranquilizers. Leave a call with the Charge of Quarters and you'll have no trouble."

He sat down opposite her and inspected her. She really would be a rather attractive woman if it weren't for the lines about the corner of the mouth and the too firm jaw line. She had a look of formidability now that would harden into something more forbidding by the time she reached forty. He wondered if she had ever had a lover or if other men saw the same forbidding strength about her.

"When will we have the probe data?" she asked.

"In about five hours," he replied. He rose and walked to the refrigerator under the galley counter, where he found a container of milk. He poured himself a glass, then returned to the table. "It seems a useless drill," he said slowly. "We know what we'll find."

"Do we?" asked Janice. "We can't afford to operate from a position of ignorance. We have to know the contamination level and how long it will last."

"So we can sit up here and count out our last hours."

"Don't be foolish. The station resources and that of the ship are still very large. You yourself know our atmosphere can be recycled indefinitely as long as the pile operates."

"What do we do? Live out our lives aboard this little doughnut? What's the point to that?"

"Point?" said Janice. "I don't know that life has ever had any point, no matter where it's lived. That doesn't stop living things from living."

"That's well enough for animals and lesser creatures. For men—"

"Men are as much a part of the mainstream of life as any amoeba."

"No, no," he said, shaking his head. "That's not true. An amoeba doesn't regret the loss of beings near to it. It has no emotional hold on other beings. It carries its own future in itself."

"Perhaps," she conceded, staring into her coffee. "We humans think the world is built about us and that nothing else matters outside the world of men. Even if higher life perishes on the earth, some life will probably continue. Some higher form will eventually arise again. The projected life span of the earth is still hundreds of millions of years."

All at once he was disgusted with her and her cold, detached way of looking at life. She seemed the very image of all of those dispassionate minds who had built the science and technology of the vanished world below, who had fabricated the tools of destruction and now could look calmly at the world of men as it disappeared into some morass.

"Damn you people!" he burst out, and was rewarded with a startled look. "Damn you people and your calculating, intellectual approach! If you'd had some humanity, some understanding of where your technology was going, we might never have faced this."

"Not us," she said. "Not exclusively us, anyway. What were you doing while the world built to this end? What was anyone doing? What *could* anyone do?"

He felt like weeping, thinking of the lost dear creatures below. It was not a simple death, he realized. Death was something he could have faced for himself, but Martha and the children. . . Their loss represented the complete, never-retrievable loss of self and immortality, and the whole future of the human race. There was nothing, he suddenly realized, in which he had an investment in the future. He and the rest were dead ends.

Up until this moment, he had viewed the demise of his race blindly. He did not dare think personally, did not dare accept that all that had filled his life and gave it meaning was gone. He rose silently, without looking at Janice, and stumbled somehow to his quarters, shut the hatch, and curled himself into a ball on his brief couch. After a moment he pulled the jumper from his body and felt the cold air from the duct play across his body. It feathered the rich growth of hair on his chest and belly as he pressed himself against the cold metal of the wall.

Martha, Gino, Anthony! Too much agony to crowd in so few symbols. No more the hot intense nights of lovemaking, the morning squabbles over toast and cereal, the piping hot dinners, sometimes hotly-spiced Cajun dishes from her youth, other times the heavy tomato-rich pastas that he loved with the real Italian sauce made from the long, lean tomatoes of Italy, not from the pallid *pomo amore* of the West.

And Martha at night. No more Martha with her marvelously firm breasts with the wide dark nipples punctuated

with a few stray black hairs, no more Martha of the great
crushing legs and the thick brush with deep, moist body
caverns in which one could lose oneself. His whole body
writhed erotically at the thought, until he realized what
she must at this moment be.

She was a marvelously hairy woman, very much true to
her French ancestry. He had persuaded her, in spite of the
style, never to shave under her armpits. She had a lush
growth there, and its clean perspiration odor had an exciting effect on him. He had never felt that with other
women, with their stubble where the hair had been and
their stinking antiperspirants that left a thin layering of
white chemical scales. How make love to that? But
Martha, Martha, warm and full and with an exciting pneumatic feel to her body that built on his basic erotic desire.

What marvels they had in bed, sometimes for endless
hours. Once stretching from a Friday night to Sunday
midday, it seemed that his energy would never flag, that he
could go endlessly again and again. He was big, much big-
ger than usual, and she gloried in it, grabbing him with
both hands and seeing that there was still more to grab.
She would groan and growl like some animal mortally
wounded as he went at her. She would push his swarthy
hairy body off so she could look down and revel in the
sheer animalness of the sight of him penetrating her, with-
drawing and going in and still further in.

He chided himself that this was basic, animal-like, un-
seemly in a civilized being who was going to the moon. He
knew better. This was basic; this was real; this was life. It
had a joy and an innocence about it that he had not expe-
rienced since he was a child.

Yes, that was the key word. Innocence.

Like his marvelous, strong boys with their backs still
curved with the curvature of youth and their little buttocks
indented with the growing muscles. How he loved to bathe
those kids, especially Gino, the youngest, who was scarcely five. He would stand him in the bathtub and pour the
soapy water over him and marvel at what he must surely
become. Strong, with a big chest, hairy and with fine nipples, arms deeply indented, and a hard pubic fold if he

took enough exercise. Beautiful hair that framed his face in tight ringlets.

What he loved most was his young penis, small and uncut. (He would not allow this supposedly sanitary surgery. "He should leave the world as God brought him into it," he insisted.) His small penis and the scrotum, only recently filled with the descended testicles, bearing in them the seed of a long line of Longos. That precious seed and the body that would become a lover's body, delighting women.

Gino would be beautiful, Longo knew. He would be a grand and glorious man, a lover of women, a proud bearer of his seed on and on and on . . . only . . .

He was no more.

And Anthony was no more.

And Martha, exciting, fecund Martha was no more.

And there was only the terrible, terrible emptiness.

No Martha, no more to delight him, to grab his fevered body with her heavy muscular thighs, no Martha with the dark and secret caverns that brought his manhood, full and swelling, to its culmination.

He heard the door open and a stray ray of light drifted across his anguished face. It was Steinbrunner. He tried to compose himself as the man came over and looked down at him.

"Pretty rough, eh," he said hoarsely.

"Yeah, yeah, I suppose so," Longo said.

"Thank God I don't have anyone."

"No one?"

"Well, there was someone, but that doesn't matter any more."

"Oh God, I envy you," Longo groaned and turned to face the wall. He felt the man's hand on his shoulder.

"Take it easy. It just takes time. We'll all learn to live with it."

"Will we?" Longo asked. "Will we ever learn to live with this?"

He lay for a long time before he found a troubled sleep.

Six

The modification of the probes was complete by 1100 hours. The nonrecoverables were launched by Georgeoff's crew half an hour later. As soon as the nonrecoverables were free of the station, they launched the programmed recoverable probes at fifteen-minute intervals. Longo was on hand for the final launches, feeling as if he had not slept a moment.

Afterwards he wandered through the station, checking on the air crew. The moonship group were suiting up for their shift on the growing craft. He wondered why Farrington insisted that they go ahead with the insane charade. Of what possible use now a launch station on the moon? Still, it kept them occupied, and he supposed that this alone had merit. He had recovered somewhat from his earlier panic, but the heavy sense of loss still weighed upon him. The depression was so deep at times that a casual breath became a deep wracking sigh. Had he been less inhibited, he might have wept and found some kind of emotional relief there. Instead he walked through the station like a dead man, thinking that indeed for practical purposes this was what he was.

Colonel Farrington had radioed the Soviet station that they were launching probes and somewhat later had received a similar message. The contact between the stations had been limited to this. Rothgate stopped Longo at one point to ask his advice on the probes he was modifying as attack missles. Longo marveled at the enthusiasm with which the man was attacking the job. He had commandeered two of Georgeoff's propulsion technicians and had armed five more probes.

"I don't think we have anything to fear now from the Soviets," said Longo.

"Mister," Rothgate retorted fiercely, "you don't know

those bastards the way I do. They're hagridden. They have an answer in their dialectic for every situation."

"Even this one?"

"*Especially* this one. It wasn't too long ago that the Chinese were quite willing to wait out an atomic war, confident that they had more people than their opponents and would eventually inherit the globe."

"Well, that was the Chinese," Longo pointed out.

"Who the hell do you think wiped out New York?" Rothgate said, as though that ended the matter.

Longo conferred briefly with Georgeoff, checking the first signals that were coming back from the nonrecoverable probes. The background they were detecting was incredibly high.

"I suppose that there'll be personnel in bunkers who will survive this," Georgeoff said, "but the unprotected population at large—" He shrugged.

My God, Longo thought, how can you take this so casually? He knew the man had a family in Detroit and parents still in Greece. Even that ancient island complex had not been spared the final atomic spasm. Part of the Mediterranean fleet had been caught by a water blast in Piraeus harbor, he knew. The resulting contamination from a two-hundred-megaton burst had undoubtedly polluted the surrounding islands. Athens, of course, was no more, and all of the faded sepia prints of the Parthenon by moonlight that had graced the schoolrooms of his youth were so much curling paper now.

He thought of the myriad lovely things that had graced the earth they had destroyed, and inevitably his thoughts came back to Martha and the boys. He tried to shake the thought, seeing that Georgeoff was waiting for an answer to some question he had asked. He mumbled something that seemed to satisfy the man, and left the launch bay.

The station had become a cold alien place to him in the last hours. He was acutely conscious of the thin membranes of steel and plastic that separated him from the alien hostile environment outside. Before, that feeling had been tempered by the thought of home and warm honey liquid days, lazing beside the pool and Saturday mornings

with the kids—playing ball, walking down dusty Florida
roads with back pack, the two boys with their light packs
running on ahead, exploring a reed-grown ditch and running off the road in pursuit of some great flopping grass-
hopper. Now . . .

Now the universe was cold and sterile and the world
was no more. He knew it, knew it as surely as if the probes
had already returned and the final death sentence of the
human race had been spelled out in so many microphotos
and traceries of intensity lines on heat-sensitive recording
paper. After that there would be little left for them in this
station and the Soviets'. True, with the resources at hand,
including their nuclear-power supplies, they could probably survive for some time, but the oxygen, even when generated electrolytically, would slowly be depleted and their
food stores, while large, were still finite.

He wondered what would happen in the end. Would
they wait patiently on the station for death, that last choking death that would overwhelm them? For himself, he
thought that he would prefer a quicker way out. There
were still the shuttle reentry bodies. Perhaps he should
take one and return to Earth. That would be the best way
to spend his last day or two. Surely it couldn't be that bad
down there. The death in the air would be invisible, and at
least he would die on good soil. And what about the others? There would be others of a like mind. Janice Svoboda, for instance. She certainly held to life as fully as any
man. It seemed only right that she should have that privi-
lege, too, of dying down there rather than in this cold cof-
fin.

He realized that in the depths of his depression he
wasn't thinking too clearly. He'd seen men in this state of
emotional shock before, and he recognized it dimly in
himself. Yet he could not throw off the depression. Better
to make his plans as soon as he knew for sure. If he cheated someone else of his chance, well, that was unfortunate,
but he knew that he had to go back. There was no other
choice, if for no other purpose than, like some wounded
animal, to make it to his home and. . . . And see Martha, if
she was still there, cold and inaccessible.

Shaking off the morbid idea, he found himself near the passage that led to Janice Svoboda's laboratory in the hub. He looked at his chronometer and found that he still had some time before checking again with Georgeoff's crew. He preferred to stay out of the way of the men after he had set up the assignment. Georgeoff was a stable and reliable engineering officer, but like anyone else, he hated a superior who stood about, looking over his shoulder. Longo needed someone to talk to. Janice was certainly a questionable choice. Still, in spite of her severe exterior, she was a woman, and a human.

He made his way through the passage to the section of the hub devoted to the biological laboratories. Here the pseudogravity was much reduced, but since the lab was on the periphery of the hub, there was still a measurable centrifugal force. This area had been assigned to the biological group in addition to another laboratory area on the rim because of their experiments in growing the new species of low-gravity chlorella. The Space Agency had developed a high metabolic plant that would provide the oxygen source for personnel in larger installations. The laboratory had been equipped with a variety of apparatus for DNA manipulation, and during her period on the station, Janice and her co-workers had made some remarkable strides in modifying the Earth-born algae.

He found her with Lieberman, who in his off-hours had become interested in her projects. They were deep in conversation, quite unaware of his silent entrance. Lieberman was saying, "It seems like the most hopeless kind of optimism."

The woman shrugged. "Yet, we still hold onto life. There isn't much else we can do. I've had the techs begin the screening already."

"We don't know that things are as bad below as all that."

"Now who's holding onto the most hopeless kind of optimism?" Dr. Svoboda challenged.

"We'll know soon enough," Longo said.

The pair looked up. "Oh," Lieberman said. "I didn't hear you come in."

"What screening are you talking about?" Longo asked.

"A crazy idea of mine," Janice said. "I'll tell you more about it if it bears fruit." Lieberman choked, as though on some hidden joke. "It would be embarrassing if it didn't pan out," she said, glaring at the older man.

"As for your special brand of optimism, Dr. Lieberman," Longo said, "I wouldn't hold too much to the hope that anything has survived below. If the radiation level gets high enough, we can probably write off most animal life and presumably a little later most of the plant life."

"I find that hard to believe," said Lieberman. "Surely something will survive."

"If the Chinese used more than a few of the Cobalt-cased bombs, or if any of the other combatants resorted to them, I think that what survives will bear little relationship to the animal and plant life we know."

"Mutations?"

"Perhaps some," said Janice. "Particularly in plants. The animals, perhaps with the exception of some simpler hardier forms, will probably all die."

"It might have been better," Longo said darkly, "if we had all been trapped below. If it hadn't been for Merklin's stupid accident, that would be me down there and him still alive on the station."

"Would you have preferred that?" asked Lieberman, eying Longo closely.

"No." Longo smiled bitterly. "No, I suppose not. Which only outlines the basic stupidity of our race."

"That's outrageous," Janice exploded. "To hear this sort of thing from another human being is intolerable. We've lost a great deal, but we still exist out here, healthy and untouched. There's no reason to suppose that the human race ends with those poor creatures below."

She stopped, seeing the look on Longo's face. "I'm sorry," she said, softening her voice. "I had forgotten that you lost your family. I had none. No one but myself, and it's hard to understand the purely personal tragedy of someone who did."

He nodded without speaking.

"You should get some rest," said Lieberman.

"Time enough for that later," replied Longo. "There's a great deal to do. Besides, it helps to keep busy."

"I suppose so," said Lieberman.

"I'll have the samples in two hours." Longo turned to go. He wished he hadn't come upon these two. The brief exchange had done little to lift him from his despondency. He turned back before entering the hatch, and saw the concern on her face. Odd, he thought, I've never seen her unbend before. It softens her face. She's really very human under the armor plate. He wondered if he would ever be able to say that to her aloud.

After Longo had left, Lieberman said, "Janice, I think we may be entering a period where you will have some very special problems."

"Me, Doctor?" she asked in surprise.

"You forget that this station is composed entirely of males except for yourself."

"Oh, come now," she scoffed. "Am I supposed to become the object of every airman in rutting season? That seems overly melodramatic."

"Perhaps," Lieberman said, "but you must recognize that there are certain fundamental responses even in humankind. The idea that the race has to go on through the individual is deeply ingrained, and the loss of a world is a shattering emotional experience."

"I think you're being simplistic," she said.

"No. A kind of panic overwhelms every other thought when men are faced with the loss of racial immortality. Look at Longo. He's been a remarkably stable man; one of our best space engineers. I'd give you odds that he's hovering on the edge of a breakdown at this point."

"Italians are often pretty emotional," she said.

"They tend to give vent to their emotions more, at least those raised in a first-generation environment. It's good catharsis and ultimately leads to a more stable individual. However, Longo is very strongly family-oriented. His wife and children represented his major reason for existence—he's lost the very backbone of his life."

"So have the others," she pointed out.

"Yes," he said, "and we may well expect some very irrational responses from them as the situation develops—at least, unless we find some real or imagined hope for survival."

"Which is precisely what we're trying to do. I can't lie down and accept this kind of end any more than you can. My great-grandmother lost her family, her husband, brother, and children, to an Indian raid and she stayed with the homestead they founded. She found herself another man and she went right on in the face of what seemed the ultimate disaster. I think we humans are still built of that kind of stuff."

"Dr. Svoboda," Lieberman said, "you constantly amaze me. Whoever convinced you in the first place that you should behave like a machine? I like you much better when you're being a woman."

"It's somewhat second nature," she said ironically.

"I'll check on the screening. It would be nice to give the Colonel some small germ of optimism."

"Thank you." She watched him leave, thinking that he was a man you could grow very fond of. A humanist of the old breed, she thought. Yet he still thought of her as Dr. Svoboda. Suddenly she felt the old pang of regret.

She had always been Dr. Svoboda, she told herself. Never Janice, not even to her closest friends, since that day years ago when she had donned the doctorate cowl on her gown and crowded into the auditorium for the June graduation ceremonies, sweltering in the oppressive St. Louis afternoon heat. The temperature outside had been 103 degrees, she recalled (Fahrenheit, she amended in her mind—since the partial changeover to the metric system, only old people still thought in terms of that archaic temperature scale). A hundred and three degrees and the relative humidity hovering between 98 and 99 percent. A typical St. Louis summer day, and under the black gown her body had felt as if it were immersed in a sauna.

How long ago was that? she thought. Nineteen seventy-four, yes, that was the year. She was twenty-four then and still a virgin, very much a virgin with a fierce determination to continue such until her special male ideal became realized. Her head bursting with knowledge and the fresh scars of doctorate orals, chanting German and Russian (her two languages) to herself, she had sat and melted and waited for that moment when she would never again be Janice but always Dr. Svoboda.

What a marvelous day that had been. Dr. Earl Sutherland, the Nobel laureate, had been there and had said something complimentary to her afterwards about her thesis. She'd introduced herself because many years before her father had been in the Coris' department when Sutherland had been there. She rememberd all the old names from the early fifties—Sutherland, Udenfriend, Hayes, Carl and Gerti Cori reigning sternly and demanding over an array of minds, rare and unique, with the other greats of the world wandering in and out—Kalkar, Georgi, Tselius—all the famous names that one read about now in the textbooks.

She had her own memories, too, of four years of the most demanding, fatiguing, near chattel-slavery graduate period, when she was in the department every morning at eight to stumble home to bed at midnight. Sometimes she'd even slept overnight in the anteroom of the big student laboratory where, during the day, she worked as teaching assistant with the medical students, watching their clumsy efforts to draw venous blood in the glucose level experiment, their near disastrous maneuverings with the Warburg apparatus that more than once scattered streams of mercury over the floor. And there were Metlan, Starkey, her own advisor Chiang (black eyes inscrutable, soft Mandarin voice precise and controlled)—and George Eyres, with his bulky male body, big hands, and sensuous lips, looking much like an early Marlon Brando in—what was it—*On the Waterfront*.

It should have been George, she told herself. Of all the men who had tried to penetrate that instinctive reserve she had, who had—wonderfully—wanted her body rather than her mind, it should have been George. She still remembered the hard male beauty of his body, and today it meant more than it had then to a rather frightened girl, completely walled away from the common boy-girl relationships.

They had both been enrolled in Goldenblum's Quantum Chemistry course. It had been quite impossible—Goldenblum, for all of his fame as a researcher, was probably the worst teacher they had ever encountered. Before he arrived for each class, Marty Geldman, whom she dimly remembered as a young man with an offensive braying laugh, would strike a dramatic pose in front of the small class, strike an imaginary gong, and intone "Goldenblum's Mystery Hour." And so it was. Goldenblum, looking for all the world like one of the Three Stooges, with an astonishing shock of undisciplined kinky hair surrounding a bald pate, would stalk to the board, begin to write an eigenfunction, and announce, "It is intuitively obvious that . . . Let's see, is it intuitively obvious?" He would then proceed to mumble to himself the rest of the hour while he filled the board with equations. Finally near the end of the hour he would look out on the class in myopic triumph and say, "Yes, it is intuitively obvious that——" and the bell would ring. It was hilarious and deadly, but somehow they'd both pulled A's in the final exam and, being the only two from the biochemistry department, they went out to celebrate.

First it was pizza and Italian sausage smothered in garlic at Lebrano's, with a marvelous mouth-puckering red wine, followed by an endless walk down the refurbished cobblestone streets (when had she last seen cobblestones?) and George saying, "I've got a great new Led Butterfly record—would you like to hear it?" She was flattered, even though she knew only dimly about the Led Butterfly, and said "Yes," and they went up a dusty flight of stairs to his apartment on the second floor. There were two rooms, which impressed her with his affluence. He had a very good portable hi-fi and a cabinet with more red wine, something thick and heavy from California.

She did not at once suspect that he might have other motives, She was remarkably innocent and when he lay down on the bed with the wineglass in his hand and motioned for her to join him, she thought nothing of it. They lay untouching, like Tristan and Isolde with the unsheathed sword between them, and drank wine and listened to the music.

She was conscious of the garlic smell about him from their dinner, and supposed that she must exude the same odor. It wasn't offensive, indeed rather close and erotic. She wondered crazily if the Italians looked upon garlic as an aphrodisiac and, considering her reaction to the odor, decided that they might well make a case for it.

He was waving his hand in the air, punctuating the heavy beat of the music, while she closed her eyes, savoring the deep somesthetic pleasure of a full stomach, a mild heady feeling from the wine, and the simple joy of being with another human being. She knew that she was rather drunk by then, but she felt little alarm at the idea.

When he dropped his hand, it fell almost naturally on her small breast. She made no move to evade it or to shove it away. Almost without predesign he began to explore her body and—marvelously—she his. She wasn't quite sure how they became nude but they were and for the first time she was holding an unclothed man in her arms. She remembered the heavy musculature of his arms, the precise triangle of coarse black hair between his nipples, his slightly protruding belly (he'll be fat in another five years, she thought, but now. . .), his jet-black hair with the high widow's peak and the full, almost pouting lips that seized upon hers frantically. She had never felt such passion before, and indeed never since, and below her out of her sight was the heavy insistent prodding of his male authority.

She wanted to touch it. For an instant she did touch it. And then she realized what was happening.

She pulled away from him, seeing his gasping form, watched his eyes plead with her as she dressed. He was crying then and she watched him with a kind of detached pity mingled with contempt. (Much later he told her that he had never done it before, but she was not at all sure she believed him.) She finished dressing and he lay watching unashamed in his nakedness.

Finally, in a kind of desperate need to clothe his bare

flesh, she reached over to the table where he had laid his horn-rimmed glasses and handed them to him. He put them on and looked at her and said, "Now, do I look decent?"

It was too much for her; she sat down beside him and started to laugh and he started to laugh and soon they were holding on to each other, he nude, she fully clothed, and laughing. She left soon after.

After that they were always very good friends but they carefully avoided touching or doing anything that either might construe sexually. He became almost like a brother to her. When, later that year, he started to experiment in a different direction and became seized with an obsession that she could only wonder at, they drifted apart. Because of his new interests and the impossible demands they made on his time and emotions, his studies suffered and he finally left the university before his last year. He did not even take his writtens. She never saw him again.

After graduation she had been very fortunate in gaining an appointment with NASA at Ames Research Center in Mountain View, California. The work had been exciting and challenging and she had quickly gravitated there and, later in Houston, to the group studying genetic manipulation. The science of molecular biology had advanced at a spectacular rate in the decade following Watson's elaboration of the genetic code. Techniques were developed in the laboratory for the tailoring of simple plants and animals. It was surprising how much the structure and the most intimate biochemistry of an organism could be changed with the new techniques. Her special interest became the development of high-metabolic-rate plants. One of these, the chlorella she was presently culturing in the station laboratory, promised to be a remarkable source of carbon dioxide uptake and oxygen generation. The apparatus the Space Agency had given her for her low-gravity work was the equal of anything on Earth, and she had accepted the assignment as the only woman aboard the station with special enthusiasm.

Now there was some special meaning for her coming to the station. The specialties she commanded would not normally have been found aboard an essentially military station. Certainly the peculiar insight she found in herself was compounded equally of being a molecular biologist and a woman. Only a woman, she told herself, would think in terms of continuing in the face of disaster. Men did not have that deep instinct for the continuity of the race.

She smiled wryly at that thought, thinking of how ill equipped she was for that primary biological function. While her medical records with the Space Agency showed this, it was not something that she cared to think about too much or talk about. Still, if she were less than able biologically to face the crisis of preserving a race that had nearly destroyed itself, she had other real and immediate drives in that direction. It was, she supposed, the ultimate substitution.

She made her way down the passage from the hub to the outer ring and turned left for Colonel Farrington's wardroom. She glanced at her wrist chronometer and noted with satisfaction that she would be precisely on time, as was her habit. That sort of punctuality always instilled something approaching awe in the males she worked with. She liked the image of precision, although she knew too well how imprecise her mind could be and how prey to self-doubt and the impossible emotions that went simply with being human.

Farrington was waiting for her. His face looked more drawn than usual, the lines about the mouth showing that in a few years his jowls would become prominent and, as age advanced, pendulous. It was an odd sight in an otherwise lean face. He motioned her silently to a seat opposite the foldout desk at which he sat and said, "Is what you have this important, Janice? There are a lot of pressing problems."

"There is only one pressing problem," she said. "Everything else is trivial at the moment."

He rubbed his hand across his face wearily but said nothing. When he looked up at her, his eyes were bleak and filled with a mixture of sorrow and despair.

"I suppose the first probe results are pretty bad?" she asked.

"Very bad," he said. "We'll have the atmosphere samples in an hour or so and then we'll know the full import of the disaster. There are still people alive below, of course. We've been in communication with several stations in both hemispheres, one in the Arctic on the Bering Straits. He says the walruses are dying."

"Walruses?"

"He's in a sealed radar shack. He's jury-rigged some fiberglass filters and that seems to be working for him for the moment. He can look out on the ice floes and see the walruses. It's their northern migration period except for the old ones who stay in the area. He says the sea is thick with their bodies. He gave us an external pickup and you could hear the bulls crying out. It was the most terrible sound I've ever heard. Comical and yet you knew the terrible consequence of those sounds. To think that there could be something comic about the death of a species."

"*All* species," she said flatly.

"I think he's done for," Farrington went on. "The fool brought in one of the pups that had strayed near the station. That pup is probably as hot as a reactor element. When Sugiyama asked him why he did it, he cut the transmission. Before he did he said that he knew what he was doing, that it wasn't good for a man to die alone."

"No," said Janice. "That's not foolish. I can understand a man like that."

"I suppose I can too," Farrington said dully. "The problem that now faces us is how we are to die."

"We're very much alive," she said intensely. "There's nothing to be gained by thinking in terms of any inevitable death for the station."

"I wish I shared your optimism."

"Between our station and the Soviet one there are a great many resources we can apply for our survival."

"The fact remains," he said, "that while we are up here

with a great many resources they are limited and finite. The stations cannot exist as closed systems forever. Eventually we must think in terms of the death of the stations or of returning below to that hell our stupidity has built."

"The stations have a greater life potential than you realize," said Janice. "Given food, our oxygen and water supplies are practically unlimited so long as our reactors work."

"The food is the critical item," Farrington admitted. "We could probably send expeditions down and find uncontaminated materials—canned goods, and the like—but our rocket fuel supplies are limited and, if the contamination has any appreciable half-life, we'd have exhausted our fuel long before we could return to the surface."

"The return to the surface is the whole key, of course."

"And we know that is not possible, or we will probably know that before the day is out."

"Colonel," Janice said intensely, "you've missed the most important single resource of the station in your assessment. A resource duplicated in the Soviet station."

"That's hardly likely. Don't you think I've spent the last hours in just such an assessment?"

"Just what has been our mission up here? Oh, I know we have a military assignment, but what has been our primary concern for the last few months?"

"The moonship," he said—and his face broadened as he realized what he had said.

"Exactly. The moonship—and the mission of the moonship is to establish a self-sustaining launch station on the moon. The Russians are doing the same thing. Now it must be obvious that a self-contained station on the moon will survive equally well on the earth. We have all we need. Equipment to set up hydroponic gardening. Atomic piles to assure use of a closed oxygen and water cycle. Completely airtight Mylar domes. Everything that is necessary to support life against the hostile environment of the moon will work to protect the personnel of these stations against the hostile environment of Earth."

"But can we get everything down? The ships weren't designed to land on a planet with an atmosphere."

"We can jury-rig shuttles. I'm sure that there's enough material stored at the Cape so that we can expand our activities, once we have established a bridgehead, and soon we'll be back in force. Oh, we'll be confined to our little world for some time, perhaps even a century, but in a planetary environment we can slowly expand our facilities and—well, a hundred years confined to the narrow limits of a closed ecological station is not my idea of fun, but the alternate is the complete disappearance of the human race."

"Yes," said Farrington, his face showing a sudden relief of tension. "Yes, it could be brought off. Earth becomes another hostile planet to us, but we can survive, and given any luck, we can grow and eventually, as the background decreases, reclaim the whole planet."

"The one thing we need now are viable foodstuffs," said Janice. "We can't depend on any plants or animals on Earth as being immediately useful to us. Indeed, if the preliminary probe findings are correct, we may have to write off all plant and animal life."

"Back to the fundamental problem of food," the colonel sighed.

"Well, we may never have the variety we once had, but there are sources. With the techniques of genetic manipulation we have in the station laboratory we can eventually expand our food sources, tailor a whole new larder for Second Earth. I've started in that direction already."

"How so?" asked Farrington.

"I've been having my technicians screen the human waste material of the past week."

The colonel looked puzzled.

"It's simple," she said. "We need viable seeds. Everything we eat aboard the station is processed to reduce the bulk and this, of course, destroys any material we might depend on. On the other hand, we had something like twenty-three people come up from Earthside in the past week. Our normal processing time for the station's waste products is five days. That means we have the accumulated feces of these people for five days in our reservoirs."

"What has that got to do with our problem?"

"How do you think seeds and grains have been so widely disseminated on Earth?" she demanded impatiently. "A lot of them are windblown or carried on the feet and fur of animals, but one of the most effective ways of widening the range of any plant is for the seed to survive the digestive system of an animal that has eaten the mother plant and to be excreted in the feces."

"I suppose I should find this funny," he said. "There's something completely insane about all this in the midst of what may well be the end of the world."

"The point is that the recent arrivals ate unprocessed food before they came to the station and in the two days' contents of their colon there may be viable seeds. Any kind of viable seed will be useful. With the genetic modification techniques we have, I can probably take a sample grass seed and, given a few months, recreate something approximating wheat or even corn."

"All right," Farrington said. "You've convinced me. I'll bring the subject up with Voroshilov in our next contact. I plan to call him as soon as we have the final probe results. He's been sending out probes also and, between us, we can probably determine just how complete the sterilization is below."

"You see," Janice said, "nothing is ever lost—really lost." She realized as she said it that her voice had an almost plaintive quality. She had been fighting off the realization of the personal nature of the problem she faced, and now it was upon her. *Oh God,* she thought, *to hold to life with such a tenuous thread.*

But, she told herself, it was the only thread they had and she would be less than human—this brawling impossible ape creature who had inherited a world and then destroyed it—less than human if she did not act as she was acting.

Very true to type, was her last thought before she left the colonel and returned to her laboratory.

By 1800 hours all of the data from the unrecoverable probes were in and had been evaluated by Georgeoff's crews. The recoverable probes returned at 2300 hours, except for one that had dipped too deeply into the atmosphere. This one had lost control and plunged to a fiery destruction. The sampling chambers were carefully detached in shielded bays and taken to the analytical laboratory. There one of Janice's technicians ran elemental analyses on the gases and the solids entrapped on the felted metal filters. Background counts were alarmingly high on the samples. Longo would have preferred more than the makeshift analysis they had set up, but it soon became obvious that the major dust component was strontium with a very high activity. From this the analyst surmised that the level of Strontium 90 in various oxides had reached a level of nearly seventy parts per million in the lower atmosphere, allowing for natural suspension of the fine particles by winds and Brownian movement.

"And that," Janice sighed, "is just about that. The level is incredibly high, an unarguable sterilizing level."

"Is there any chance of a mistake?" asked Longo. They were in the rim laboratory while Blaisdell, her technician, ran the last of the determinations on the chromatograph.

"It doesn't seem likely," Janice replied wearily. "I suppose we'll be getting confirmation from the Soviets soon. Now that the situation is this desperate I imagine all of the rules of this stupid war will be suspended and we'll reestablish contact."

"Not if Colonel Rothgate has his way." Longo bit his lip. "He's armed about ten of the remaining probes and he's dead set on launching an attack against the Soviet station."

"Good God, to what end?" she exploded. "Doesn't he realize that the game is over, that there's nothing to be gained, that only our mutual cooperation will mean anything?"

"He's obsessed with nothing but revenge now," Longo said. "Only Farrington's likely to talk him out of that project."

"Is it likely that he will act unilaterally? We'll have to demand some kind of restraint on him if that is so."

"No," Longo replied. "He's acting well within his orders and I doubt that he will attempt anything without Farrington's say-so. The technicians won't go along with it any-way, that I'm sure of."

"It's hard to believe that men can behave so insanely," she said sorrowfully.

"Not for me, it isn't," replied Longo. "I can understand his motivation all too well." He felt the sudden tension in his throat and he sighed deeply, feeling the faint giddiness of hyperventilation. It was too much to bear, he thought bleakly, to be standing here in this insulated world and talking of menace and the death of that distant world and trying vainly not to think of what that meant. If he were a small boy again, he could go off by himself and cry, but the sobs remained stilled in his breast and the choking sadness wadded in his throat. It had been like that when his father died, this feeling of standing unguarded in the cold winds of the world, menaced with no protection against that undefined hostility. Now, it was so much worse.

She reached out and touched his hand where it rested on the plastic laboratory table. The sudden warmth on his fingers broke him from his inward thoughts and he looked at her strangely, seeing the sudden concern, the eyes wide with sorrow and understanding.

"I'm sorry," he said. "There's so much——"

"Sorry for being human?" she asked. "What is so dis-graceful about sorrow, about tears? I've seen men struggle against this for years and I've always thought that kind of image of manhood was the worst creation of our species. It's part and parcel of the same unreal pride that brought whole nations to the point of self-destruction! Isn't it pos-sible to forget pride, to be human and weak and needing the help of another human being once more? Pray God, in our new world we may have learned that pathetic lesson."

"There is no new world," said Longo.

"Yes, there is," she said angrily. "There will be. Do you think we can give up this easily? It will be a terrible period in our history and there will be more deaths, but we can't give up. We aren't built this way."

He shook his head. "One of the techs committed suicide about two hours ago."

She gasped. "I hadn't heard."

"We're trying to keep it quiet, but I'm sure it's all over the station. Airman 2/C Renault, one of Georgeoff's men. After the data came in from the nonrecoverables, he wandered off to the NCO shower and cut his wrists. A pretty thorough job of it, deep cuts and very bloody."

"I suppose there will be others," she said sadly.

"Yes," said Longo. "Yes, I'm sure there will be."

Blaisdell, the technician, came over and handed Janice the printout on the chromatograph. She inspected it slowly, nodding to herself, then said, "Very heavy in nitric oxide and aldehydes. That coupled with the heavy strontium and alkali metal analysis from the inorganic run and the high count pretty well confirms it. We'll have to take thorough decontamination precautions if we venture back on the surface."

"To what end? Man can't live in a suit forever down there."

"Man can live in a great many uncomfortable ways if he must," she declared. She was interrupted by the buzz of the lab intercom. She walked over to it, spoke briefly, and returned. "The colonel wants us on the bridge with him. He's about to renew contact with the Soviets."

"For what purpose?" Longo asked dully.

"That you will see in a few moments," she said, her eyes aglow with her secret knowledge.

They made their way through the passages to the commo bridge, passing silent figures of crewmen moving about their work. There were no greetings, only a hasty shifting of the eyes. As if we share some collective guilt and it's better not to acknowledge it even by a glance, thought Longo. Once he fell behind Janice to allow a group to pass and his hand brushed her back lightly. She looked around at him, her eyes wondering. They were eyes that were very much alive, and he saw concern written in them. Was his emotional state so obvious? he wondered. But surely then he was little different from the other men of the station who had lost their homes and their families.

A silent group awaited them before the colonel's communication station. He nodded at Steinbrunner, who stood apart, dark and unreachable, and at Lieberman, who was sucking on an unlighted pipe. Farrington acknowledged their presence silently. Then he said, "Sugiyama."

The man hurried over. "Yes, sir?"

"I want all personnel not essential to the contact to leave the bridge."

"I can handle it by myself as soon as we establish contact," Sugiyama said.

"Very well. What we're about to say is strictly classified for the moment. It won't do to let the news out until we've definitely established a working agreement with the Soviets."

"Very well, sir," he said and went back to his post. He spoke briefly with two other communication men on duty. Some seconds later, the screen before Farrington flipped several times and then steadied as the image of the Soviet commo chief appeared. Behind them the two commo technicians left the bridge. Sugiyama remained, the sole outside member of the group.

"One second," the Soviet commo man said, and the screen blanked and reformed in the image of Colonel Voroshilov.

"Good day, Colonel," Voroshilov said without preamble. "If you will be patient for a moment, we are removing all personnel not directly involved in our discussions. I would suggest that you do the same." His eyes looked worried, Longo thought.

"We have already done so," said Farrington.

"Good. There are some things that are to be kept to ourselves," said Voroshilov. "Do you wish the others of your staff to be present?"

"Yes," answered Farrington. Rothgate beside him fidgeted and glared at the image. Longo could imagine the killing hate the man was generating at this moment.

Voroshilov sighed deeply. "We too have sent out probes, as you know. Our results are perhaps more complete than yours by the nature of our equipment, but I believe we have reached the same conclusion."

"That the background count is high enough to sterilize Earth in a matter of weeks?" said Farrington. "Yes, we have reached that conclusion."

Voroshilov sighed, then smiled wanly. "Well, my friend, we seem to have made a very bad job of it."

"We?" Rothgate snorted. Farrington favored him with a silencing glare.

"I know, I know," Voroshilov said. "There are recriminations, so many recriminations, but these seem a senseless waste of breath now. So much is lost."

"This is exactly why I have contacted you," Farrington said. "We may be reasonably sure that within a few weeks, the sole representatives of the race will be in our two stations. We have both nearly completed our moonships for the launch stations. In addition we have extensive genetic manipulation equipment aboard, while you, Colonel, have a near monopoly on the one factor that makes the plan I'm about to propose feasible."

"Yes," Voroshilov said. "You have, of course, been thinking in the same terms as we have. Fortunately half of our complement is female." He smiled bitterly. "Otherwise, there would not be too much use of this discussion."

"In a moment I would like you to have your biological sciences chief discuss some detailed steps with my Dr. Svoboda. The essence of our scheme, however, is that we combine the resources of the two stations and the two ships with an eye to establishing a completely self-contained Earth colony. I grant you that it will be perhaps as much as a century before man can venture out on the surface unprotected, but we believe that it can be done. It's the only solution, Colonel."

Voroshilov sighed again, more deeply and despairingly. "If this could only be so," he said.

"What other choice do we have?" Farrington insisted. "The odds are long, but there's no alternative."

"You must understand," Voroshilov said. "There are factors below of which you are unaware. My own special military knowledge and the evidence of our deep atmospheric probes have convinced us that we dare not return to the surface."

"What do you mean?" Janice demanded.

"You are Dr. Svoboda, I take it?" asked Voroshilov.

"We are most familiar with your remarkable reputation. However, the war we have witnessed these past days has not been merely a nuclear war. It has been much more, disastrously much more."

"Oh, God," Janice said.

"You must understand the enemy we faced," Voroshilov persisted. "Vast stretches of land and a population of gigantic size. Granted they were less technically developed than we, but one does not defeat such a country by conventional ground war, and we had no idea that this war would escalate in this fashion. I myself argued against such a weapon, but I was overruled and it was developed."

"A bacteriological weapon?" Farrington asked.

"No," Voroshilov said. "It is rather a rickettsial disease, but one so mutated that it may infect through a variety of entrances—the lungs, an open cut, the digestive tract."

"Its vectors will die," Janice objected.

"Alas, Doctor, they will not," Voroshilov said patiently. "The disease is airborne. Its spores are resistant to dehydration and may persist for years, decades. It is no use. The surface of the planet is denied to us.

"It's a trick," Rothgate declared. "Surely you can't believe this?"

"I can, and do," said Farrington. "Our Intelligence knew something of this."

"We can protect an Earth colony from this," Longo protested. "After all, we have to build a completely sealed colony anyway."

"No," Lieberman said. "The risk is too great. Ordinarily, if an accident occurs, if the seal is broken in a suit or in a chamber of the colony, we lose those people and we can regroup. Make no mistake, breaks in our system will occur, but in this instance one break would be fatal to the whole colony."

"That is the way we have analyzed it," agreed Voroshilov.

"So we have done a good job of it," Farrington said despairingly. "What do we do now—simply sit and wait to die?"

"No, that is not the way," Voroshilov said. "We offer you an alternative, a new venture with us, with our full partnership."

"What alternative is there?" Farrington asked, and then his eyes widened as Voroshilov's meaning penetrated.

"Of course," Janice said. "It doesn't matter where a self-contained colony is located, just so long as it has access to certain minerals, a supply of water even in such things as gypsum—"

"The moon!" Longo exclaimed.

"Yes," Voroshilov said triumphantly. "This is what we propose—that we transfer these pitifully few remainders of the human race to the moon. There, the fates willing, we may live and hold onto our heritage against the time when we may return to the poor Earth below."

Seven

"The question foremost in my mind," Colonel Farrington said, "is whether it is feasible to mate the two ships as a single vehicle or whether we should proceed in two separate vessels. In terms of fuel consumption and life-support systems, there's a great deal to be said for the single-vessel concept. We have enough points of technical overlap as a result of the early technical discussions under the MilLimS treaty so that I suspect a single vessel is possible."

Georgeoff looked at Longo, who nodded silent assent. "I think that this may be the reasonable approach," he said. "We will cannibalize both stations during the final phase. We must take along as much of the station installation as possible. This means that we will be jury-rigging a completely new vessel in any event."

"The problem here," said Longo, "is whether we have enough fuel and oxidizer for the extra mass. We can establish a parking orbit, of course, and use our and the Soviet shuttles to ferry down material, but we'll need an extensive computer run to determine the reaction mass requirements. This means we'll have to mate our computers with the Soviets' since we can't handle the problem in a reasonable time on our own shipboard computers."

"There might be an alternate solution," Steinbrunner said slowly.

"To the computer problem?" asked Farrington. "I don't see how. Our facilities are severely limited."

"The facilities at the Cape are not, and we have done remote programming from the station before. If we can put the computer system at the Cape on ready, perhaps our people can handle the problem from the station by remote control."

"Is that possible?" Farrington asked Lieutenant Rodrigues, the station computer center chief. Rodrigues, a rather heavy man with an oily dark skin and deep black eyes, shrugged his thick shoulders.

"It is possible," he hazarded. "The Cape systems are always held on stand-by. They are never shut down because of the problem of deterioration of the monolithic circuitry on repeated start-up."

"Good," Farrington said. "I'd like a complete report on that as soon as you've talked with your people. I need also a complete survey as soon as possible of station facilities and an estimate on the material we will take with us. The Soviets are doing the same."

"You know, there were several shuttlecraft on stand-by at the Cape when we left," said Steinbrunner. "We should get a survey of their cargo and decide if we can possibly salvage that material."

"But that would mean that someone would have to return," Janice exclaimed.

"That's right."

"But that would be very dangerous, perhaps suicidal!"

"I'm quite aware of that," Steinbrunner said flatly. "Nevertheless it is a risk that should be taken."

"Would you be willing to take such a risk?" asked Longo.

"I'm certainly the logical one to do it," Steinbrunner replied.

Rothgate had been brooding silently at the end of the table. "Do you honestly believe that you can trust the Commies to honor this agreement?"

Farrington sighed. His voice was patient but his eyes spoke his annoyance. "Jeb, there is simply nothing we can do but take them on trust. They have as much to lose as we do by any double-dealing."

"I question that," Rothgate said fiercely. "You haven't read as much as I have of the writings of their dialecticians. This sort of situation will bring only one response from them, a very careful ordering of the situation so that they will eventually inherit everything. That's the whole key to their thinking—even on the brink of disaster their whole operation will be directed to the elimination of us as a political entity and perhaps as a physical entity."

"I think you're going to extremes, Colonel," Janice protested.

"No, perhaps he is not," said Steinbrunner. "I have lived under them, as you know, and their ways are very subtle, particularly in any détente arrangement. They follow the rules until it is convenient to violate them."

"Ah, yes," said Lieberman. "We have had more than one sampling of what your German philosophers called *Realpolitik*."

"I think you're out of order," said Farrington.

"The times, my dear Colonel," Lieberman said sadly. "The times are out of order."

"The one underlying purpose of this project," Farrington persisted, "is the preservation of this race of ours. If there were no other argument to advance for cooperation with the Soviets, it is the simple fact that they have all the women."

"Bluntly, succinctly, that is it," agreed Lieberman.

"Not all the women," Rothgate said fiercely.

Janice colored. "I'm not at all sure I'm flattered at being considered breeding stock."

"There was no offense intended," said Rothgate, "but this is a reality we must face."

"And so is the reality that one woman cannot carry on the human race alone," Farrington objected.

"At one point in the past a single one did."

"I won't hear any more of this," Janice said angrily. She rose to her feet. "I have a great deal of work to do and I don't feel that I can contribute to this justification of the male rutting instinct."

"Please, Dr. Svoboda," Farrington said gently. "I'm sure that no one has anything but the highest regard for you. Jeb certainly intended no offense."

"I'm sorry," added Rothgate. "The facts are difficult to live with, but there are many difficult facts to live with in the next months."

"I think we can get to our various tasks," said Farrington. "A great deal remains to be done. I think I'll try to schedule a meeting with Voroshilov in twenty-four hours."

"Is that wise?" Rothgate asked.

Farrington ignored him. "Thank you all for your time and we'll meet again in six hours. Jeb, stay behind. There's some additional work you can do for me."

The others filed from the conference room, dispersing to their stations, while Farrington sat silently, looking at the solid figure of his second. How can I go about this? he wondered. This was always the problem of command, and he had never successfully solved it in all of its ramifications in his years of service. You needed the initiative and the talent of your staff officers, but you needed their loyalty more. Granted, you couldn't stifle disagreement, but the disagreement had to be nurtured in such a fashion that it did not become destructive, that it was always hidden by the military formalities. More than this, you had to assure yourself of that continuing loyalty while exercising the autocratic military control.

How do you do this? he thought. Do you play God, or do you in some fashion reach the inner human understanding of every human being? Certainly, you do not do this with Jeb Rothgate, who is a man with a terrible hatred, a man obsessed. But a valuable man and one capable beyond the capability of most of the men he had had in his command in the past.

"Jeb," he said slowly, counting his words, "I'm concerned about you."

"About me?" Rothgate said. "I can't see why."

"This obsession of yours about the Russians. I understand that you have little reason to love them. Neither do I. But I think you should consider that it is just this unreasoning hatred that has brought us to this crisis."

Rothgate laughed bitterly. "No need to worry, Colonel. I'm not about to do anything unilaterally. Sure, I hate the bastards, but they are still our flesh. Out of them and their women we can build another world and still save the essential way of life that we think is best."

"Do you mean that?" asked Farrington. "Do you really believe that?"

"I shoot off my mouth," Rothgate said. "I know that, but I'm not such a fool as to compromise the last chance this race of ours has for existence. I'm only pleading with you to recognize that they will not change their basic way of thinking. They believe that they will inherit the earth—well, the human race now—and they will keep that uppermost in their minds in every negotiation with us."

"All right,"said Farrington. "I'm afraid I did you an injustice, but I worry when you come out with some of your wild statements. We will need every appearance of good will in the future to bring off this project."

"You can count on me," Rothgate assured him. "This is the way it has to be. No one knows that better than I."

"All right," said Farrington, his fears still nagging at him. "You can go now. I want your survey in as soon as possible."

"We can get some help from down below."

"That's surprising. How so?"

"We still have sporadic contact with someone on the Cape. Everything's intact. Apparently they suffered a near miss in the ocean. There's a woman who has apparently shut herself in one of the computer buildings. They're all air-conditioned, you know. I think she's suffering from the first stages of radiation poisoning, but Sugiyama has been able to raise her on three occasions. Everyone else is dead or has been evacuated."

"Follow that up," said Farrington excitedly. "She may well be the solution to our exposure problem."

"I doubt if she can help us with the computer systems below."

"Find out," Farrington ordered.

"Yes, sir," Rothgate responded with apparent enthusiasm. He turned and started for the hatch.

"Jeb—"

"Yes, sir?"

"I'm sorry if I seemed to lose confidence in you. It wasn't that, but I have to be aware of the inherent weaknesses of every member of my command."

"Think nothing of it," Rothgate assured him, and vanished through the hatch.

In the passage, his inner fury almost mastered him. The

fool, Rothgate thought, the utter fool. Couldn't he see
what was about to happen? They would take the resources
of the station and make them their own and in the end all
that the Americans had fought for, all that they had held
on to through the decades of cold and hot wars, would be
lost by simple fiat. It had always been this way, the bleed-
ing hearts who were so willing to barter away their heritage. Well, it would not happen. He promised himself
fiercely that it would not happen.

He went to his quarters to freshen up. At the wash-
stand, he looked in the mirror and saw the naked hatred in
his eyes, the hatred that he worked so hard to disguise
when he passed among lesser men. Yes, that was the term.
Why not admit it? Lesser men. He had always been the
exceptional man among lesser men from the days when he
had graduated at the Command School first in his class.
And a reservist at that. He should have been a full colonel
now, perhaps even in command of this station, had it not
been for the tragedy that had dominated his life.

He remembered the terrible nights after his wife and
child had been killed, the agony-filled nights when he
could sleep only after downing an inordinate number of
pills. The flight surgeon with the legation had worried
about that, but he had been a patient man, an understanding man, and he knew the shattering impact of losing
your whole life in one terrible instant.

For a long period, for months in fact, Rothgate had
been sure that he was going insane. The terrible depres-
sions, the ceaseless unreasoning rages that turned not only
against the swine who had cost him everything in life, but
finally against his own co-workers, the men with whom he
had daily contact. He had finally gone into limited therapy, but it had done no good. Instead he had learned to disguise his emotions, his aching loss, his secret rage. It
wasn't that difficult to trick the therapist, who was, after
all, overburdened himself. Still, it was that short period of
therapy that had appeared on his records and had given
rise to the doubts that held him back. He outranked Farrington by five years, and yet here he was in the intolera-

ble position of being second in command to the man. Farrington was capable enough in an ordinary command situation of course, but he was weak, incapable of acting with decision at this terrible crucial moment of history.

Rothgate stared at the face in the mirror before him, at the heavy lines that cut through the subcutaneous fat of his massive features, and promised himself there would be no compromise, no final defeat before this implacable enemy.

For a moment he thought of the years before and the terrible night in Karachi. Then, as had happened so many times in the past, his face dissolved before him and the silent tears flowed from his eyes. Oh, he thought, the terrible ache, would it never end? For a searing moment, his mind was filled with a disordered series of images—the faces of men contorted in the grip of mob passion, the oily red of torches, the stench of fire and above it a deeper more pervading stench of organic matter charring, the distant shout of voices and then of screams. All the old, terrible memories—sight, sound, smell, smell most of all— washed back over him.

He had seen them die. He had just returned from one of his confidential trips when, at the airport, he had heard of the attack upon the consulate. There were many Europeans in Karachi at the time, and no one noticed him as he pushed through the mobs in the street. He felt unclean as rank, unwashed bodies brushed against him. He felt repelled by the mobs but he pressed through them, abandoning his cab when it became apparent that one could proceed only on foot. God, how he hated these dark creatures with their blue-black hair, their unshaven jowls, and their smelly rags.

Still he pushed ahead. He made it to the periphery of the mob that surrounded the consulate. He saw other white faces, and they seemed equally as dazed as he at the violence and the hatred that ran through the mob like a living tide. Yet not one of the mob noted his face and his European dress, not one thought to turn part of his hate against the isolated white face in the sea of shouting, hating, lusting olive faces. They were intent upon the building and upon the two lone M.P.s who had retreated to the relative safety of the iron-fenced consulate enclosure.

It was a moment before he realized that the smell of fire came from the building, that it was burning, that indeed the flames had already spread to the second floor.

He realized what was happening and his whole body erupted in a fury. He shoved and pushed and when the tight-pressed bodies did not yield before him, in a manic hysteria he began to beat against them. He struck a swarthy face that turned to him and as the man fell he ground his foot into the man's chest, feeling with a wild joy the crunching of bone, He saw a grey mass of hair and a seamed female face before he struck and brushed the tattered thing aside. He must get to the building, find his way to the second floor where the living quarters were.

It was amazing how they drew aside before his fury. They who had created this chaos were no match for his blind fury. They bowed their bodies before his implacable anger, falling and groveling before his blows until he was in the front ranks of the mob. He looked up and then—just for an instant he saw her. She stumbled to the window, her lovely eyes blinded by smoke. She was clutching something, he dared not imagine what—or whom. She looked out on the sea of faces, painted blood red by the flames. She seemed to be screaming but no sound came from her distorted mouth. Then she seemed to fall back and a wash of flames curtained the window.

He screamed. He must have screamed. He was sure he screamed as the world dissolved about him. Many of the consulate personnel had escaped and they fled into the crowd—the strange, quiescent crowd that, having worked its chaos, became vulnerable to the first lone assault. Several of the consulate personnel who knew him forced their way to him, sorted him out of the crowd as a sheepdog sorts out blind animals, and led him away. He lost track of where he went or what he did. He only knew that the beings most dear to him had appeared in that gate of hell, that window, and then had dissolved forever in flames.

It was far too much for one man to accept. He descended into a special private hell and now, seeing his face of agony in the mirror, he realized that he-would never ascend to light and faith and love again. That he was forever pent in these nether regions of his aching soul.

He was quite unprepared for the low buzz from the door. It cut into his pain and for a second disoriented him. He was suddenly again in this space and time and staring with anguished eyes at his image. The buzzer cut through the silence again and he grimaced. He splashed water quickly into the basin, washed his face, touched the button that sucked the water with a whoosh from the basin, and dried his hands and face. Then he walked to the desk and keyed the door.

Outside Steinbrunner said, "I hope I didn't disturb you, Colonel.

"Not at all," said Rothgate. "I was just washing up. Come in, Lieutenant."

Steinbrunner entered and the hatch slid silently closed behind him. He stood silently for a moment, his large form looking gigantic in the small room. He was staring at Rothgate with a strange look, compounded half of concern, half of amusement. Rothgate realized he must have made some sound in the last moments that had reached the lieutenant's ears.

"What do you want, man?" he demanded, too loudly.

"I have some papers here that need your signature."

"My God, do we still go on with the bureaucratic charade?"

"Regulations." Steinbrunner shrugged.

"I'm sorry," said Rothgate. "Of course, we have to preserve the routine even now. Otherwise—"

"Systems are always important," Steinbrunner agreed. He paused. After a long moment of brow-wrinkling: "Colonel, is there anything I can do?"

"I'm not sure what you mean," Rothgate said, stiffening.

"I mean, I understand your concern."

"Do you?" Rothgate demanded. Then, "Well, of course. I want to thank you for saying what you did earlier."

"I'm a practical man," Steinbrunner said. "I wouldn't have survived in my life if I were not."

"Nevertheless, I want to thank you. There are too many people ready to believe that my suspicions are dictated strictly by my—by what has happened in the past."

"A man may bear wounds for a long time. This doesn't mean the source of the wounds isn't real," Steinbrunner said slowly, feeling for words. "I grew up in East Germany, you know."

"Yes," said Rothgate. "I know something of your past. I've seen your dossier. I heard how you escaped."

"I was just nineteen then. But I learned to hate them and distrust them."

"What—" Rothgate broke off at the look on the distant-eyed face of the man before him.

"They destroyed someone I loved, too. I escaped. It's a memory hard to erase. It's a loss hard to forget. You find someone like that only once in a lifetime."

Rothgate looked at the man in wonder. This was the first time he had ever heard him utter more than a few words, and these were uttered so coldly, so dispassionately that it was hard to realize the agony behind them. He felt an instant bond with the taciturn German, a sudden realization that in diverse ways they had indeed become brothers.

"It may be that they are sincere," he hazarded.

"It may be," Steinbrunner agreed. "There are good men on their side."

"But after a lifetime of conditioning—?"

"The conditioning will always win out."

"Then we should do what we can to urge caution in this coming venture; we should be alert to every possible treachery," said Rothgate.

"If I can help, I will."

"I have no idea how you may. I have no idea of how I can influence the commander," Rothgate said slowly, "but I will count on your support, even if it's only moral."

"I suppose that moral support is about all I can give."

"Thank you for that," Rothgate said fervently. He

reached out his hand, then realized that he had been too forward. He felt vaguely compromised.

Steinbrunner drew himself up and saluted very stiffly before taking the outstretched hand. "The colonel may trust my judgment," he said stiffly.

How odd, Rothgate thought, in the midst of an almost intimate contact of spirits, the German spirit asserts itself, the acute sense of propriety.

"Thank you," he said formally.

"If the colonel will look at these requisitions." Steinbrunner offered his clipboard.

"Of course," said Rothgate and began to scan the sheets. Inside he sighed, wondering at the momentary touch of two persons now suddenly isolated by rank and the rigid codes of male behavior. A cold man, he thought, a product of his conditioning. Always proper. He wondered if he would ever be that close to Steinbrunner again.

Colonel Farrington told Longo, "I want you to come with me to the Soviet station. We'll need your special know-how in these earlier discussions."

"Why don't they come over here?" Longo asked.

"I suspect their EVA equipment is not as efficient as ours. The one time that Voroshilov visited our station, he pretended that his EVA equipment was all occupied and we sent him one of our bugs. You know how proud the Russians are."

"It may be a simple matter of range. After all, without EVA equipment, they wouldn't be able to work on their station. Have you seen their bugs, by the way?"

"Yes, at the station. They look very crude, very boiler plate, but all Soviet equipment looks the same way. I don't know how they're powered."

"They overengineer," said Longo. "Still, that has its virtues, not the least of which is low cost, since they use off-the-shelf components."

"I don't think we'll be troubled with the problems of expense from this point on," Farrington said wryly.

"No." Longo shook his head. "No, I suppose that will be the least of our troubles."

"I'll let you know as soon as I establish a time for the visit," said Farrington. "Will you tell Dr. Svoboda I'd like her to go with us?"

"Very good, sir," Longo said, and left the colonel's wardroom.

He made his way through the passages, stopping at the launching bay to watch the final decontamination of the recoverable probes. He complimented Georgeoff and Kurman on the manner in which they handled the assignment, and was pleased at the way Kurman beamed under the praise.

When he reached Janice Svoboda's laboratory on the rim she was sitting at a small desk, writing in a journal. He paused, seeing her wrinkled brow and air of concentration. If she noticed him, she made no sign, but continued to write for some minutes. Finally she looked up and said, "Thanks very much."

"For what?" he asked.

"For letting me finish. I wanted to get this down while it was fresh in my mind." She closed the book. "You're quite unlike most of the men I know. They'd have bulled in without thinking."

"Well, it seemed that you were doing something important."

She smiled and Longo noticed again how the expression softened her features. He realized that he had been staring at her without speaking, so that the silence became an uncomfortable gap.

"The colonel asked me to give you a message," he said at last. "He'd like you to come with the party that visits the Soviet station."

"I expected that he would want that," she said. "The biological end of the mission becomes quite important, and I'd like to see what resources the Russians have." She frowned and bit her lip. "I'd like to get some of their thoughts on the feasibility of this project."

"Well, it's quite feasible from the propulsion end and I think we can handle the establishment of the physical plant. Is something bothering you?"

"Nothing that I can document at this moment."

"But something *is* bothering you," he insisted.

"I suppose it's the problem of growth. I can't help feeling that in restricting ourselves to such a barren world, we have circumscribed any chance we have for growth of the colony."

"You're probably quite right," Longo agreed. "The whole idea of the project is to construct a holding colony until we can return."

"Which may be for up to two centuries. I've been making some calculations, based on the information the Russians sent us and it seems unlikely that we could consider a return to the surface in less than that time. I have no idea, of course, if the rickettsial spores will still be viable then. That's a completely unknown quantity."

"At the moment, we'll have to assume that we can find ways of dealing with them if they are still about," Longo said slowly. "I know it's the vaguest kind of optimism, but our only alternative is to continue to live aboard the stations, and I don't think that's a workable solution."

"Nor do I," she admitted. "The problem I worry about is—well, call it 'historical decline.'"

"You've been reading too much Toynbee," he laughed.

"No, I'm quite serious," she insisted. "Toynbee isn't what I had in mind, but his analysis of what he called 'arrested civilizations' could very well apply to our situation. There are challenges that a society can meet but only at the expense of every available bit of creative energy available to them. There's nothing left over for growth, and a society that isn't growing must either stagnate or decline."

"The moon is a harsh environment, I grant you," Longo said, "but we'll have mineral sources that we don't have in space."

"But we'll always be confined to the colony as we establish it. All of our energies will be devoted to simply keeping alive. We must establish some kind of rigid birth control, since it seems unlikely that we can extend the physical limits of the colony significantly."

"I suppose we can tunnel under the surface and extend the physical limits of the colony in that manner."

"At the expenditure of how much energy?" she objected. "And there are few materials that we know of that we
can use to expand our life-support systems. There's no
place other than hydrophonic labs where we can grow food.
We'll be confined like moles to a burrow for two centuries,
and I shudder to think what this will do to any human
community. This assumes, of course, that we will have
maintained our technology at a level where we can indeed
return."

"We can make provision for that."

"Two centuries is a very long time," Janice observed.
"The decline in technology and in our society would be
subtle, but the cumulative effect of two centuries could
well be fatal."

He shrugged. "I suppose it's a moot point. There's no
reasonable alternative other than returning to Earth now."

"I'm almost tempted to argue for that solution," she
said. "With the genetic manipulation techniques we have,
we might be able to develop plants that would concentrate
the radioactives and eventually drop the background to a
reasonable level."

"Is that possible?"

"I think so."

"But there's still the plague."

"We might find a solution to that."

"At what risk to the colony?"

"Yes," she admitted, "I suppose so. It's an unknown
danger, and from what the Soviet biologists have told us,
one that we're not likely to conquer in a short while."

He felt the need to change the subject. She was obviously depressed and he could sympathize with that emotion.
"How'd your screening program go?" he asked.

"We're still finishing the reservoirs," she said, brighten-
ing. "You know we have to use a great deal of water, and
that has to be recycled before we place too large a strain
on the station resources. Nevertheless, we've managed to
find a variety of seeds, some of which may be viable. It de-
pends on the cooking heat they were exposed to. Then
we've vacuumed all of the suits and come up with some
grass seeds and things of that sort. Thank God, the white-

room discipline has declined over the years. We made one marvelous find. Someone must have had popcorn before coming up."

He felt his face flush. "Popcorn?"

"Yes, there were a number of unpopped kernels and I suspect they'll be viable." She looked at him more closely. "You're blushing," she accused.

"I guess I give myself away too easily. The kids and I had popcorn the night before—" His voice broke at the mention of his sons. He saw the look of concern on her face and turned away.

"I'm sorry," she said. "I wish there were something I could do."

"It's all right," he said, fighting for control. "It's all right; it's all right."

He felt her light touch on his back and smelled her faint feminine clean scent and for a second he could almost close his eyes and pretend.

"Please . . ." she said. Her voice was soft and concerned.

He turned and took her hand in his, marveling at how small it was in the grip of his black-bristled fingers. For a long moment they stood silent. Then he said, "Thank you. You're a very remarkable woman."

"So I've been told," she said wryly.

"I didn't mean it that way," he said.

"It's nice to have someone remember that I *am* a woman," she said. "Perhaps I've worked too hard building the image that I am not."

He looked at her, seeing the eyes filled with hurt and thinking how close two people could become with scarcely a word being passed. For a second he was tempted to touch her face, but the image of Martha intruded and he could not.

"No," he said. "That cold clinical image isn't one I could have of you. You're very much a woman."

She stood expectantly, as if waiting for something. He smiled rather sadly and said, "I'll call you as soon as we have a schedule for the visit."

Not trusting himself to speak further, he walked to the hatch. He turned at the last moment to look at her. She was standing with her eyes half-closed, a faint expression of pain on her face.

"Thanks again," he said.

She nodded but said nothing. He turned and left the laboratory, thinking that the warring emotions in him were more than he could bear. Martha so soon gone, and he was thinking these things. He grew angry with himself and tried to force the thoughts from his mind. They persisted nevertheless.

Eight

Two hours later Colonel Farrington called Longo to tell him that the station-to-station party would be leaving in hours. Longo passed the information to Georgeoff, Steinbrunner, and Janice, all of whom had been included in the party. Longo wondered at the conclusion of Steinbrunner, who was still on casual status with the station, but he assumed that Farrington had something in mind about the hybridization of the American and Soviet control systems. It would naturally require close collaboration with the senior pilots of the two stations, he thought.

He had brought along his annotated log covering the survey of materials still available at the Cape and an estimate of the probable facilities and launch equipment still available to them, should it be decided to make one final expedition below to recover as much material as possible. Inserted in the log were brief message flimsies from their sole remaining contact on the Cape. He had listened to several of the transmissions and his emotions had been touched by the forlorn tone of this lone survivor in a dead world.

She was a senior computer technician, named Karen, who had somehow managed to seclude herself in one of the air-conditioned launch buildings just before the general evacuation of the Cape. One warhead had landed northeast of the Cape, spraying the countryside with hot water so that most of the fleeing technicians had been trapped. The attack had occurred just as a storm front approached the Cape, and the greater part of the radioactive material from the blast had been swept past the station. As a result the residual activity in the area was lower and of distinctly shorter half-lives, as contrasted with the air contamination, which was already building to a long-term high that would not decay for centuries.

Karen had been invaluable to them in their survey. She assured them that she knew how to switch the Cape computer system on stand-by to the station net so that they could use the Cape facilities for many of their calculations. Not once, Longo reflected sorrowfully, had she voiced any hope of her own rescue. In the past twelve hours, their local machines had begun already to feed data to the Cape for the final trajectory calculations and for the needed reaction mass-payload data. The final data would come from the Soviets, once their engineer and Longo had estimated the probable thrust of their final configuration and the amount of useful payload that could be cannibalized from their station.

The group assembled in number 3 hub lock. In his great white suit Farrington would have been obvious even without the command antenna rigged on his helmet. He carried himself, Longo thought, with the air of a man who had held command so long that leadership had become second nature to him. The idea that there should be a contest of his authority was so completely beyond his adult experience that Longo was sure that the thought had not intruded even into his subconscious in years. He wondered what problems this would present now that there were two senior commanders in the project. For that matter, the inevitable conflict of American and Soviet authorities in all areas, including his own, was a worry that he could not avoid. He had thought to speak of it to Farrington in their last conversation, but decided against it. He was sure that Farrington recognised the problem intellectually, if not emotionally, and would discuss it with Colonel Voroshilov.

They boarded two of the cargo tugs and at Farrington's signal Longo, who was pilot of the second, opened the throttle. Georgeoff, who piloted the first, did the same within a fraction of a second and the two craft moved out, their wakes filled with the dancing pinpoints of condensing steam and other small debris that caught the bright sunlight. The first part of the flight was blind with one of Sugiyama's technicians feeding them course corrections over the radio. The vectoring thrusters on the tug underside flared again and again as they changed their thrust attack and sought a new orbit, changing their velocities and the orientation of their orbit slightly. On the last correction Longo tapped Janice on the shoulder and pointed. In the distance the bright spot that was the Soviet station stood out against the blackness like a new star, its image flickering as new surfaces caught the light. Far above, the Soviet moonship revolved around the station center, its raw beams looking like gossamer at this distance.

They drifted toward the station as in a dream ballet. Now the details of the star became visible. It looked like a monstrous spiderweb with masses of silent creatures caught in its strands. The individual masses, of course, were the personnel compartments, and the cross-members of the web were the personnel passageways that connected these capsules. The radial arms of the web were the nylon retaining cables that held the whole structure together against the outward centrifugal force of the ranked personnel capsules. The station was more versatile than their own in many ways, since it permitted easy expansion by a modular approach. Moreover, any imbalance in the web through the loss of an individual component would not be nearly as disastrous. While the web would undoubtedly be disrupted, the individual compartments would not fly off into space. Only the fragile personnel passages would be ruptured in the sudden shifting of the center of gravity. They could recover rather rapidly from such a disaster with far less personnel and equipment loss than would the American station, with its more rigid construction.

As they approached the station, patiently trimming their trajectory, Longo saw several bright points of light detach themselves from the station hub. The points of light drifted slowly toward them and he saw that they were man-shaped. Guides coming out to meet them—or guards on the alert for any suspicious move, his inner thoughts corrected him. He had heard that the Soviets' EVA equipment was clumsier than the American equipment, and this became apparent. They were large torpedo-like structures that moved rapidly toward the American bugs on tongues of bright yellow flame.

The flame color was unusual. Longo wondered what sort of fuel they were using for their propulsion—certainly not the colorless peroxide that the Americans used. The color reminded him very much of the emission spectrum of either sodium or lithium, but he discarded that idea. No one was using lithium for propulsion, not even the Americans, who had the requisite liquid fluorine technology. Even though the use of the metal would have amplified the energy yield of their present system, the American propulsion people preferred to incur the energy loss of forming hydrogen fluoride as a propulsion species rather than mess with the highly dangerous powdered lithium metal. You didn't use blowtorches in a gasoline dump, he told himself.

The torpedo shapes circled the American bugs now, warily, as though inspecting for hostile intent. Which was just what they were doing, Longo realized, and felt his face flush at the thought. That was exactly what he would have done in Voroshilov's shoes, he told himself. The mass destruction below was too recent. The possibility that a parlay party might indeed be an attack party was something you could not, as a responsible commander, ignore. As the torpedo shapes circled them Longo saw that the expanding wake from the motors was hazy, as though part of it were a white smoke. They must indeed be using a metal in their motors, he thought. Somehow they had learned to throttle a solid over a wide range and the thought excited him. If only it would be possible to jury-rig that solution for their exodus ship. Perhaps they had a store of motors sufficient for what he had in mind. He fervently hoped so, since one of the severe problems they would face would be the ferry problem—how to get the incredible masses of supplies down to the lunar surface without mishap.

The heavily suited figure in the first torpedo raised an arm and gestured. Longo increased the pressure on the tug tiller and closed with the figure as the torpedoes moved out in a wide arc. They formed an escort for Longo's bugs. The first torpedo took up the lead and the scattered formation moved in frustrating slowness toward the hub of the station, then descended slowly on a heavy air lock in the top of the hub.

Longo and Steinbrunner moored the tugs at a distance of twenty feet from the hub while the torpedo shapes circled ominously. Longo followed Farrington as he pushed from the tug and used his suit back pack thrusters to maneuver himself across the intervening distance. Behind Longo the other members of the American party followed suit. He looked behind to see them moving in scattered formation under the watchful eyes of the Soviet escort. The implications of the escort disturbed him. What if Rothgate were indeed correct in his distrust of the Russians? Treachery was no more improbable than that a supposedly intelligent and rational species should have in one spasm of madness laid waste to its world and most of the members of that species.

His feet touched the surface of the hub lock and he rebounded for an instant. His timing was off, he saw, a sure sign of mounting fatigue. The emotional drain of the past days had left him inattentive on more than one occasion, and this coupled with the natural fatigue could prove dangerous. In space it took only a small miscalculation to bring you quickly into a dangerous situation.

Farrington reached out to steady him and he saw a small worried frown through the colonel's faceplate. Did Farrington realize how much his inner reserves had been drained? Longo wondered. No matter, there was little that the colonel could do. There was no replacement for Longo. He'd have to find the strength he needed somewhere within him. There was far too much at stake. He reached out to help the next suited figure that touched down on the hub and realized with a small flush of pleasure that it was Janice. He saw her quick smile through her faceplate and the lips moving silently to say, "Thank you."

As soon as the party was complete, Farrington spoke through the command net and waited. The lock door opened ponderously. Like much of the Russian equipment, it was massive and overdesigned by American standards. A matter of different engineering philosophies,

Longo told himself, but he couldn't help smiling at what
appeared at first glance to be a more crude approach to
the sealing problem than he would have taken. Then he
realized that the flange and gasket arrangement on the
outer door could compensate for a number of seating ir-
regularities in the seal, so that any casual damage to the
sealing surfaces would not result in a disastrous depres-
surization. Indeed, the seal was so designed that the construction of the air lock door need not be to exacting
standards. Where the American design emphasized costly
precision of design, the Russian design was more rugged
with a greater safety factor. Even after this time, their
ability to machine to high tolerances was limited to a relatively small number of installations. While the workman-
ship was excellent, they had chosen to design away from
such demands, knowing that each extra high-tolerance design placed a new strain on their limited industrial facilities. He had to admire their ingenuity in solving the logistics problem of space travel.

As soon as the lock had cycled, Farrington signaled and
began to remove his helmet. Longo had a moment of
doubt, thinking how easily they might be eliminated at this
stage. Well, there was nothing they could do but trust their
hosts and hope that Voroshilov had made his own inner
ideological peace in deciding to embark upon this collaboration. After all, it was he who had suggested the joint
moon colonization venture. There were some very good
reasons for the collaboration from Voroshilov's end,
Longo suspected. The Soviet station was probably so completely devoted to the military end of their mission that
they did not have some of the nonmilitary resources of the
American station. Well, they would see soon enough.

The first thing he noticed when he removed his helmet
was the oppressiveness of the atmosphere. It was not that
it stank exactly, although there was a distinct odor that he
found unpleasant. The air tasted somewhat metallic on his
tongue, and the smell was musty, as though the air were
blowing from some dank and moldy cavern. The temperature was perhaps three or four degrees below that to which
he had become accustomed in the American station.

He removed his bulky suit, following Farrington's lead, and helped Janice from hers. "Thank you," she said. "I haven't had the practice with these things that I should have." There was a touch of the old harshness in her voice, as though she were annoyed at herself for needing help. But this wasn't a matter of a man helping a weaker woman. He would have done the same thing for any inexperienced male. He wondered why it had been so important for her to excel in this world of men.

She leaned close and said in a whisper, "I hate being ineffectual, even in someone else's area. I didn't mean to sound that way."

"I understand," he said, and realized that because of that small concession. For an instant he looked at her and saw the small frightened girl in the overpowering world of strong men looking out through the guarded eyes of the adult. Good God, he thought, has she never learned that we're all frightened and trying our best not to show it? He winked at her and was rewarded with a remarkably warm smile. She seemed to relax.

Longo looked up to find Steinbrunner eying him with a faint twisted smile on his face. Damned kraut bastard, Longo thought. What did he find so funny about all this? He stopped the thought even as it formed. He was getting tense, he realized. That was the major problem they would face in the coming weeks, this abrasive feeling of so many people packed in tightly with no place to go and an almost unbearable work load. Steinbrunner saw his sudden intense look and the smile faded, to be replaced for an instant with a look so wistful that Longo felt himself drawn to the man. It was remarkable the way the anger evaporated before this other, gentler emotion. God, he thought, what's happening to me that I can feel a killing hate and a tenderness toward the same human being within a matter of seconds?

A young woman in severe coveralls met them as they passed into the inner chambers of the hub. "Gentlemen," she said haltingly, "our Comrade Commander offers you his greetings and will welcome you in person if you will follow me." She turned stiffly and moved down a passage, holding to stanchions along the way. They followed her, feeling the centrifugal gravity build up with each yard of movement. After the initial impression, the stale odor of the air seemed to have retreated. More likely, Longo decided, he had simply become accustomed to it.

The passage bloomed ahead in a bellowslike horn over which an expanding catwalk led to another sealed door. The bulk of the module they were entering spelled its earlier origin as one of the Soviet massive capsules with which they had initially established their five-man space laboratories. Unlike the Americans, they continued to use shelf hardware if it could be adapted rather than commit large sums of money to the development of completely new units. The Salyut IV capsule had proved admirably suited to its earlier mission and now functioned well as a part of the larger station module. He supposed the capsules still had their reentry ablation shields and retro rocket equipment. It would be typical of the Soviet approach to retain such equipment against the need of evacuating the station. Because of several disasters in the past, they had become more sensitized to safety-inspired redundancy in their designs than had the Americans.

They descended through four levels of the capsule and found themselves on a deck from which radiated six passages. The girl conducted them along one of these and through a flimsier passageway that was obviously one of the connecting passages from one capsule module to another. Finally they entered the second capsule, and moments later they were on the counterpart of their own commo bridge. This enclosure was about twice the size of their own, with the walls covered with communication and radar equipment. The overall effect was of sterile efficiency with none of the colorfulness and, the odd comparison came to Longo, coziness of the American station. It was strictly a no-nonsense room that presented an odd massiveness in its appearance. Longo felt that the place was more appropriate to a fire-control center in a modern battleship than to a space station.

Voroshilov had been waiting behind a metallic desk for

their appearance. He now rose and crossed the deck to meet them. He seemed somewhat less squat and massive than he had appeared on Sugiyama's monitoring screens, but there was a bull strength to the figure that found its echoes in the massive chords of his neck and the thick boniness of his wrists. He had quite the largest wrists in proportion to his body that Longo had ever seen. His face was markedly Oriental, with a strange delicacy to the otherwise hard lips. He could as easily have been a poet as a demonic murderer with that face, Longo thought. It was a disturbing hybrid of the sensual, the sensitive, and the violent.

"My welcome to our People's Station," Voroshilov said, extending his hand to Farrington. "I am sorry I wasn't on hand to meet you." The fingers too were thick, but tapered rapidly to almost feminine tips with full flushed nails. Behind the colonel a taller, darker man with dusky blond hair streaked with grey smiled and waited.

Farrington grasped Voroshilov's hand. "Thank you for inviting us," Farrington said. "Don't apologize. In a situation such as we are facing, there's little time left for elaborate courtesies. We have a great deal to do."

"I appreciate your attitude," Voroshilov said. "Let us then get to business immediately. You have met my Major Bucholtz?"

"Yes," Farrington nodded, motioning Longo abreast of him. "On my last visit. Captain Longo, my engineering officer."

"Major Bucholtz," Voroshilov said. Bucholtz saluted stiffly. "The major is my second here and, of course, our engineering officer as well."

"I am pleased to meet you, Captain," Bucholtz said. His face was reserved and controlled but there was a hint of sardonic humor in his eyes. "We will, I think, get to know each other very well in the coming days."

Longo nodded and waited. Voroshilov was introduced to the rest of the party. He favored Janice with an almost courtly half bow. "Yes," Voroshilov said. "We have watched your work with great approbation, Dr. Svoboda.

My own staff does not include anyone so talented as you,
but we may be able to offer you some adequate support in
your part of the mission."

He in turn introduced a woman in her late thirties, a
Comrade Captain Alexandra, who was in charge of life-
support systems under Bucholtz and who commanded the
small team of biologists that monitored the early data
from their probe program. "Now," Voroshilov said,
"please come with me to our briefing room, where I will
have one of my engineering officers describe the arrangement of our orbital station." Voroshilov smiled at the expression on Farrington's face. "Please, Colonel, it is now
time we forget our past rules and become perfectly open
with each other. There can be no such thing as military secrecy among us now. Too much is at stake."

"Of course," Farrington agreed. "I was concerned that
this step might be a difficult one for both of us."

"No, no," said Voroshilov. "I am senior commander
now—alas, probably supreme commander of all our
forces. This is my decision and I ask that you tell me if
there is any problem due to reticence of my people. This is
my order to them and they have all been impressed with
the need of full cooperation."

They followed Voroshilov to the briefing room where a
Comrade Sonya, whose military rank Longo could not dis-
cern, gave them a short thorough briefing on the general
plan of the Soviet station. There were copies of deck plans
on flimsy duplicating paper and a number of hastily prepared descriptions in oddly phrased English.

"We will have compiled for you a complete inventory of
supplies and equipment as well as general facilities in another twenty-four hours," Voroshilov declared.

"I believe that our own survey will be complete within
that period," Farrington told him. "There remains a second survey of standby facilities and material at our launch
station in Florida. We may wish to consider salvaging
some of this."

Voroshilov frowned. "This would be a most serious and
dangerous undertaking. I am not so sure that it would be
wise. In any case, our own facilities no long exist. There is

one booster intact at our launch station in Kapustin Yar but our boosters are liquid, as you know, and I fear that it may no longer be trustworthy. In any event its upper-stage cargo holds have not yet been loaded."

"Very well," Farrington said slowly. "Then we may assume that only those Orbiter assemblies presently on pad at Cape Kennedy and fully loaded are of interest to us. We have some data on these, which Captain Longo can turn over to you."

The conference continued in this matter for half an hour, when a young enlisted man appeared with a tray holding a steaming metal pot of hot tea and a number of plastic cups. They broke into individual groups then to continue their discussions. "I will instruct Comrade Alexandra to take your Lieutenant Steinbrunner to meet our chief of pilots," Voroshilov said, hesitating on the last phrase. "He has been detained on other duties until now."

Longo and Georgeoff, with Steinbrunner trailing them, followed Bucholtz from the briefing room and along a dimly lighted passageway to his quarters where other members of his staff were assembled. Farrington remained behind with Voroshilov, while Janice Svoboda and Comrade Captain Alexandra made their way through passages to an adjoining capsule where much of the probe biological work was done.

When the groups had left and they were alone, Voroshilov sighed, "Well, my Colonel, we are at least into it and, pray God, we may work with harmony so that we will not repeat the madness of the past week."

"My people will give you every cooperation they can," Farrington assured him.

"Come to my quarters and let us talk," Voroshilov said, rising. "I have some excellent Spanish sherry, a great indulgence of mine from my days in that bright land." His face clouded. "It is so hard to believe that it too is gone. I loved that rich country almost as much as my own homeland."

Farrington nodded, not trusting himself to speak. They moved along a deserted passage. Voroshilov stepped aside to offer Farrington entrance to a small complex of two rooms. The suite was somewhat larger than Farrington's in the American station, but it was Spartan in its simplicity. At Voroshilov's invitation he sank to an outstretched bunk. The Russian pulled a table from hidden fastenings in the wall. A stool swiveled from under the table to a comfortable position. Then he procured a bottle wrapped in a loose burlap sacking from a wall locker, with two glasses. As soon as he had poured the sherry, he raised his glass in a silent toast. Farrington followed suit.

"To success, and to the solution of our greatest and most pressing problem."

"The problem that I'm sure has concerned you as much as myself," Farrington said, nodding.

"It is true," Voroshilov said sadly, licking the sherry from his lips. "It is no discourtesy intended, my Colonel, when I confide in you that my people do not trust you."

Farrington laughed ironically. "Nor do mine trust yours," he said. "I guess it's better to state it as bluntly as that."

"The time for the niceties of the politician is over," Voroshilov agreed. "They have had their day and we are the worst for it."

Voroshilov reached behind him to procure a thick folder from a wall file. This he placed on the table precisely in front of him, absently scrubbing at the ring left by his glass. "I know a great deal about you, Colonel," he remarked.

"And I about you," Farrington said. "Your folder in my quarters is as thick, perhaps thicker."

"Then it remains for me to decide if you are indeed the man I have found in here," Voroshilov said, tapping the folder. "It tells me much that I would want to know and a great deal that I do not wish to know. Nowhere does it tell me the most important things upon which I must base eventually a most difficult decision."

"You are anticipating me," Farrington said. "I had not intended to bring up that problem at this time."

"No, no," Voroshilov said, gesturing. "It is our most basic organization problem and one which we must face as soon as possible and solve. This does not mean that the solution may be freely transmitted to our subordinates without a great deal of emotional preparation, but we must think in these terms, Colonel."

"I wonder if it may not be simpler to talk of a joint command."

Voroshilov laughed bitterly. "At another time, what I say would be considered politically dangerous, but I tell you that government by committee does not function. Certainly military command does not. We have learned bitter lessons in experimenting in that direction."

"It was a thought," Farrington said. "I confess that I didn't believe in it, but we at least had to voice it. I agree. With so much depending on a close joint effort, there must be a single command."

"And it is for us to say who it will be," Voroshilov said, pouring more sherry. "Ah," he said sadly, "one can taste the sweetness of the sun on the grapes of that far-off land. It is a treasure, this bottle, and when it is gone there will not be another. So much lost, so many small and valuable things."

"So very much lost," Farrington agreed, remembering other lost things. Over Voroshilov's shoulder, in the open compartment from which he had procured the file, Farrington saw a sepia photo taped to the back wall. It was partly hidden by several logbooks but he could see that it was of Voroshilov—somewhat younger, somewhat less beefy, with a smiling lean woman and two children.

"So much lost," he repeated solemnly, "and we both must be assured that nothing further is lost." ·

Voroshilov nodded and sighed deeply. For a long moment they sat silent, sipping the rich, fruity sherry, and each contemplating his own private thoughts. Farrington, who had lived his life in the loneliness of command, found himself drawn as by an invisible bond to this other man. Odd, he thought, that they should be so much alike. Yet not so odd, for a certain type of personality rose to command positions, regardless of country. It was a personality compounded of ego, self-control, an eye for infinite detail, and—if the man was a good commander—a carefully preserved integrity and compassion. One could not command without compassion. Failing this, one became the most brittle of martinets.

He raised his glass once more and the two men toasted each other silently. But in the silence, Farrington thought, there was a wealth of communication.

Nine ━━━━━━━━━━━━━━➤

Janice Svoboda found some difficulty at first in communicating with Comrade Alexandra. Janice had not spoken Russian in years and her accent was strongly larded with a Midwestern flavor, while Comrade Alexandra who had grown up in the metropolitan area of Moscow, spoke with a peculiar crispness and speed that was quite foreign to Janice. After ten minutes of careful conversation, however, Janice began to catch several of the distinctive regional pronunciations that had at first given her difficulty.

They passed through the lower decks of the command capsule and moved along connecting passages to an adjacent capsule. From there they progressed to a third before they finally ascended one deck to the large rather drab workroom where Alexandra was quartered and worked. While she was primarily concerned with the programming and launch of the planetary probes and most recently the Mars probe program, Alexandra explained, she worked closely with the station biologists, since a major part of the program was the mapping of any planetary biological resources.

It was this approach in the Soviet probe program that particularly fascinated Janice. The American program had been largely geology and planetary physics oriented. Implicit within that program had been the assumption that the planet was dead and of little other than scientific interest. The Russians, on the other hand, had taken an almost mystical approach to exploration, stressing the life sciences. As they walked to the place where they were to meet the personnel of the probe program, Alexandra talked at length about their continuing hope of finding some evidence of life with their planetary probes, or at least the conditions for life.

This seemed to Janice to be at odds with the purely de-

terministic bent of a Marxist state, but she realized suddenly that the existence of life independently on another
planet would fit very well into the Marxist lexicon. After
all, determinism implied the implacable inevitability of
historical processes, and by extension all natural processes. To find life arising independently on another body
would imply that life was inevitable and from this that the
development of life, in all of its ramifications, was inevitable and predetermined by the natural biological laws that
function alike on Earth and Mars. She ventured some such
remark to Alexandra as they entered the final capsule and
proceeded to the workroom. In spite of her halting Russian, Alexandra understood the subtle point, and her face
lighted with enthusiasm. She clearly approved of the for-
mulation and Janice was, in spite of herself, pleased that
she had fathomed a basic motivation in their work.

There were three men and another woman waiting for
them. The eldest of the men, whom Alexandra introduced
as Dr. Konyev, was in his late fifties with aristocratic thin
cheekbones and intense eyes. Konyev assumed control of
the meeting, introducing his colleagues in terse, clipped
English. There was Koenig, a molecular biologist—he was
the shortest of the group, with round youthful features and
straw-blond hair—and Yeremenkov, an analytical chemist
with a soft look and a distinct Asiatic eyefold. The woman,
whose name was Chernevsky, seemed withdrawn and in-
ward-directed throughout the meeting. She was a planetary
ecologist, which surprised Janice and, in view of their present problems, delighted her. Konyev rather dryly agreed.

"You understand," he said, "that I am not completely
in agreement with this decision. Nevertheless, the
Comrade Commander has committed us to the project and
we will expend our best efforts to work with you."

"Thank you," said Janice, picking her words carefully.
Konyev was a proud man, she saw, of the sort who guarded his position and prestige carefully. She would have to
walk a tightrope with him or risk the complications of a
personality clash. "I must confess that I have definite res-
ervations myself. Nevertheless, we must consider how we

can complement each other's efforts in establishing a viable colony."

"You are very young to have such a reputation," Konyev remarked.

Janice colored. She had so long ago ceased to apply that adjective to herself that to be called "young" again was disconcerting. "I hope you will find it deserved," she said modestly, and was rewarded with a somewhat frosty smile. Well, she thought, grit your teeth and get on with it.

Koenig described the results of their screening program, which they had started shortly after Janice's conversation with them. It had been disappointing, although Koenig thought they did have at least one strain of rye that might germinate. The most encouraging part of this report was quite unexpected. Voroshilov was accustomed to breakfasting on eggs, an unusual habit for a middle European, and these were brought up periodically in the station supplies. He insisted on fertile eggs, and they now had about ten such eggs incubating. Assuming that they might experience a 20 percent sterility, that meant at least eight chicks. It was a bonanza she had not expected. She had, of course, considered the problem of tailoring subsequent generations from the few laboratory animals aboard the American station, but to have chickens to add to the larder would be an unexpected bonanza.

"With these as a base stock," she said excitedly, "we can do some remarkable things to supplement our animal protein supply in three or four generations."

"So soon?" Comrade Chernevsky asked, her eyes mirroring doubt. Janice explained some of the techniques and equipment available to her.

"But this is better than I dared hope," Koenig exclaimed. "You have complete genetic tailoring facilities. This makes our task much simpler."

"I confess that I do not understand the full implications of this or of your enthusiasm," Konyev said coldly. "I presume, Comrade Koenig, that you will brief me after this meeting? For the moment I will accept your assessment of our good fortune."

They discussed various ways in which they might collaborate, and slowly Janice brought Konyev to an agreement that they would exchange biological materials. She would have preferred to have all of the fertile eggs for her laboratory, but she detected a heavy undercurrent of suspicion from Konyev and carefully maneuvered to avoid an overt statement of that suspicion. Koenig was delighted with the facilities she described and offered to come to her laboratory to work with her.

"This we will have to discuss among ourselves for a later decision," Konyev interrupted. Janice nodded reluctantly. "Nevertheless," she said, "we offer our full facilities to your personnel. We need every talent available to us if we are to survive."

"I am well aware of that," Konyev said, "and I have my instructions from Comrade Voroshilov." He pursed his lips. "Subject to my interpretation and final approval," he added primly.

The conversation shifted to a discussion of probe data from the moon and how they might best acquire last-minute data on the landing place finally selected. The principle problem was to identify those areas rich in minerals with water of crystallization, since water was a prime necessity. Comrade Alexandra reviewed this operation and suggested several launch missions that they might undertake in the next two days.

"Of course," she said in halting English, "it is awkward because our vehicles are designed for planet-probing."

"This would mean a redesign of the retrorockets," said Yeremenkov in a silky-soft voice.

"Our propulsion team can tell us if this is indeed possible," Alexandra said. "I will convey this information immediately."

"Please do so," Konyev ordered. Alexandra looked startled, then excused herself.

"We cannot afford the luxury of delay or extended conversation," Konyev explained, as Janice raised her eyebrows. "Our people understand the nature of such discipline."

"If the Comrade Academician permits," Koenig said

slowly, "I would like in the remaining time to acquaint Dr. Svoboda with some of the results of the planetary probes."

"I am not in agreement with your ideas," Konyev said, "but we have exhausted the main subject of this first contact. If you will excuse me, I will report to the Comrade Commander." He rose, as did the others, and walked from the room without further comment.

"A most formidable man," said Koenig nervously. "Still, he is our strength in this great challenge."

"Of course," Janice agreed, wondering at the statement.

Comrade Chernevsky cleared her throat nervously and looked embarrassed. Koenig turned silent eyes to Yeremenkov, whose round Asiatic features betrayed no clue to his thoughts. Finally Koenig said, "We are interested in your view of this project."

"My view?" Janice asked. "I don't understand."

"Do you believe that it is valid in the long run? Can we truly preserve our species while holding to a technological level that will allow us to return?"

"I too have had my doubts," Janice said slowly, "but I haven't voiced them."

"Yet the doubts persist," said Koenig. "We have discussed them among ourselves and we are concerned that we may be pressing ourselves into a strait-jacket, that all of our energies will be expended in a closed-cycle survival."

"Perhaps we are not daring enough in our thoughts," Yeremenkov ventured. "Until your arrival we merely speculated on an alternative. Now it may seem possible."

"Your unexpected genetic tailoring facilities are a source of great encouragement," Koenig observed.

Janice laughed wryly. "I did not dare hope that someone else would think in these terms."

"Yet, such unthinkable things must be thought," said Koenig. "Moreover, we have information that you do not and that information makes it more than possible that the alternative we discuss is more attractive than the cold future that awaits us on the moon."

"We have barely an hour to talk," Janice said, consulting her watch.

"It is more than enough," Koenig said, producing a folder. "I have assembled all the information to take with you. For the moment, let me tell you about a remarkable series of observations that will excite you as it has us."

Longo, Georgeoff, and Steinbrunner had proceeded with Major Bucholtz to their meeting with the Soviet propulsion group. Longo had found Bucholtz at first taciturn and wary, but the excitement of seeing some of the Soviet hardware had brought forth Longo's natural ebullience and soon Bucholtz was responding in appreciation. Nothing pleases an engineer more than to have his designs admired by a competitor. Bucholtz had soon shaken off his earlier reserve and was responding with the same enthusiasm he saw in Longo. In the same manner, Georgeoff had quickly forgotten their late rivalry and was deep in a discussion of the intricate thrust vectoring controls of the Soviet main moonship engines with Bucholtz's second engineer, a surprisingly young esthetic-looking man whom he addressed as Comrade Gregor.

Steinbrunner remained apart from the group, his dark eyes taking in all of the details of the propulsion system as Bucholtz and Gregor alternated in their expositions. He frowned slightly as Longo unrolled prints of their own system and began to show Bucholtz whereby they might mate the two systems in one rather clumsy-looking unit for maximum use of their thrust capabilities. Longo looked up once at Steinbrunner, and was rewarded with a remarkably opaque expression that seemed to carry hints of disapproval. To that moment Longo had forgotten Steinbrunner's early history. He wondered as he talked if the man might harbor the same kind of unreasoning hatred for the Soviets that Rothgate had shown so violently on occasion. No, he decided, Steinbrunner was much too cold and phlegmatic a man to nourish that kind of intensity. What had happened to the man in the past, Longo wondered, to have carried him so far into this cold shell of almost inhuman reserve?

Comrade Gregor, at Georgeoff's prompting, began a discussion of the propulsion devices that had powered their EVA vehicles. The motors were, surprisingly, neither solid nor liquid, but rather hybrid propulsion units, using a liquid oxidizer and a solid fuel. The liquid oxidzer in this case was liquid oxygen and the system could be throttled over a wide range, far wider than was possible with an ordinary liquid system, without any danger of combustion instability. The fuel system of the hybrid itself was a remarkable achievement.

In the past the Americans had used small hybrid systems for thrust vectoring and orbital correction. These had generally been simple tubes of polymethylmethacrylate—Plexiglas—down which an oxidizer such as liquid oxygen had been injected. The Plexiglas tubes served themselves both as the combustion pressure chamber and fuel. Frequently the tubes had been fabricated to include finely divided aluminum that increased the enthalpy change of the oxidizer-fuel system, but the nature of the combustion processes in a hybrid had severely limited the amount of metal the fuel tube could contain.

Unlike a solid propellant system in which heat-yielding thermal processes in the solid itself gassified the fuel and drove the reaction, the hybrid fuel normally depended on heat transferred from the flame above the fuel surface. Since gases were being constantly evolved from the fuel surface, the heat transfer had to operate against this "blowing," and the resulting mass injection from the fuel was fairly low. While solid propellants could be fabricated to yield burning rates well above an inch a second and in some special instances up to ten inches a second, a hybrid fuel system rarely ablated—"burned" here was not a proper term—at rates faster than 0.05 inches per second.

The Soviet fuel system had solved this in a remarkably direct manner. The fuel was basically a polybutadiene rubber matrix, enclosing particles of elemental lithium. Heat reaching the surface from the flame established at the fuel gas-oxygen interphase initiated a solid phase reaction between the lithium and the rubber. The result of this reaction was a significant amount of drive heat plus the reaction products: lithium hydride, lithium carbide, and elemental hydrogen, all of them excellent fuels. The Soviet processing technique had managed to encase each lithium particle in a pocket of polybutadiene rubber that effectively insulated the particle and moderated the disadvantageously low melting point of the metal. There was some softening of the surface on shutdown, Gregor said, as the thermal profile established during the motor operation diffused through the fuel tube, but they had moderated this effect to a manageable degree by their insulation techniques.

"This is a marvelous basic system," Georgeoff exclaimed.

"Doesn't the fuel reaction continue once it's initiated?" Longo asked uncertainly.

"It would, of course," Gregor explained haltingly, "if we did not modify the fuel system to dilute the heat content below the activation energy of the fuel phase reaction."

Georgeoff shook his head. "But then you sacrifice energy."

"Not at all," Bucholtz interjected proudly. "We use lithium hydride, one of the 'ashes' of the reaction, and this itself is an excellent fuel."

"The overall fuel reaction isn't very efficient, however," Longo pointed out. "I'm no thermochemist, of course, but I do know that your combustion products are solid lithium oxide among others and this is a low-energy way to use the metal."

Bucholtz shrugged. "We have had to sacrifice energy for convenience. Our liquid oxidizer technology has been built largely around liquid oxygen and our logistics have dictated the oxidizer-fuel combination."

"You know," Georgeoff said excitedly, "we will need some versatile propulsion systems for ferrying and maneuvering when we achieve circumlunar orbit. How many of these units do you have?"

"Well over five hundred fuel cores in the warehouse," Bucholtz replied, "with propulsion hardware for about fifty flyable units. But I don't understand. The acceleration of the system is relatively low."

"I think it can be upgraded," Georgeoff said. "You

have variable throat nozzles so that we can increase the mass flow from the motor without redesign. With our liquid oxygen-fluorine combination, FLOX, we can upgrade the performance of the units remarkably. Instead of forming low-yield lithium oxide, now your combustion product would be high-heat-yield lithium fluoride. The oxygen-fluorine balance could be adjusted, of course, since our basic stores are pure fluorine for use with liquid hydrogen in our F-5 motors."

"Yes, yes!" Gregor exclaimed. "It is daring, but I think it may be done. We must, of course, protect the nozzle throats from such a violent exhaust composition, but we have alternate inserts that can stand up, I think."

"First we should run some computer calculations of optimum mixtures," Longo said, "and we need a prediction of the thrust level we may achieve with the new combination. Then a few test firings."

Georgeoff laughed. "You realize," he pointed out, "that we are rather casually trying a combination that on Earth would be the subject of a year-long development program."

"Of course," Bucholtz said, shrugging his shoulders expressively. "Only we do not have such luxurious time leads and we must sacrifice the optimum design that we would try to achieve in that year."

"By bailing wire and Scotch tape," Longo laughed.

"I beg your pardon?" asked Bucholtz, his voice puzzled.

"An American expression," Longo explained, feeling suddenly stimulated. "By the shakiest of jury-rigging we will get to the moon."

"Of course," Gregor said seriously. "We must."

They turned to the major thrust structure of the combined ships, and Steinbrunner entered the conversation. He had an excellent knowledge of basic propulsion frame engineering, and offered several telling suggestions on engine mounting and control. Excitement activated his features for the first time as he dealt with the difficult technical problems before them. He feels more for machines than he does for people, Longo thought. Well, he had met people like that before. With his own natural emotionality, he did not understand them, but he could feel the aura of excitement emanating from Steinbrunner as he probed more deeply into the control and servotechniques that the Soviets had designed for their ship.

They were so deeply involved in the discussion that none of them noticed when another man entered and stood silently, listening to their discussions. Bucholtz was the first to become aware of him. "Gentlemen," he said, straightening up, "this is our chief pilot, Comrade Captain Rudenko."

Rudenko was a tall, muscular man in his thirties with wide, almost innocent-looking blue eyes, sandy hair, and remarkably even features that might well have belonged to an actor. He smiled almost boyishly and acknowledged the introduction. In the next instant the smile seemed to wipe itself from his face as if by magic, and a distant cold look invaded his eyes.

Steinbrunner had been bent over the table, his two hands outspread to prevent the prints before him from rolling up. When Rudenko had entered, he had ignored him, indeed had probably not even been aware of him. Now he straightened slowly as Bucholtz spoke. The prints before him, freed of his restraining hand, snapped together with an unnaturally loud slithering sound. His eyes met Rudenko's. The silence of the room suddenly became oppressive. The others sensed the abrupt tension and Bucholtz looked at Longo questioningly.

"Do you know each other?" Longo asked.

"Yes, yes, of course," Rudenko said.

"Yes, Rudy and I met long ago," Steinbrunner confirmed. "Long ago in Berlin."

"It's good to see you again," Rudenko said uncertainly.

"And you too," Steinbrunner replied darkly. "Particularly since I had heard that you were dead."

Rudenko laughed nervously. "It takes a great deal to kill me, I think."

"So it seems," Steinbrunner replied.

"I'm sure we can find time for you two to renew acquaintances," Bucholtz said nervously, eying the cold Rudenko. "For the moment we still have a great deal of work to do."

"Of course," Rudenko said. "I am at your disposal."

Steinbrunner nodded silently. He looks as if he could kill the man, Longo thought. No, it's more than that. The emotions that had flickered across the normally reserved Steinbrunner's face were the oddest combination Longo had ever seen. Certainly shock, and anger, but something else, something softer, moderating the violence of his sudden recognition.

"Would you join us?" Georgeoff said and Rudenko advanced. He moved past Steinbrunner, carefully avoiding touching the man. The tension that filled the room was almost tangible.

Some three hours later the American party took leave of their hosts and proceeded through the hub to the spot where the two EVA tugs were moored. Longo felt curiously elated. His admiration for the brute engineering approach of the Soviets was augmented by his realization that the more subtle American approach would complement their technology in unexpected fashions. The final moonship would be a horror to an Earth-based engineer, if one still existed, but the beast would fly and it would accomplish their mission. The configuration they had agreed upon was a compromise, ungainly and hardly the image of the streamlined ships of his youthful imagination, but then one did not have to worry about streamlining in space. The only requirement was that the ship frame be able to transmit the thrust of the motors and that the motors themselves be aligned to give balanced thrust through the ship's center of gravity.

Longo strapped himself into the tug behind the one piloted by Steinbrunner. Far above them the ungainly shape of the Russian moonship flickered as its slowly spinning members caught the light momentarily and reflected it back like facets of a giant diamond. Longo looked up and saw small dots that resolved themselves into the figures of suited men. Two groups were towing objects that he decided must be small thrust units. They were already about it, he saw with approval. Fitting the ship with thrusters to modify its orbit. That was the first task he must apply himself to, so that the two ships could be brought close enough for the engineering crews to work on them. The logistics of the collaboration would be impossibly demanding in the next week, but he and Bucholtz had already arrived at a workable compromise for the two ship structures. Fortunately, both had been somewhat circumscribed in their design by the MilLimS agreements, so the crossbreeding of the two systems was not as formidable as it had first appeared.

As Longo took the tiller, Farrington leaned back behind him in an attitude of fatigue. Longo was glad that he did not have the man's responsibility. Farrington was in the unenviable position of having to make innumerable critical decisions, any one of which might compromise the whole project. Someone had to do this, but the strain would tell on even a strong man, Longo knew.

Janice strapped in next to him. The first gentle acceleration pressed him back as he activated the motors. He was conscious of Georgeoff and the others behind him in Steinbrunner's bug. Janice sat staring distantly into space. Once he touched her on the shoulder and she turned to smile at him. Her eyes seemed focused miles away and there was an atmosphere of excitement about her that puzzled him. What had happened on the Soviet station to stimulate her so, he wondered?

As the EVA bug accelerated and the Soviet station receded, he watched as Steinbrunner's bug drew abreast of his. The man's free hand clutched at the tiller before him, grasping it rigidly. Longo wondered if he should discuss the incident in the propulsion lab with Farrington. He was reluctant to do so, it smacked of tale-carrying. However, he decided, it was important in some obscure fashion and he supposed Farrington should know. He was thinking in this manner when Steinbrunner turned in his place and stared across the distance at Longo.

The others could not see through his faceplate because of the side reflections but Longo saw the man's eyes, pleading with him. He wanted Longo to keep still about the incident, Longo realized. What had happened between those two so many years ago in Berlin, Longo wondered, to inspire such a continuing hatred?

All at once Longo realized that the reflections on Steinbrunner's faceplate were not playing tricks. The faint gleam of light that he had mistaken for a reflection from the receding station was not on the exterior of the suit. The reflection proceeded from inside the suit. From small points around the silent German's eyes.

Steinbrunner, Longo saw with wonder and concern, was weeping. Not from sorrow, for his face was twisted into a mask of anger. He was, Longo thought, weeping from sheer frustrated rage.

Ten ➤━━━━━━━━━━━━━━━━━━━➤

The collaboration began smoothly enough, surprisingly smoothly in Longo's view. He had expected a great deal of carping from the propulsion and spaceframe people over the somewhat clumsy compromises he had accepted, but all of them seemed to perceive the necessity of these compromises to build a single flyable unit. The technical problems at first glance seemed remarkably simple, a problem of jury-rigging rather than any need for innovative solutions. Granted the final vehicle would be anything but aesthetic. It would certainly not make the most efficient use of the propulsion equipment available to them.

"The bird will fly," Georgeoff assured him, "and that's all that's important—that and reaching escape velocity."

"Will our thrust-mass ratio give us the velocity we need?" Longo demanded.

"That's still debatable," answered Georgeoff. "Remember, we plan to take as many of the resources of each station as possible, which wasn't a part of the original plan. The model studies have given us several alternate solutions, but we haven't translated these into specific requirements yet."

"I'd suggest we compile an A, B and C list of the escape packages we want," said Longo. "The first list is obviously composed of the necessities, including the ship and fuel load. The B package will contain those items for which we will, if necessary, make certain sacrifices. The C list will have to consist of the items we can do without and may conveniently abandon. In that way, when the final printouts become available, we'll have a list of modules that we can take or abandon to fit the escape velocity solution."

"That presents some personal problems," Georgeoff pointed out. "A lot of people will be unhappy at having their special pet pieces on the C or even the B list."

"I've thought of that," Longo said. "I've asked the colonel to set up a joint review team of our people and the Soviets. They'll have to pass on the priority of each module as well as any internal ranking."

"I'm glad I'm not a part of that," Georgeoff said wryly.

Longo laughed. "I hate to tell you," he said, "but you are."

Georgeoff made a face. Thank God, we can begin to laugh again, Longo thought. Now that something positive is happening, you can see the optimism growing again.

"We'll need some first approximations for planning," said Georgeoff. "Can we divert the Cape machines for about a half-hour run?"

"I'll see," Longo promised him. "How soon do you need it?"

"In about two hours," Georgeoff replied. Longo left him, thinking that it felt good to be doing something. Exciting, in fact, although they were literally betting all of their lives, and the future of the race, on a single roll of the dice. They must be sure of their calculations, for once the stations had been cannibalized and the complete ship assembled, they could not waste further time on more elaborate calculations or on last-minute modifications. They either had the requisite total impulse to achieve escape velocity with their mass, or they were marooned forever. The problem was that they had to make so many assumptions about thrust efficiency, and their safety factor was alarmingly low. The failure of one motor to reach full thrust would surely doom the project.

In the passage to the commo bridge he met Janice, who said, "Quint, could you help me?"

"If I can," he said. He wondered at the almost furtive look in her eyes.

"I'd like to get some modifications programmed for the on-board machine. DNA structure alterations. The basic program won't handle them but I've already written out the modifications." She showed him a sheaf of programming notes.

"Is it really necessary?" he asked. "Both the Cape and the on-board machines are pretty well tied up in the propulsion and spaceframe designs."

"They're very important," she said. "I wouldn't ask if I didn't think they were terribly important."

"Can you tell me what they are?"

"I'd rather not just yet," she answered. "I discussed them with several of the Soviet group and we feel they are quite necessary. Can you trust me with a blank check?"

"I'll try to help. Of course, Lieutenant Rodrigues has final say-so on budgeting of computer time."

"Thank you," she said. "May I go along with you?"

"Of course," he answered, rather pleased that she had asked.

As they moved down the passageway, he was conscious of the faint hint of perspiration odor about her body. For an instant a distant image flickered in his mind. He thrust it aside, feeling disloyal, then angry at himself. Life went on and men had lost their women before, he told himself. Martha would always occupy a special part of his memory and that memory would be something deep and private, holding all the emotions of their long nights and days together, the special joy of their children. But a man had to continue living. Nevertheless, he felt a sudden surge of anger at Janice for bringing him to these thoughts. This he quickly suppressed, and wondered at the emotion. Janice was a fine woman, he thought, unnaturally pressed into a professional strait-jacket that had prevented her too many times from being the rich human being that he knew her to be.

A part of him continued to taunt him. There was a time when you didn't care for the woman, when you even actively disliked her. Now you romanticize her because she's patted you on the head. You wag your tail like a puppy. Surely, a man's emotions are more than the effusions of his gonads?

"Is something wrong?" he heard her ask. She had

glanced behind her as they proceeded up the passage and had seen the silent war written on his face.

"Nothing," he reassured her quickly. "Nothing, really. I suppose we all have these moments."

"At least you have a personal investment in all that's happening," she said sadly.

"Don't you?" he asked.

"Yes, I suppose so," she said, "but not in the same way." Her eyes were suddenly lidded and secretive. He wondered what silent thoughts churned behind those impassive eyes. Suddenly, insanely, he wanted to make love to her, and he felt the physical evidence of that desire growing. He felt his face coloring, and he gestured for her to continue. Inwardly, watching her slight figure move down the passage, he raged at himself.

Rodrigues was seated at a small printout console in the far end of the computer station. His olive features were hidden as he stared into the printout viewer, but Longo recognized him by the bright orange coveralls that he favored. He looked up as they approached and gestured for them to be silent. Then he turned to the transmitter before him and said softly, "The auxiliary corps are in, Karen."

The speaker before him crackled and through heavy static a female voice said thinly, "I thought I could make the switchover."

"Did you have to leave the bunker?" Rodrigues asked softly.

"It was the only way," the woman said. "Don't worry, I wore a white suit."

"I wish you hadn't, damn it," he said.

Karen sounded tired and very distant. "It was the only way, and you need the capacity."

"It was very dangerous," Rodrigues persisted.

A faint laugh echoed through the room. "Danger doesn't have too much meaning, does it?"

"How are you holding up?" Rodrigues asked.

"Tired, of course," the woman's voice responded. "But I'm tired quite a bit lately. Don't worry. I can keep the remotes going for you."

"Thank you," Rodrigues said quietly. "Good night."

"Good night, Julio," the voice came back faintly. She used the correct pronunciation, Longo noticed. The word "Hulio" sounded like a caress from the scratchy speaker. Rodrigues turned to him, his face composed and controlled.

"More of your stuff, Longo?" he asked. "You've got us almost at capacity now."

"It's necessary," Longo said, spreading out a folder before him. "What's the problem?"

"It's Karen, the girl down at the Cape," Rodrigues said.

"How's the poor thing holding up?" Janice said.

"That's just it," Rodrigues said. "She's showing signs of fatigue and possibly something more."

"Radiation?" Longo asked.

"That and something else," Rodrigues said. He paused and then added, "It seems she's also pregnant. We just found that out last shift."

"How far along?" Janice asked.

"Seven, maybe eight. It's causing her a great deal of fatigue." Rodrigues shook his head. "God, and she never once whimpers. You'd think she'd at least wonder if there was a chance of rescue."

"No, no," Janice said. "She knows there's little hope for her."

"And the baby?" Rodrigues asked no one in particular.

"No hope," Longo said dully.

"There would be if she were here," Janice said. "We could probably detoxify it even if we couldn't save her."

"But she's not," Rodrigues said flatly, and turned to the folder. "There's a whole bank of stand-by cores in the building a mile from Karen," he went on. "I wish we could switch them in."

"Can she do it?" Longo asked.

"Of course not," Rodrigues snapped. "What can you expect from a lone girl? She's done remarkable things already."

"I'm sorry. I didn't mean to sound inhuman," said Longo.

Rodrigues tried to laugh. "It's my place to apologize," he said. "You wouldn't know. It's just that I have had to live with this, knowing how lost she is, seeing how brave she is. A remarkable girl." He shook off the mood and went on, "Yes, I think we can give you the approximation you want in three hours. Will that be sufficient?"

"It will have to be," Longo said. "Dr. Svoboda would like you to handle an on-board reprogramming if you can."

Rodrigues now seemed subdued. "I will do it myself, Doctor."

"You look awfully tired yourself," said Janice.

"There's time enough to rest later. You don't look as if you've had too much sleep yourself."

They talked for some minutes while Longo stood apart, thinking of the lonely girl somewhere down below. He wondered what she looked like. Blond? Brunette? Pretty or plain? It mattered little. He wondered if he would have the courage she had shown, or would he simply open the door and walk out into the deadly night? It was something he would never know, but his quiet admiration went out to her. Humans, he thought, were a remarkable breed.

When Janice had finished her business with Rodrigues, he asked, "How about a cup of coffee?"

"Not that stuff in the mess," she said. "Come back to the lab and I'll brew you a special cup."

"That sounds ominous," he laughed.

"Not at all—I'm quite a good cook and that extends to coffee."

They made their way back to her hub lab and he sat at one of the laboratory tables while she heated a beaker of water and set up a filtration funnel with fritted paper. Into this she measured coffee. "Brought this up when I came," she said, showing the can. "None of that powdered stuff for me." She laughed. "I suppose that I'll have to become accustomed to it after this is gone."

Longo sniffed appreciatively. "That's the first real coffee I've smelled in weeks." Not since that last morning, when he had brewed himself a pot and left part of it for Martha when she arose. He remembered the way the smell filled the kitchen and how he had sat at the breakfast bar, sipping the black brew and thinking of her in the bedroom

sound asleep. She would have gotten up and brewed it for
him but he had decided to let her sleep. She'd had a hard
day before, preparing for his departure, and the boys had
been a special trial. Now he wished he had spent that final
hour with her but it was too late, and the might-have-
beens had become too much a part of his thoughts the past
week.

He rose and began to wander idly about the confines of
the lab, thinking to shake off the first hint of depression.
There were several new pieces of apparatus set up on the
far bench. He saw an incubator with the shells of several
eggs showing, and next to that a small container with
Cyrillic writing. The container was empty, but within a
desiccator, he saw a glass container labeled in Cyrillic.
Inside the container was a black igneous mass, and he wondered what this could mean. Near the desiccator a flask
rested in a cooling bath. Some of the black material was
inside this flask, but the black material was frothing and
the gas from it was being collected in a container to which
was affixed a pressure gauge. A small laboratory pump
was exhausting the flask into the pressure container.

"What's this?" he asked.

Janice looked up from pouring water over the coffee
grounds and frowned. "An experiment," she said casually.

"Is this some of the material from the Soviet Survey?"

"In a way."

"It looks like it's fermenting."

"Yes, thank God," she said. She returned to the coffee
and tried to look noncommital.

"At a pretty rapid rate, too," he said. "Come on, why
the secrecy?"

Janice returned the flask of boiling water to a hot plate
and looked at him for a long moment. "Please, Quint,"
she said. "Don't ask any questions right now. I'll explain
in due course. For the moment I've agreed to keep this between me and the people at the Soviet station. Even their
own supervisor doesn't know about this."

"That bothers me," Longo said slowly. "You know, all
of our efforts are occupied in completing the ship and I assumed yours were by the need to develop viable food

sources. Yet you seem to be occupied with something quite apart from that. I'm not so sure I shouldn't insist."

"Don't be stuffy," she said. "I know you're third in command and that you have a responsibility to the total effort, but please trust me. This is something that's terribly important to our survival and I'll report on it as soon as we're sure of the results."

"When will that be?"

"Two or three days, a week at the most."

He paused, debating his course of action. "All right," he said. "I won't say anything for the moment. Tell me, the reprogramming Rodrigues is doing—that a part of this project?"

"Yes," she said slowly. "Yes, it is. An important part. I have to know if I can manipulate certain DNA molecules in the way we need."

"I don't understand your reluctance to talk about it."

"Please," she said. Then, "Come, drink your coffee."

He crossed and sat again at the table while she poured.

"I'm sorry, I don't have any cream. There's some sugar, though."

"I prefer it black," he said.

She sat down next to him with her own cup of coffee and they sipped at the brew silently for a long time. Longo again was uncomfortably aware of her warmth and her odor. Thoughts came to him and he pressed them down, thinking that she had been right to worry about the male rutting instinct. Was that all it was really? He had never missed sex before during his station tours, mainly because there was always the exciting image of Martha before him, waiting patiently for his return. Unlike some of the station personnel, he had never even felt the need for recourse to onanism. He was patient; he could afford to wait. It was as simple as that. Now the physical pressures were becoming almost an obsession with him.

Was it as simple as that? Or was there something more? His view of her had changed through the last week of crisis; more and more he saw into the secret self that she had hidden from the men of her world. What he saw touched him, and for the first time he knew that he would find

someone else. Martha was already dimming in his mind
except as an abstract object of grief. And Janice?

Romantic schoolboy nonsense, he told himself. Yet, the
fact remained that there were Janice and the women
aboard the Soviet station, and beyond that he was a biological deadend. That in itself disturbed him, for he had
always thought of himself as a part of a long chain of
Longos stretching into the unseen future. "You're basically a peasant in your outlook," Martha had told him once,
and he supposed that this was true. It was an attitude he
had learned at his father's knee, and it had become so
emotionally ingrained that no intellectual examination of
it would change the basic need.

"You look like you're somewhere out on the edge of the
universe," Janice said, interrupting his thoughts.

"In a way," he answered. He stared moodily into his
cup, swirling the last of the coffee.

"More?" she asked, starting to rise. In so doing, she
brushed against him. His reaction was unplanned, purely
automatic.

He reached out and touched the hand that reached for
his cup, then grasped her arm and quite automatically
pulled her toward him. She resisted for a moment and then
relaxed. He half rose, pulling her to him, and in that awkward position tried to kiss her. His hands were doing remembered things. She tried to push him away once and
then was responding clumsily, unsure of herself.

"Not here," she said.

"Where?" he whispered. "Where?"

"Not here," she said and moved back away from him.
He stood, suddenly feeling embarrassed but wanting her
still. She colored and then closed her eyes as though in
final decision. She reached out and took his hand, pulling
him along.

"Not here," she said softly and, quite without understanding the inner force that propelled him, he followed
her without question.

Eleven

During the next week the work on the hybridized ship proceeded rapidly. The problems of mating two dissimilar propulsion systems, each with its own special oxidizer tanks, presented few of the difficulties Longo had envisioned, largely due to Major Bucholtz's inventiveness. The man was a marvel at jury-rigging a workable design, Longo admitted. Their talents complemented each other in unexpected fashions, particularly on the problems of mounting motors on the massive double frame. They had provided for mounting within the framework so that whole components of both stations could be transferred at the last minute when the station installations themselves would be cannibalized.

Bucholtz had assigned several of his technicians to Georgeoff to work on the adaptation of the hybrid motor systems for use with the fluorine-oxygen combination oxidizer. The preliminary firings showed that the resulting makeshift system would provide much of the needed versatility for ferrying supplies down to the surface of the moon. "Fit the damned birds with lifting surfaces," Georgeoff chortled, "and we could fly the beasts right down to the surface of Earth itself."

As for Longo, his whole sense of worth expanded in the new task and in the special relationship that had developed with Janice. He laughed at first at the secret they shared. They managed to find a variety of ways to sneak away to her quarters without anyone apparently suspecting. Then Longo began to realize from the envious looks he received that they had become very obvious. It seemed suddenly as if everyone were involved in a conspiracy of silence in which they all knew the secret.

"You know," he told her one sleep period, "everybody knows we're shacking up."

"Is that the term?" Janice asked.

"Oh, you've heard that before," he accused her.

"Of course." She laughed in the dark and pressed close to his body, rubbing her hand over the heavy growth on his chest. "Only it seems an odd term for doing it on a space station."

"Would you rather do it in a spacesuit?" he whispered, biting her ear.

"I remember a writer named Heinlein," she said. "He wrote about a song called 'A Spacesuit Built for Two.'"

"I've never tried it in freefall," he teased.

"If I know you, you'll find a way."

A week later they were in the hub laboratory and he did. It was a completely insane experience. He expected Lieberman or someone else to walk in at any moment, but Janice suddenly quite literally attacked him. There was no place to do it but on one of the tables, hanging from the bulkhead with a row of animal cages near at hand. He found it perversely exciting, especially when the hamsters seemed to catch their excitement.

After it was over and they had smoothed their clothing, he sat on the floor, holding to a stanchion when he tended to drift, and laughed like a man possessed. She started to laugh too, and soon they were both howling like maniacs. She told him about George and the time she handed him his glasses to make him feel clothed, and that set Longo off into a fresh spasm.

"God," he roared. "I can't wait until you and I can have a kid. What a monster we'll make!"

She lapsed into silence at that and the mood evaporated as though it had not been. He tried to find out what had oppressed her but she seemed to withdraw. There was a certain coolness for at least a day, until this too evaporated in the new excitement they were finding together.

While he had buried himself in his work except for those hours they spent together, she had become increasingly absorbed in her own projects. He found her on more than one occasion deep in conversation with Lieberman. When he approached, Lieberman would start almost guiltily and then raise his voice as though he had started on a completely different conversational track.

Finally, Longo asked her, "What's up? You and Lieberman act as if you're hatching a conspiracy against the Grand Duke."

"Just work," she said casually.

"It's more than that," he accused. "Sugiyama tells me that you spend an hour each day talking with the Russians and that you insist that the conversations be private. That's rather suspicious."

"Quint," she said. "There's some new data developing. We want to be very sure of ourselves before we go to our separate commanders."

"New data?" he asked. "You're supposed to be developing a new food supply for the colony. You know we should start that as soon as we land and get the first pressure enclosures built."

"We're doing that, of course," she said, "but there's a great deal more. I can't tell you just yet, but it's important."

Her secrecy bothered him. He had felt that they were growing closer together. After all, he told himself, you can't cohabit steadily with a woman, especially under these restricted circumstances, without developing a special emotional empathy. Yet she was hiding something, and he felt annoyed. He supposed it was his male ego that was injured. He felt a more personal responsibility, knowing how much the energies of the two stations were being channeled to the completion of the ship and the extensive planning for the moon station.

Steinbrunner had become more and more involved in the final assembly of the ship. Of all the workers, he had probably had the most experience in extrastation activity, and his EVA know-how became particularly important in those days when they began to position the great plastic and metal fuel tanks. The problem of transferring the highly reactive liquid fluorine lay ahead. Longo knew that this would be the most critical of the operations. The LOX from the Soviet stores would be comparatively easy. The

problem lay in the complex metering job from the two dissimilar oxidizer tanks.

The Russian fuel was essentially the same as the American JP-2, hydrocarbon jet fuel. The Soviet system used
this in combination with pure liquid oxygen—the American engines used a similar material with a combination of
LOX and the liquid fluorine, while primary engines were
fueled by pure liquid hydrogen. The end result was a primary propulsion system of twenty dissimilar motors that
operated on three distinct oxidizer and fuel combinations.
It was quite impossible to switch the Soviet oxidizer system in spite of the greater energy that they might achieve
by the use of LOX-Fluorine—FLOX—with the Russian
fuel. Their engines simply could not handle the higher
combustion temperatures, and even had they been able to,
it was unlikely that combustion acoustic instability could
have been avoided in the rocket chambers without extensive testing and redesign. Longo remembered with a shudder the early days of the development of the J-3 engine,
when every test ended with the standing acoustic waves in
the chamber literally ripping the great motor apart.

He ended his shift each day with a kind of dull fatigue
that invaded his muscles and, more, his brain, making it
feel like wet pudding. Whenever they could, he and Janice
sought some secluded spot and often sat or lay for hours
without speaking. It was the animal comfort of sheer exhaustion soothed by mindless rest. Steinbrunner had the
alternate shift, so Longo could bring her to his quarters.

She seemed restive now and more and more excited,
but he could pry nothing from her. He knew that the collaboration with the Russians had become more intense
and Rothgate had taken him aside to ask about it. "Well,"
Rothgate pointed out darkly, "her name is Svoboda and
she does have relatives in Poland."

"No, I think you're worrying needlessly, Colonel,"
Longo said.

"She's getting awfully close to those people."

"Not all of them," Longo pointed out. "Colonel Farrington has received some kind of formal protest from
their Konyev. He seems to think she's jumping channels."

"Oh, she's a good one for that," Rothgate said. "Damned civilians never seem to understand military protocol."

Longo thought that he had never seen Rothgate looking so bad. His eyes were sunken with lack of sleep and he seemed to have developed a slight tick in the corner of his mouth. He had, of course, been driving himself, as had the other members of the station, but the tensions seemed more tightly repressed in him than in the others.

"Colonel," he said, "I know it's none of my business, but it might do you some good to get a little more sleep. You've been putting in more hours than most of the men and—well, that sort of fatigue can warp your judgment."

Rothgate seemed to draw himself up stiffly for a second while sudden anger blazed in his eyes. Then his expression softened and his face seemed to flow for a second like melting wax. "Yes," he said. "Yes, I suppose so. Thanks for your concern, Quint."

Longo frowned. The speech somehow didn't ring true to his ears. Rothgate was not like that at all. He was usually mildly arrogant and very careful of the relationships of rank. Now he seemed to invite a closeness that was completely out of character. Longo saw that the man was watching him carefully, waiting for his response. What the hell does he expect of me? Longo wondered.

"I know I'm sticking my neck out—" Longo began.

"Not at all, Quint," said the other man, his eyes bright and waiting.

"It's just that we all have to be concerned about each other now."

"Of course," murmured Rothgate.

"We depend on each other's talents for survival."

"I appreciate your consideration," Rothgate said. "I've probably been pushing myself. Just as you have. The same advice could apply to you."

"I've been bearing up under it pretty well."

"Well, of course—but then you have obvious advantages that we others do not have."

Longo stiffened. An innuendo? He scanned Rothgate's face closely, considering his possible reactions to the colo-

nel's statement. Finally, he decided that he had best ignore
it.

"Not obvious ones, Colonel," Longo said somewhat
stiffly. "Just that this kind of work is good therapy for
me."

The emotional exchange, whatever it had been between
them, was fading. It was like watching the lights being
turned out in a darkened upper room, slowly, one by one.
In the same manner the half need reflecting from the colonel's eyes faded, with only the flicker of wariness remaining. In some subtle fashion, Longo saw, he had offended
the other man, and the rapport was at an end.

"I have some final reports to make out before I go off
watch," he said, saluting.

"Of course," Rothgate replied. "I've been watching
your progesss with great interest."

"Thank you," said Longo. There was more than wariness in Rothgate's gaze now. There was something else,
something indefinable. A sort of slyness compounded with
a clear suspicion, even a faint distaste.

Longo left his quarters, and paused in the hall. A nagging intuition quivered in the back of his mind. Well, perhaps it was merely the emotional strain of overwork. He
thought of mentioning the conversation to Farrington, but
then he realized that he had little beyond that vague intuition to repeat. God knows, all of them had been acting in
emotional patterns that were exaggerated and often atypi-
cal these past weeks. He shook his head and tried to dismiss the colonel's face from his memory. For a long time
the image of those wary eyes persisted.

He spent the last hour checking final inventory lists for
the moonship. He wished that they had at least one more
propulsion unit so that they might take more of the station
gear from both stations. As it was, the C list had grown
very large and Longo knew that much of the material
would be left behind with little chance of salvaging it later.
The harsh demands of the moon colony would strain their
technology to the point where it seemed highly unlikely
that they would be able to mount a return mission within
several decades. Whatever they took with them now would

be the basis for the tenuous hold that the human race had on continued existence.

Later, when he and Janice lay on his bunk in his darkened quarters, he said, "It's going to be a very bleak existence. I wonder if it's worth it?"

He felt her nude body stiffen beside him. "Worth it?" she said fiercely. "Of course, it's worth it. Just keeping alive is worth it."

"I've wondered these last days. There really ought to be more to human life than the kind of embalmed existence that we're planning."

She laughed softly and kissed him. "You men," she said. "You're always striving for complexity, for some deeper subtler philosophy. Has it ever occurred to you that the whole object of life is simply living?"

"We've spent a lot of our history finding something more than that."

"Yes, and we've developed a hundred contradictory systems that lay every kind of restriction on humankind. We've never yet learned that basic principle that we are alive simply because we are alive and we remain alive simply because it's better than being dead."

"That's an almost monomaniacal philosophy," he objected. "I can conceive of many instances in which it would be better to be dead, in which the human race might better pass from existence."

"I won't accept that," she said. "We daren't take such a decision on ourselves. We don't have the prescience of gods. We can't know the ultimate good or harm of simply going on. It's a matter of a sort of ingrained optimism. We have to assume that keeping the race going yields an ultimate good, if not to us, then to our descendants."

"I suppose so."

"Of course. That's why it's worth taking chances, simply because the alternate is decline and death."

"I don't understand this attitude of yours," he said. "You speak of an optimistic future in one breath and then worry about the historical strait-jacket that the moon colony may become."

"It's not such a contradiction," she said quietly, "as you shall see."

"Never mind," he said, touching her, then leaning over to smell the sweet-sour odor of her body. It was a most exciting perfume and it brought back old memories, memories that seemed less charged with pain than they had been a short while ago. "Whatever we do, it's for us—and for what comes from us. For a bunch of gangly kids growing up on the moon."

Her body shuddered under his hands and she turned away from him. Her back against his belly was suddenly cold and dank with perspiration. He touched her and she seemed to shrink a bit.

"What's wrong?" he asked.

"Nothing, nothing," she said. There was a quiver almost like a sob in her voice.

"Tell me," he insisted.

"I can't now," she said. "Later, later after it's over and it all has some other meaning. For the moment I want this."

"You've got what you want," he said, putting his arm around her. He felt her breath fan the hair on his opposite forearm. "Come on, come on," he whispered. She was in his arms then and her lips were pressing fiercely, possessively against his as though this might be the very last time.

"Hey, hey," he whispered, soothing her, but the words only brought her to a greater frenzy, a frenzy which he had not seen in her before. He felt his own body respond to it, frantically, almost hysterically, and they mated in the dark like two lost souls. All the while he was building to that violent shuddering orgasm, he kept asking himself, *What's driving her? What's driving her?* Afterwards, he lay drowsily, his head cushioned on her soft arm, and listened to her even breathing. Several times she drew deep sighing breaths and he thought of trying to find out what was bothering her, but he was reluctant to disturb the tranquility of the moment. In the end he dozed and when he awoke she had dressed and was gone.

He did not see her again for two days. She seemed almost to be avoiding him. When he called her, she pleaded a heavy work schedule. Once she was closeted with one of the Soviet scientists, Koenig, who was ferried over from the Soviet station. He brought a large case of printout sheets and another of what appeared to be biological samples which he carefully shepherded. He would allow no technician to touch them until he and Janice were in her laboratory, with only Lieberman as a witness.

Lieberman himself seemed to be undergoing some subtle emotional change. On the several occasions when Longo met him in the mess hall, his eyes were bright with an ill-concealed excitement and he seemed to lapse into a deep introspection in the middle of a conversation.

Over coffee at the start of the first watch of the second day, Longo said, "Hey, Doc, why the deep study?"

Lieberman started and then quickly gulped at the coffee before him. "Am I that obvious?" he said.

"You've been walking around in a fog for several days."

"Well, I've been very preoccupied," Lieberman admitted. "It's a rather difficult problem."

"Care to tell me about it?"

"No, not just now," Lieberman said. "It's a sort of a moral problem as well as a technical one. Rather like trying to decide which horse to bet on."

"So far as I know," Longo said slowly, eying Lieberman for a reaction, "there's only one horse race."

Lieberman frowned and finished his coffee. He started to rise. Longo reached out a hand to restrain him. "There *is* only one horse race, isn't there, Doc?" he asked.

"Probably, probably. We'll all know soon enough," Lieberman said.

"Look, I'm a little concerned about Janice," Longo said, delaying him still further. "She seems emotionally— well, not disturbed exactly, but unpredictable."

Lieberman sank to the stool before the table and looked at Longo for a long time without speaking. Finally he said, "Look, Quint, do you love her?"

Longo frowned. "Love? I don't know. Is it important?"

"Probably not," Lieberman said, "but she's made an

emotional commitment to you that she has never made to another man in her life."

"You make me sound like I'm using her," Longo said.

"Aren't you?" Lieberman asked. "Oh, I don't mean in a completely self-seeking way, but aren't you using her as an emotional prop for your own loss?"

"Perhaps," Longo said slowly. "Still, isn't that a part of any male-female relationship, this mutual propping?"

"Yes, but precisely as you define it," Lieberman answered. "You take strength from her and you give her strength. The problem that concerns me is that in the long run you may not give her the strength she needs."

"She's a strong woman."

"But she *is* a woman," Lieberman pointed out, "and she's vulnerable in certain uniquely feminine ways."

"I wouldn't hurt her," protested Longo.

"But you will," Lieberman promised. "It's inevitable that you will. The only question is when. Right now, her need for you is very important, even though she knows that hurt is inevitable."

"Do I impress you as being that insensitive?" Longo demanded angrily.

"I'm not trying to insult you," Lieberman said softly. "But I know you and I know what moves you in this relationship and I know Janice."

"You sound like there's something more basic to be afraid of."

"From her standpoint, perhaps," Lieberman said. "If only you weren't so goddamned Italian."

"I don't remember ever regretting that," Longo said.

"Perhaps you will someday," Lieberman said, and rose to his feet. Then he laughed and said, "Forget it, Quint. You're a good solid male with more admirable traits than you've a right to. I guess everything will shake itself out."

After he left Longo sat for long moments. For the first time in weeks he wished he had a cigarette. He drew a second cup of coffee and mulled the conversation over in his mind. Its melodramatic overtones bothered him. Then he remembered the first part of the conversation and Lieberman's veiled answers to his horse-race question.

"Well, there is only one horse race, isn't there?" he asked himself. He was quite unprepared for the answer when it came.

The answer came twenty-four hours later. His first suspicion that something was up was when Georgeoff reported at the beginning of the watch that Voroshilov had requested a station bug to ferry him to the American station. Longo wondered at this, since the modifications they had now made to the Soviet EVA equipment had extended their range considerably. However, he ordered Georgeoff to dispatch the vehicle. It returned within the hour with Voroshilov himself and several of the Soviet scientists. Janice and Lieberman met them at the hub after they entered the lock.

She ushered the group through the lateral passages to Farrington's wardroom and shortly thereafter Longo heard the intercom page Rothgate. "What's happening?" Georgeoff demanded.

"I wish I knew," Longo said, "but something big is up."

They returned to their work. Longo was on the station monitor, watching the transfer of liquid FLOX from the great reservoir to the ship tanks. The process would take at least a week because of the touchiness of the material, and he wanted to make sure that nothing menaced the operation. He finally turned the task over to Georgeoff after two hours and went looking for lunch.

In the messroom he sat down next to Sugiyama, with a small platter of reconstituted meat and vegetables. Sugiyama nodded and continued to eat. There was a scattering of personnel around the small room. Because of the prepackaged nature of the rations, there was no definite dining hour and each group took care of its own debris.

"How is the girl?" Longo asked.

"The girl?"

"Karen, the computer technician below."

Sugiyama made a face. "She's bearing up well. She's done quite a marvelous job, but it seems very tragic. Surely we could do something to help her."

"I wish it were so," Longo said. "You know the risk involved in that. It would take a greater motivation than rescuing her to mount a return flight."

"That seems pretty brutal," Sugiyama said.

"It is," Longo admitted. "Only what alternative do we have? She's probably suffering already from radiation sickness and we don't know if the plague has spread to the Western Hemisphere yet. We don't dare find out."

"It's still brutal," Sugiyama said.

Longo was about to answer when the paging system crackled and a voice said, "Captain Longo, report to Colonel Farrington's wardroom."

"Now we find out what's happening," Sugiyama said.

"I hope so," Longo said, depositing the ration packaging in an incinerator chute. He hurried through the corridors to Farrington's wardroom and knocked on the door.

When the door opened he entered to find the group ranged around the retractable desk which was filled with printouts and several bound reports. Rothgate was standing apart from the group, his eyes flashing angrily.

Farrington looked up and said, "Quint, I think it's time we get your advice on all this. It will probably come as something of a shock."

"Yet it is a very serious proposition," Voroshilov said slowly. "Otherwise I should not have come personally."

"I must confess that I am halfway convinced," Farrington said.

"Convinced of what?" Longo demanded.

"They've taken leave of their senses," Rothgate snarled angrily.

"Jeb—" Farrington said sharply.

"I don't give a damn, Colonel," said Rothgate. "You know as well as I do that it's insane."

"What's insane?" Longo demanded.

Janice looked at him with wide eyes and smiled. "Not too insane, Quint," she said softly. "It's just that we want to go to Mars."

Twelve

In the silence that followed, Longo was suddenly aware of the chorus of sounds that the group made, the tiny sounds of breath slowly expelled, of rustling clothing and the crinkle of flimsy paper, the faint cry of warped plastic as Farrington shifted weight in his chair.

"I'm sure you must be serious," Longo said at last, "but do you realize what you're saying?"

"Of course, Quint," said Janice. "Believe me, we haven't brought up the proposal without being fully aware of how radical it is."

"Radical," Rothgate snorted. "I protest, Colonel. We all have too much work to be wasting our time on such outrageous proposals."

One of the Soviets, the scientist named Konyev, cleared his throat. "I am of your opinion, Colonel Rothgate, although Comrade Colonel Voroshilov has asked me to reserve my final judgment in this matter."

Rothgate's face was cold and unyielding. "I must commend you on how well-disciplined your technical men are, Colonel," he said, addressing Voroshilov.

Voroshilov smiled coldly and turned to Farrington. "I believe we should review the recent data upon which this recommendation has been made. Perhaps then Colonel Rothgate will not think us so very rash."

"I think it's pretty well out of the question, regardless of your reasons," Longo said. "We're in a pretty unfavorable orbital position relative to the planet and we'll need quite a bit greater velocity than that we're planning to achieve to intersect its position in a reasonable time. Our oxygen supplies, for instance, would probably be close to exhaustion."

"There is a solution to that with the new chlorella," Janice said.

"Regardless, you're asking for a great deal that our system cannot give you."

"Can you be sure of that?" Farrington asked.

"No," Longo admitted. "That's only intuition, of course, but I don't think we have the computer capacity to find out for sure. The problem in celestial mechanics plus the other logistic problems would place too great a burden on our facilities."

"Yet, we must find out if we can," Voroshilov said. "A first approximation with our on-board machines—can we not have that?"

"If you're willing to sacrifice several days in the present project," Longo said. "Rodrigues will have to be the final arbiter on that. I simply don't know enough about his operations."

"Then," Voroshilov said slowly, "let us review for the moment the information we have and then prevail upon you to give us some more guided opinion on whether the project is feasible."

Longo spread his hands silently and found a seat. Farrington's eyes silently thanked him for his restraint.

"We have all considered the problems of establishing a moon colony," Voroshilov began, steepling his fingers and gazing into space. "It would be foolish to ignore the most basic problem of such a colony—that of growth. The moon has few resources and during our stay we would always be confined to a few enclosures; our resources severely strained by the mere act of survival."

"Yes," Longo admitted, "I've discussed this with Janice. But the colony would survive. That seems reasonably sure."

"But in survival, what would happen to our carefully preserved technology? Would it grow?" Voroshilov laughed wryly. "I think not, and I thought that when I proposed the project. Still it seemed the only solution at the time, at best a gamble."

"What you propose now," Longo objected, "seems even more of a gamble, even assuming we could make the journey."

"We've thought about the journey," Janice said. "There are ways of handling some of our more basic problems."

"More of that in a bit, Janice," Farrington said. "Let's talk about what happens when we get there and why we should go there."

"The reason is simple enough," Koenig said excitedly. "We now believe that we can make the planet habitable in less than two hundred years."

"A whole planet?" Longo demanded. "With a sea level atmosphere of barely fifty mm. of mercury, no water—with a mean temperature at the equator below freezing? You'd have to retailor the whole atmosphere in two centuries."

"We nearly did that very thing accidentally on Earth," Koenig pointed out. "The pollution problem in three quarters of a century of industrial revolution—remember? There we retailored a planetary atmosphere without trying."

"All right, all right," Longo said, "but we had resources with which to start."

"And so we have on Mars!" Janice broke in. "The last Soviet probes have given us data that show very clearly that what we propose is possible. Oh, Mars will never be the paradise the earth is, and we will want to return, but we can remake Mars into something that is livable for humans and in which a human culture can grow."

"Let me tell you about Mars," Koenig said, his eyes almost mystical. "It is not at all as we once supposed. It is a planet in the throes of rebirth. It once had an extensive carboniferous period much like our own, and the planetary land masses covered vast peat beds that are scarcely more than ten million years old. We have sampled around the planet extensively and these peat beds are universal, lying scarcely fifty meters below the surface in many places. It is a planet in the grip of a new wave of vulcanism."

"Volcanoes?" Longo demanded. "You want to plant a colony in the midst of a mass of volcanic action?"

"There are safer areas," Koenig insisted. "We will

choose one of these. The important thing is that the volcanic action is intensive. It is already modifying the atmosphere at a fantastic rate. The atmospheric pressure has increased twenty millimeters within the last two decades."

"What kind of gases, though?" Longo objected.

"Carbon dioxide mostly," answered Janice. "A great deal of that and some sulfur dioxide. Quite a bit of ammonia and methane from the peat beds."

"A primordial atmosphere," Koenig said, "being formed at a fantastic rate. Already large parts of the poles are covered by frozen carbon dioxide, but as the hothouse effect grows this will disappear."

"And water?" Longo asked.

"Tons of water," Janice said. "Vast underground lakes of water driven off by the internal heat and condensed in lakes near the surface."

"I fail to see how this is so attractive."

"This is where we come in," Janice said. "I have developed a strain of bacteria, using Koenig's probe samples, that will attack and ferment the peat beds, converting much of them to more water and carbon dioxide. We calculate that we can accelerate the formation of a planetary atmosphere by several hundredfold."

"We can't breathe carbon dioxide," Longo objected.

"But we have the chlorella! We can grow it in fantastic abundance with the water we have—we can harvest sugars and oils on vast chlorella lakes and convert the carbon dioxide to oxygen. Other strains can split the methane and the ammonia. We know how to do this, and cultivating these plants on a planetary scale we can speed the evolution of the planetary atmosphere. What would take five to ten thousand years naturally we can do in a century and a half. Out of our work can come side products to feed a growing technology. In scarcely a hundred and fifty years men may walk on the surface of the planet in an atmosphere of over three hundred millimeters, of at least forty percent oxygen."

"I find this all difficult to accept," Konyev said. "At least, I did until I saw the printouts from the computer study."

"That's why I needed Rodrigues's help so badly," Janice explained.

"It will work," said Konyev. "I am against the terrible gamble of the trip but should we arrive safely, it will work."

Longo leaned back and shook his head. In his mind's eye he saw the vision that now animated the others. A cold inhospitable planet with scarcely an atmosphere, made to bloom in a bare century and a half by the work of men. It would be hard at first but with the growth of the colony population—a growth that was forbidden them in the hostile environs of the moon—the work would accelerate and the age-old dream of a second home for man might indeed finally be realized. It seemed fantastic that a planet might be terra-formed in so short a time, but as Janice had pointed out, they had almost made their own planet unliveable by atmospheric pollution, and—he still had to remind himself—with the power of atomic fission, they had finally indeed denied humankind one planet.

"What about fissionables?" he demanded.

"We don't know," Voroshilov said. "We think so from some of the background counts, but that too is a gamble."

"Can we land on the planet if we arrive?" asked Farrington.

"Yes, I think so," Longo said slowly. "It would require modifying the Soviet bugs with airfoils, but this is not the problem it might seem. The big problem is getting there."

"Forgive me," Janice interrupted. "I know this is probably stupid, but won't we reach escape velocity when we start for the moon?"

"Yes," Longo said. "I wish it were as simple as that."

"Won't escape velocity take us to Mars?"

"To Mar's orbit—eventually. The problem is twofold: Would we still be alive and would Mars be there when we wanted it? We're quite a few years out of inferior conjunction and the trip is long. We have to have enough velocity to rendezvous with the planet in a reasonable time before our oxygen and food supplies are gone. The trip would take anywhere from six months to a year. I don't know without running a detailed study."

"Janice has a solution for some of those objections," Farrington said slowly. Longo said nothing. He was becoming infected with the subdued mood of excitement and he wanted to maintain control of himself. He must not be swept along with the sudden excitement to the point where he lost his sense of judgment. The voyage they were proposing was incredibly complex. They would have to abandon not only their C list but probably a good portion of their B list to make it. Even then he did not know if it were possible. It would take a long study to correlate all of the factors and converge on a solution.

"There are two approaches to the problem of an extended voyage," Janice said. "We can supplement our food supplies with the use of our on-board pile. With the electricity we can synthesize simple sugars and amino acids from waste products. The techniques were developed back in the seventies. However, this cannot be the complete solution. The other half will simply involve placing a large part of the crew in hypothermia."

"You can't be serious," Longo protested.

"I *am* serious," she insisted. "We've been able to hold volunteers at ten to fifteen degrees centigrade for a year with no apparent brain damage. The drugs are available aboard the station and there's no dearth of cooling. We would simply bypass the circulation of the patient and cool the blood externally, returning it to the body for circulation. Of course, we would have to depend on external pumps, but I think we could solve this problem by combining all of any one blood type in master reservoir. This would mean only four or five pumps."

"It is a daring solution," Voroshilov admitted. "I am not so sure that we have enough skilled personnel to monitor the vital functions of our sleepers, but——."

"We will lose perhaps ten per cent of these," said Konyev.

"How many will we lose otherwise?" Koenig demanded. "Surely the risk is worth it?"

"Is it?" asked Longo. "Is it really worth the risk?"

Farrington sat silently for a moment, and finally sighed. "Yes. If we can make the trip, I believe it is."

"And I too," Voroshilov said.

"I think it's insane," Rothgate said. "We have a slim enough chance as it is and you want to throw this away for what no sane man would even consider."

"It is an historical process that determines all this," said Voroshilov. "I believe the long-term survival of the race is better assured on Mars than on the moon."

"You Reds love to talk about 'historical processes,'" Rothgate said, his voice rising. "What have you really got in mind? There's something more than meets the eye here, Colonel."

"That's enough," Farrington snapped. His face flushed with anger and he visibly sought control. "Jeb, there is no further room for that kind of thinking. We are no longer Americans or Soviets. We are human beings trying to preserve our race. Personal ambitions, personal animosities— they all have to be forgotten. For this reason, I think this as good a time as any to tell you that Colonel Voroshilov and I have agreed that he will command the ship that makes the trip."

"There is, of course, more to the agreement that that——" Voroshilov began.

"I'm sure there must be," said Rothgate, his face a study of conflicting emotions. Before Voroshilov could continue, he turned from his position by the wall and strode through the hatch.

"Colonel!" Farrington shouted after him. Voroshilov reached out a hand. "No, no," he said. "I understand much of his feeling. You forget that I know of his past and his overwhelming hatred for us. Perhaps it is justified. Both of our peoples played deadly games in those days and many of us have been injured."

"Nevertheless, he's a military man first," said Farrington.

"Yes, and he will remember it in time. I have great faith and pity that so many of us in our lifetimes have had to learn this discipline. It is not, I think, the proper frame of mind for the best of men. Still, it is useful in such emergencies and we must give it the credit it deserves."

Remarkable, Longo thought. Was this the enemy he had

been fighting all his life, this eminently civilized man?
Well, perhaps Voroshilov was one in a hundred thousand.
Still, Longo thought, they were all fortunate to have him
rather than some prancing martinet. What a tragedy that
would have been.

"What is important is that no two men can master the
voyage and the details of the final colony," Voroshilov
said. "We have decided that I will command the voyage
and Colonel Farrington will exercise military control of
the colony until such time as other more reasonable political arrangements may be made. Each of us will in turn be
assisted and watched by a group of our—" He smiled.
"What word can we use? Counternationalities? I wish that
we might now forget this but it will be with us for some
time, perhaps even a generation."

"The important thing now," said Longo breaking into
the sudden silence, "is that we determine if this new
voyage is feasible. I need hardly point out that the calculations will place a terrible strain on our facilities. We may
well endanger the moon project without getting a satisfactory answer."

"We've considered that," Farrington said. "We feel that
it is worth the risk."

"I wish I had your confidence. However, I think at this
point we'd better call in Rodrigues. He will have the information we need next. After that perhaps I can give you
some early answers."

Rodrigues listened impassively while the project was
outlined. Longo found himself pleased with the no-nonsense attitude of the computer man. If he was surprised by
the sudden turn of events, he gave no sign. He sat and listened, taking notes periodically. Once he produced a device that looked like a circular slide rule and made several
quick calculations. Finally, he said, "I'm sorry. It simply
can't be done. We don't have the capacity within a reasonable time to do such a complex convergence."

"Even if we abandon the calculations for the moon
flight?" asked Farrington.

"I have assumed that we will do that," Rodrigues said
quietly. "You must remember that we have to balance

thrust and reaction mass against a variety of payloads, depending on the percentage of the packages. We have to calculate an intercept path with something like twenty basic variables. In addition there are alternate, somewhat longer flight paths that would in the long run save us reaction mass. All of these have to be explored. This means an array of several hundred simultaneous equations to be solved. We have to establish a convergence margin that is fairly narrow because of the large variation in thrust data. The engines have never been worked in this array before and we have to allow for wide deviations in thrust alignment and general performance efficiency." He shook his head. "It's a calculation of much greater complexity than the ones we are doing now."

"Wait!" Longo interrupted. "You mentioned several days ago that there were unused banks at the Cape."

"The new monolithic core assemblies?" asked Rodrigues. "Yes, they're on standby, but there's no way to tie them in."

"You mean there's no communication?"

"No," said Rodrigues. "I mean that someone has to go over there physically and activate the banks and give them the proper orders to tie into the main array."

"What about your girl at the Cape?" asked Farrington.

Rodrigues favored him with a pained look. "Colonel, we've got everything we can out of Karen. She has done things I did not think physically possible. Now she is ill and weak and in an advanced stage of pregnancy. She simply could not make it."

"There is a way," Longo said, checking the notebook he had carried with him to the meeting. "If we can send someone down to activate the complex."

"That would be a solution," Rodrigues admitted. "I have only one man besides myself who is qualified, however, and I don't know that I can spare him."

Voroshilov spoke. "Besides this man may have to double as pilot in case of an accident. I perhaps have a solution in keeping with our spirit of cooperation."

"I can brief anyone you decide to send if he has a good basic computer background."

"The mission," Voroshilov said slowly, "will be a very dangerous one, I think."

"We are not sure that the plague has reached the continent yet. I think it unlikely at this point. The only thing to worry about is radiation and we know how to protect against that."

Longo said, "My inventory shows that there are several loaded shuttles at the Cape that may be launched by the same team that does the job."

"Are you indeed that automatic?" Voroshilov asked in amazement.

"Steinbrunner knows enough about the setup to do it," Longo replied. "We have two shuttles ready for launching. One contains two J-5 engines and the other was topped off with liquid FLOX. Probably a good quarter of it has boiled away by now but the rest will help supplement our tanks. The extra engines and oxidizer will increase our margin of safety. We have more fuel than oxidizer."

Farrington laughed incredulously. "Like rabbits out of a hat!"

"Don't knock it," Longo told him wryly. "Not when you're having trouble making rabbit stew."

"The capacity from the new array would enable us to do the calculation in a matter of days," Rodrigues said.

"Then we must talk with Steinbrunner," Farrington said. "It's not something you easily ask a man to do."

"My chief pilot, Rudenko, will be of great help here," Voroshilov said. "He has a background in computers. You know that we have always required a secondary speciaity."

"Then, if we can ask them to make this trip—?" Farrington said.

"Yes," Voroshilov said. "It is a terrible thing to ask, but then we are faced with terrible decisions on an hour-to-hour basis."

When Steinbrunner reported to them, he agreed without comment. "I've been expecting it," he said quietly.

"You don't have to do it," Farrington pointed out.

"What else can I do with my life?" the man said, and lapsed into silence. The discussions continued for another hour and the atmosphere became charged with a new and moving excitement.

That evening Janice spent two hours with Longo in his quarters. "I can't believe it," she kept saying.

"You engineered it," he said. "I can reconstruct all of your thinking as I look back. This whole decision is the product of your work."

"I know," she said, shivering against him. "And now I'm terribly frightened."

"Frightened?" he asked sleepily. "Why?"

"Because," she said, sounding like a very small child in the dark, "because I'm not *that* sure it will work."

Thirteen

For Steinbrunner the dangers of the coming flight to Earth were of no great consequence. He had long ago lost that particular spirit that made life something to be held onto with fervor and tenaciousness. It was not that he wanted death or even that he was tired of living, but he had found so little joy in life that the mere act of existence had become an automatic thing, something that you allowed to continue and whose termination brought no great joy or sorrow.

He did at times consider the way in which he might end. He hoped that it would be with dignity and courage, that he might expire in some fashion that held special masculine significance for him. Dying was a special ritual in an ordered life in which one tried to order the factors so that one's death was worthy of a man. This was important to him, this business of dying as a man should die. He had often thought that he did not wish to grow old and expire from trivial degenerative disease between white sheets and amid the impersonal ministrations of nurses and doctors.

He would have objected to the idea of dying in what his new American countrymen called "a blaze of glory." He'd had enough of what passed for glory in his life. Many of his closer acquaintances had marveled at the tales of his escape from East Berlin and his subsequent life before he had received his visa for emigration to the United States. He rarely talked about this part of his life, however. All that had happened had become very much a part of his inner character and his image of himself as a man.

Had he formed any close friendships, he might have found himself accused of an exaggerated *machismo,* an elaborated sense of manliness and what constituted a male orientation to the world. Fortunately, he had avoided such close associations and the few casual intimates he had found since coming to the United States had, if anything, admired the special masculinity that he cultivated. It was not really a self-conscious masculinity, as a casual observer might have concluded. Rather it was an intense sense of pride. Steinbrunner liked being a man. It was the greatest gift nature had given to him and he wanted to live the role to the fullest.

It was not that he despised women. Indeed, he found their forms comely and aesthetically exciting. While he did not have the exaggerated breast fetish of his native-born fellows, and tended to sneer at the grotesques he found in the centerfolds of male magazines, he liked the subtle curves and exciting soft structure of a woman's breasts. A woman's ass was particularly attractive to him as, indeed, was the complex musculature of a man's. The soft interplay of gluteus maximi under stress was a source of often purely nonsensual excitement. He would have slept with more women in his life, admiring their bodies as he did, if he had not been so thoroughly disenchanted with the female personality.

Actually, he often amended this observation in his own mind, carefully stressing the personality of American women. He had been too young and innocent when he left Europe at eighteen to fully appreciate the intricate power ploys of European women in the sexual contest. He only knew that American women were brash and aggressive and their overt will-to-dominance offended him. He found he could easily assume a dominant role with the men he knew, but never with the women. Their will to power was too subtle, too devious for him to counter. In his love affairs, he had found women impossible to relate to except on a power-contest level. His love affairs with men had been, for the most part, an attempt to recapitulate the one moving, traumatic period of his life when he gave himself for the first and only time to another human being.

He did not think of himself as other than an ordinary if talented man, avoiding in his own mind the labels that his new countrymen adopted so readily. He was a man with wide tastes and that was simply that. Above all, he was always a man, and he liked his women to be completely women and his men to be completely men. In his newly adopted country he was too often disappointed by continuing confusion in both sexes on sexual roles. This, perhaps more than anything else, had been responsible for his growing withdrawal. It was largely ennui—funk—as he saw that the individual of either sex with whom he could relate completely was rare indeed. The only one he had ever met who fulfilled this special need was dead and had been dead since that tragic September when he had, in a wild frenzy, mounted his bike and braved the hail of bullets at the wall. After that important death, nothing had ever really mattered and he had proceeded quietly and competently about life, knowing that the simple process of living had no special meaning for him.

He prepared for the flight in a competent and mechanical way, learning the more extended layout of the Cape. He knew the launch pads fairly well and he was sure that with a little cramming he could operate the automatic launch stations. These had been highly automated over the last decade and were generally manned by a five-member team, of whom only one was really needed. As for the activation of the new core building, it had been decided that Rudenko, with his special computer training, would be the logical man for that job.

In the last two days before the mission, Rudenko had taken up residence in the American station. They saw each other occasionally but spoke little. Rudenko's English was fairly good, but he relied on one of Sugiyama's interpreters for much of his conversation with Rodrigues's men and for his periodic contacts with the girl Karen at the Cape. Once, after talking with her, he remarked to Steinbrunner, "It is sad." When Steinbrunner tried to continue the conversation he retreated into his native language, unable to express the special pathos that he felt.

The whole thing bothered Steinbrunner. He had little affection for Russians generally except for one who was now dead. Rudenko, whom he had known earlier, had been the object of fury initially and later simple rejection. He had not known the man well enough before to dislike him and their paths had crossed in such a secondhand fashion that he could not bring other emotions to bear on him. He was not even sure if he had any right to hate the man. Steinbrunner was, in all of his inner dealings with himself, completely committed to a rational outlook. He prided himself on that and he did not hate without a clear and ordered reason for hating.

He was quite unprepared the evening before the flight when Rudenko appeared in his quarters. Longo was on duty, and they had the cabin to themselves. The Russian looked confused and worried. "I would like to come in," he said.

"Then come in," Steinbrunner said, masking his annoyance. He noted that the Russian's accent was purer than before.

"It is time that we talked," Rudenko said.

"You speak English quite well," Steinbrunner accused him.

"Yes, very well," Rudenko admitted, shrugging his heavy shoulders.

"You have been pretending to be weak in the language. Was that orders from Voroshilov?"

"No, no. I thought it perhaps best. Unlike many of our people, I am not yet convinced that this—this cooperation will work."

"And you thought you might overhear something incriminating," Steinbrunner said accusingly.

Rudenko sank to the bunk Steinbrunner indicated and said nothing. He looked embarrassed. He stared at his interlocked fingers for long moments. Steinbrunner could see the massive musculature of his arms clench and unclench under the sleeves of the coveralls he wore. Absently, he wondered if the man still worked out to maintain such biceps. They were easily seventeen inches around.

"I wish it were possible for us to talk," Rudenko said at length.

"Talk?" Steinbrunner asked. "Why talk?"

"We will be working very closely together. Our lives will depend to a great extent on each other's efforts during the ground work and on the return flight."

"Is that what's worrying you?" Steinbrunner said coldly. "Are you afraid after all these years that I would do something like that? I could have stayed behind, had I wished, and found you."

"I thought that you had for a long time. Every night when I walked through the streets I looked for you."

"Were you afraid?" Steinbrunner demanded.

"Not afraid for myself," Rudenko said. "Afraid for you, perhaps. Afraid that you would do something in your anger and your sorrow that would damage you as much as me."

"Yes, I'm sure that concerned you a great deal," Steinbrunner said sarcastically. "What happened to me must have given you a lot of sleepless nights."

"It's true," Rudenko said. "I know you think I was responsible for Vasile's death, but it wasn't so. I knew he would not want you hurt."

Steinbrunner turned and stared at the wall, trying to master his anger. He felt the other man's eyes on his back. The intensity of Rudenko's stare was like a heavy weight between his shoulders. Yes, he thought, there was a time when he might have wanted to kill him, but that was long past, lost in the welcome anesthesia of years that had deadened the cruel pain.

"I doubt," he said tiredly, "if you cared very much what Vasile wanted."

"But I did," Rudenko said. "Do you think that a man turns his back so easily against his own? I watched him grow and fished him from the river one winter when he fell through the ice. I wiped his nose and brought food to his house when his father died and all that time he was like my own brother to me. What he wanted I wanted and since he would not have you hurt, I would certainly not have been the agent for it. Besides, my own survival was at stake; you have no idea how difficult it was to assure my future career against an investigation that might have entangled me in your tragedy."

"We both seem to have covered our tracks rather effectively," said Steinbrunner.

"We would not be here now if that were not so," Rudenko said. "It is perhaps best now to let the dead bury the dead."

Steinbrunner rubbed his hands over his eyes. "I'm tired," he said. "It happened a long time ago and I don't want to talk about it any more. I know what you did. He sent me a letter before they arrested him and he knew that you had been the one who betrayed him. But it doesn't matter any more."

Rudenko sighed heavily. "I loved him very much."

"And you killed him," Steinbrunner said softly.

Rudenko rose angrily, then stopped. His eyes mirrored the hurt and Steinbrunner saw that he had struck the man's emotional vitals. It was enough, he supposed. He waited silently until Rudenko walked to the door. At the door he paused and started to say something, then turned away without speaking.

After he left, Steinbrunner sat on the edge of the bunk, his eyes closed, his body rocking back and forth as he marshaled the long years of training, trying to master the war raging within him. The old anger was still there, the old clawing need to hurt. Only it would not accomplish anything any more. But that Rudenko should have escaped and risen to such esteem in his own country—Vasile had been worth a hundred of him, and Vasile was dead in those now ruined ashes of Berlin, his body a mass of corruption for nearly two decades. He had been barely eighteen. It had been such a damned waste, such a cruel and disgusting waste.

The last briefing meeting before the flight was held at H minus five hours. Steinbrunner and Rudenko joined Farrington and Rothgate in the messroom. Rodrigues reported briefly on his first approximating calculations. He had done a thorough job, even considering the influence of Toro, the quasi-moon, which was again approaching perigee. Then Rodrigues spread out a map and schematic drawings of the activation consoles that they would use to bring the new core array into the main computer hookup. The activation of this complex was Rudenko's job, while

Steinbrunner would attempt to launch the two stand-by Orbiters. The one with the liquid FLOX he would launch immediately, while the second would carry them and its precious cargo of engines back to orbit.

"This is the step that concerns me," Steinbrunner said. "I am sure that I can program the first launch. I know enough about the automatic pad equipment. But the second presents some problems. I will have to jury-rig some sort of timing device."

"The important thing is that you get back," said Farrington. "Longo says that he needs those extra motors. We can probably pare our payload to compensate for the FLOX if you fail to salvage that, but we need the extra motors."

"Thank God for the launch automation," Longo said. "A decade ago this would have been impossible. Even now, if we were depending on cryogenics, there'd be no point to the trip. The oxidizer would have boiled away by now to the point where the launch would have to abort."

"There's another task we'll ask you to try," Farrington said slowly.

"I'm completely against this," Rothgate put in. "Colonel, you're asking these men to take an unnecessary risk, besides endangering the station itself."

"It is the girl, I suppose," Rudenko said. "I have heard the conversations with her and have spoken once with her myself. A lonely and terrible vigil she keeps."

"Can you bring her back?" asked Farrington.

"What about the radiation poisoning?" asked Steinbrunner. "She must have picked up some contamination by now."

"Dr. Svoboda thinks we can handle that," Farrington said. "She thinks that a combination of hypothermia and a new chelating agent that has been pretty successful as a bone and tissue scavenger might clean up most of the problem."

"While she lies here, potentially to infect the whole station with the Russian biological agent," Rothgate protested.

"We can keep her in sterile enclosures until we know," said Farrington.

"She will probably die in any case."

"But there is the child. Perhaps we can save the child," said Longo.

"My God, man," Rothgate protested. "How many children died down below only a short time ago? You'll risk everything for one poisoned woman and an unborn child?"

"If you can do it," Farrington said, ignoring him, "try to bring her back. If it jeopardizes the mission, you'll have to abandon her."

"Karen will understand," Rodrigues said. "That sounds very cold-blooded but she'll understand. She's that kind."

Rudenko sighed. "It is perhaps time that we recognize that we have been too involved with the idea of personal death. I have often thought that you Americans had so exalted the role of the individual in your society that your concern for personal death outweighed your sense of survival."

Farrington frowned. "Perhaps you're right," he said. "Yet the individual is important to us and if we can rescue the girl, without sacrificing the larger needs of this survival group, we will do just that. It's a matter of faith with us, I suppose."

"I am not objecting to this," Rudenko said. "I will certainly respect your wishes as I would my own commander's. It is just that we must reach a point now where we learn to think in the manner that our Asiatic brothers have for years—that the pain of death is after all transitory and a life may sometimes be spent most valuably by giving it away."

"I think that's disgusting," Rothgate said. "We are not barbarians. We cannot accept the needless death of one of us without the whole being the poorer."

"The time for dying comes soon enough," Steinbrunner said, staring pointedly at Rudenko. "For myself, I promise you that we'll get her back. If Rudenko does not agree that the effort is worthwhile, then—" He left the sentence unfinished.

"I think you do not understand me," Rudenko said.

"I understand you well enough," Steinbrunner said and lapsed into silence. He was acutely aware of Rothgate eyeing him oddly. What could be going through the man's mind? Steinbrunner wondered. He did not identify with Rothgate's general hatred. His own hatred was too concentrated, but certainly it did not burn with the mindless intensity of Rothgate's.

"Do you understand the mechanics of tying in the new core array?" Farrington asked, pointedly changing the subject.

"I would appreciate an hour of review before we leave," Rudenko replied. "Can you spare the time, Lieutenant Rodrigues?"

Rodrigues laughed. "Everyone seems to be asking me that question these days. Yes, of course. I'd suggest, unless there's anything else to be decided, that you and I get our heads together for an hour now."

Farrington signaled that the meeting was at an end and the group began to break up. Janice was waiting in the corridor as Steinbrunner came out. "Could I see you a moment?" she asked.

He saw that the mess would be empty in another few moments and gestured her inside silently. As soon as Farrington had left, she sat down at the abandoned table. "I don't know quite how to put this," she said. "It may be that you will not be able to rescue this girl Karen."

"I'm afraid that this is very possible," replied Steinbrunner.

"Then I wish you would give her this," she said, extending a small plastic box.

"I expected as much," said Steinbrunner. "Poison?"

"No, not poison. Not in the usual sense. A depressant. She will simply go to sleep and from that pass into a period of low vitality."

"Which will end in—?"

Janice said nothing, but her solemn face told all that needed to be told. "Thank you," Steinbrunner said. "I know that this costs you a lot, but I think it is the only human thing to do."

"Who knows what is human any more?" she said. "No, we know what is human to do. We've only to look below. I think it's rather the animal thing to do, and we might be better off if we abandoned our much-vaunted human thing."

"You sound very bitter."

"Just fatigue and a little funk," she said.

"And you're frightened," he accused her.

"I suppose so. Aren't you? You have a lot more to be frightened about than I in the immediate future."

He laughed. "I haven't been frightened in years," he said. "Oh, a little flirt from adrenalin, but not fear. Long-term fear comes from a realization that you will lose a life of value, and I—"

"I'm sorry," she said.

"Don't be. You've just started to find something of value and fear is the natural consequence. Hold on to it; it's an emotion to be cherished."

"I haven't heard that many words out of you since I've known you."

"Perhaps I'm getting talkative in my old age," he said.

After they parted, he thought, she is turning into a rich human being. Remarkable what love can do to the cold and withdrawn ego. He remembered what it had once done for him. For an instant ancient grief warred with a present fury.

He made his way from the mess and down the endless corridors to his quarters. Fortunately, Longo was nowhere about. He drew his chest of personal belongings from the locker in the bulkhead and began to sort out those that he would take along. After some moments, oppressed by a sense of foreboding, he began to separate purely personal effects into a small pile with the intention of sealing these into a package that would be destroyed if he did not return. He paused lovingly over a small Kodachrome of himself in black leather astride his Norton. How he missed that machine and the marvelously lonely trips, roaring up the back lanes of decaying Florida highways. There was also a photo of himself, young and looking exceedingly well washed, taken just a week before he had embarked

for the United States. He wished that he had a photo of
Vasile, but he had never owned one. He could still sum-
mon a mental image of his blocky young face, eager and
stern alternately, with excited eyes that seemed to take in
the whole new world. It had been like that for him, the
first time outside of his native country and indeed the first
time he had gone more than a hundred miles from the village in which he was born. He and Rudenko had enlisted
together and the close emotional ties that held them together had persisted through the first year of their service
until they had both been stationed in Berlin.

Although they had been very nearly the same age,
Steinbrunner was emotionally older and more sophisticated, having existed on the rootless periphery of society
since his parents' early death. He was wise in the devious
ways of the East Berlin world, knowledgeable in the black
market, and facile in turning the most casual circumstance
into a way of lining his own pockets. With them at first it
had been merely business. He had bought rations from the
young Rudenko and then from Vasile. The young man
had a special kind of innocence which had delighted Steinbrunner, for all of his own youthful cynicism. The boy
took to him in spite of their conflicting social roles, and
soon Steinbrunner was showing off to his impressionable
eyes. He took him for rides on the motorcycle and showed
him the back alleys of the city and found him girls and got
him drunk. Rudenko, with a furious kind of protective-
ness, tried to stop it, and Vasile told Steinbrunner about it.
Steinbrunner finally demanded the reason for Rudenko's
special concern one night when Vasile had drunk too
much. Vasile told him. It was then that Steinbrunner knew
that he might have what he had increasingly desired to
have. It was a crude seduction with no subtlety but its impact on Vasile was enormous. Its impact on the cynical
Steinbrunner was even greater, when he realized the innocence and trust that had become his responsibility.

He had not known that he could feel such emotion. He
found himself restless, waiting for the weekends and for
the occasional pass that the boy managed. He became so

wrapped up in Vasile that his normal sense of danger waned. He was unaware for a long time that they were on occasion followed. When he finally realized it, it was too late. He sought to warn Vasile but that night a boy brought the message.

It was Rudenko, Vasile thought, who out of frustration and vengefulness had confided his suspicions to one of their officers. There was no room for such deviation, especially with one of Steinbrunner's kind, and they arrested Vasile. The arrest and the disgrace were too much. He slashed his wrists with a metal strap from his prison bunk the next night.

Of course, they came for Steinbrunner, but he was already alerted. He hid for two days, debating his course in the midst of the most terrible anguish and sense of loss. He longed for revenge, for the chance to smash that hated face. In the end, he did the only thing that meant anything to him who was, after all, strongly conditioned through the years to survive. He scouted the wall, found a low spot where the barbed wire had not been repaired and, using a high ramp from a nearby warehouse, he made his leap. The landing shock, amid the spatter of automatic weapon fire, wrenched his back and broke his leg. The Americans on the other side dragged him to safety and he spent three months in a West Berlin hospital before he was finally discharged.

There was little left but to go on. He found his way out of Berlin and into Germany, where after several months he applied for a visa. In this he had the help from a consular officer whom he had met and who wanted, finally, rather badly to get rid of him. It was a fair bargain and nine months after his grand leap, he sailed for New York.

Vasile was a year away, a decade away, and finally as Steinbrunner became more deeply involved, after pilot training, in his astronaut courses, a dim lifetime away. He never quite forgot, never quite found any real human contact again. The pain was there, dulled but never truly forgotten. Sometimes, when he had too much to drink and became maudlin, it washed out over him, threatening the iron composure he had so painfully learned. He carefully buried the hurt under work and a mindless involvement in the day-to-day details of his job.

It had been this way for years, until Rudenko appeared. Now the old passions were welling up again, threatening his control. The old hatred, the mindless need to take revenge for that ancient hate was upon him. He despised the feel of hatred in his guts, but he could no longer ignore it.

He turned out the light and lay on his side, staring at the bulkhead. He needed to rest before the takeoff next watch but his body was tense and the thoughts teemed in his mind. He could not rid himself of the racing images that chased each other in an endless, repetitive circle. Finally he caught himself dozing with the sound of his own snores in his ears starting him again to wakefulness. This happened again and suddenly he was wide awake.

There was something in the darkness, he thought; no, not something—someone—outside. Longo? No, he would be busy with the final countdown on the Orbiter. Someone was standing outside the hatch, breathing heavily. In menace? No, more like indecision. He waited, listening, hearing the faint rustle of clothing. Finally he heard a distinct intake of breath. This was followed by a quiet knock on the door.

He rose, zipped up his coveralls, and felt his way through the darkness to the door. It opened silently at his touch. Rothgate stood outside, his face a study in indecision and conflict.

"Can I come in, Lieutenant?" he asked.

"Of course," Steinbrunner said, standing aside. "Just a moment while I turn on some light."

"No," Rothgate said. "Leave it dark. I can find my way."

Steinbrunner said nothing but waited until he saw that the colonel had found a seat on the opposite bunk. Then he closed the door and carefully made his way across the small enclosure to his own bunk. He sat, leaning forward and listening to the colonel's hard breathing. Except for this sound and the pounding of his own heart in his ears, there was nothing for several moments.

"How do you feel about this trip?" Rothgate asked at last.

Steinbrunner shrugged, and then remembered that the colonel could not see him. "Feel? How should I feel?"

"I mean, are you scared? What's your reaction?"

"A certain amount of uneasiness," Steinbrunner admitted. "Nothing very positive; nothing very noteworthy."

"Even with Rudenko? Oh, I know there's something between you two. You look at him as if you could cut his throat. You knew him before?"

"I knew him before."

"And you don't like him?"

Steinbrunner said nothing.

"You know, this Mars project is insane. You must realize that we are throwing away our only chance for survival. And the agreement Farrington has with the Red commander. God, to think that I would see the day when a Red commanded men of mine."

"I suppose it was a necessary compromise," Steinbrunner said.

"Compromise, hell," Rothgate said fiercely in the dark. "You can't compromise with those monsters and you and I both know it. We know it far better than anyone on this station."

"I have no reason to love them, as you know," Steinbrunner admitted.

"If the core assembly is not activated," Rothgate said slowly, "we will have to continue with our original plans."

"To land a moon colony? I suppose so. I personally think it's the best idea, but I'm not making the decisions."

"There are decisions you can make," Rothgate said slowly.

"That's Rudenko's job. He's the one to activate the core assembly."

"That's true," Rothgate said. "You'll take care of the launches of the other vehicles. We need the motors and the extra oxidizer, of course, regardless of where we go. You must do that."

"But you don't want the core assembly tied in to the main array?" Steinbrunner asked. "That would be difficult to stop with Rudenko along."

Rothgate sighed and paused, apparently considering his next step. Finally, he said, "If you agree that the Mars project is a bad decision—"

"For the moment say that I do," Steinbrunner said.

"Then you must stop Rudenko."

"There's only one way to do that," Steinbrunner said.

"Does that seem so distasteful to you?"

Steinbrunner grunted, savoring the thought. Once it was done, there was little they could do about it. "What about the Russians?" he asked.

"We will have to handle that carefully. First, you must launch the two vehicles and I will see that the one on automatic comes to our orbit under our control. Then we may well bargain."

"And if we can't?"

"There are ways of handling them."

"What about the women? You can't move against them without endangering the women."

"Always that little ace in the hole," Rothgate sneered. "Well, we can play a few tricky games also. I've been in charge of scheduling, you know. The transfer of the female personnel to the outer shell of our station begins this watch. We start to disassemble the Russian station in two watches with sections of ours going the same watch. Once we have their female personnel aboard—"

"Yes, I can see that it might work."

"Well?" Rothgate demanded. "Shall we sit by and let them finally win out?"

"No," Steinbrunner said doubtfully. "Still, it's a terrible risk."

"The first thing is to prevent Rudenko from activating the new assembly."

"That I can do," Steinbrunner said, leaning back.

"You know what you must do?"

"Yes," Steinbrunner said tiredly. "I know. It's something I should have done years ago, but now is perhaps best. Even that death should be useful."

"It's all a part of the game they like to play."

"No," Steinbrunner said with sudden fierceness. "No, this time it is my game."

Fourteen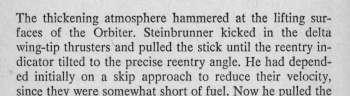

The thickening atmosphere hammered at the lifting surfaces of the Orbiter. Steinbrunner kicked in the delta wing-tip thrusters and pulled the stick until the reentry indicator tilted to the precise reentry angle. He had depended initially on a skip approach to reduce their velocity, since they were somewhat short of fuel. Now he pulled the nose down slowly, watching the nose temperature sensors as they entered the denser upper atmosphere.

Beside him Rudenko spoke softly into the throat microphone, calling out readings from the instruments before him as he had learned in the past days of drill. His role was purely secondary. Steinbrunner could have flown the mission without him, and indeed had done so many times. However, the flight was so critical that Longo and Farrington in the station far above were monitoring in an override function.

The temperature rose slightly as part of the ablative shield tore away. This happened occasionally if there was an undetected fissure in the plastic layer, but there was no great cause for alarm. So long as material remained to boil away from the nose and leading edges of the delta wings, its high latent heat of vaporization and heat of decomposition would carry away the frictional heat that might otherwise melt the leading surfaces.

The airfoils began to bite into the air now, and Steinbrunner detected a sluggish response to the stick. He checked his fuel gauges and debated starting the jet engine. He decided against it, preferring to fly the vehicle by the seat of his pants and conserve fuel by a careful maneuvering of reentry path. They were at 150,000 feet now, and swinging across Montana. It was time to increase the reentry angle. He did so, and noted only a three-degree temperature rise.

Seventy-five thousand feet now. He touched the button and in the rear the prime engine caught. He felt a faint surge of lowered deceleration but kept the thrust of the engine low so that their air speed was dropping still more with each passing moment. At 40,000 feet they dropped finally to Mach 4.0 and he brought the Orbiter under full-powered flight. The controls were sluggish but they responded satisfactorily.

Over Mississippi they dropped to Mach 2.5 and he held that velocity as they moved south down the peninsula toward the Cape. Time dragged now at this velocity but he was pleased that the full entry into powered flight had come as smoothly as it had. He looked over at Rudenko in his heavy suit. Rudenko managed an approving smile, which he ignored.

Some fifteen minutes later he dropped altitude sharply as the sickly green of the Atlantic appeared ahead. Through the scudding clouds he could make out the traceries of service roads and the discolored patches of launching pads. They dropped quickly moving over the old Titan III C assembly buildings that still served for smaller boosters, and turned out over the ocean to enter their glide path.

There was no instrumentation from below and he had to depend on his own sight. The Cape area was covered with rotted-looking clouds, colored with overtones of purple and brown. He spotted the Prime III runway which he had used so often before and moved the stick to enter its glide path, cutting power slowly and carefully. The approach was good, if a bit too fast, but he eased the air brakes down, feeling them tug like clawed fingers at the turgid air. Contrails broke from the wing tips and whipped to the rear.

Over the whistle of air biting the delta surfaces, Rudenko said, "I have the girl Karen." His voice sounded strained in the suit earphones.

"Don't bother me," Steinbrunner said harshly.

"She can talk you in."

"I don't need her," Steinbrunner snapped.

They were flashing down the runway now as he applied

the air brakes and cut power. They were almost at stall speed and still twenty-five feet above the runway. Damn it, what was wrong with him? He'd never been this skittish on a landing before. He eased the stick up and applied brakes still more. The craft flashed a bare foot above the runway and he cut power below stall speed. The undercarriage touched, squealed, bounced and touched again. They bounced almost a foot into the air before he brought it down to contact again. Then the craft settled and raced across the runway as Steinbrunner applied full air brakes. In the last instant he saw that he would need the forward thrusters.

He hit the button before him without warning and the peroxide jets flashed at full power. The sudden deceleration threw Rudenko against the control panel. The craft shuddered to a halt, just fifty feet from the end of the runway. They sat silently as Steinbrunner cut the power. He looked over at Rudenko, who pointedly looked out his window.

"All right, it wasn't a good one," Steinbrunner said.

"We are here. That's all that matters," Rudenko said.

Steinbrunner felt a surge of anger at his offhand manner. And here you will stay, he promised himself.

He signaled for Rudenko to open the hatch. Rudenko leaned forward uncertainly and pressed the wrong button before Steinbrunner could stop him. In the belly of the Orbiter, electric motors cranked open the clamshell doors to the cargo hatch. Rudenko looked ineffectual for a moment and then pressed the proper button. To their rear the pilot's air lock went through its now useless cycling noises and then opened to the outer atmosphere. The inner door was hand actuated. Steinbrunner unbelted and pushed it outward. He dismounted, bundling the extra spacesuit with him. Rudenko followed him and they alighted on the mist-damp concrete of the landing strip.

A cold wind whipped across the flat terrain, tugging at the heavy material of their suits. Overhead the tattered cloud layer twisted in swirls of brown and grey and purple, the color of rot. Nitric oxide, Steinbrunner thought, seeing the brown—so much nitric oxide. It didn't seem possible.

Across the wide expanse of churned earth and black macadam and lean concrete strips, rank on rank of giant buildings seemed lost in the mist that curdled over the launch complex. He pointed to a spot near where three electric cars, painted a bright red, stood waiting.

"Do you know how to operate those?" he demanded.

Rudenko shook his head.

"Come along," Steinbrunner commanded. They approached the first car and Steinbrunner touched the main switch, checking the charge indicator. The car was dead. The next two showed three quarters and one half charge respectively. He spent five minutes, carefully explaining how the simple devices operated. Finally he drew Rudenko aside and knelt, spreading a map out on the damp concrete. He ignored the way the moisture quickly penetrated the map. They would need it only once.

They knelt before the map and he pointed out the core array building, ignoring the touch of the man's shoulder on his own. Finally, they arose and Rudenko took the electric car with the three-quarter charge and haltingly drove off. Steinbrunner watched him go, thinking that now would have been the best time to stop him. The unreality of the situation suddenly hit him and he wondered if he was truly capable of going through with it.

He shook off the mood and mounted the remaining car, storing the extra suit intended for Karen in the rear. He turned on the power key and touched the accelerator. The electric motor emitted a low whine and the tires sprayed ground water. He guided the car out onto the landing strip and headed south, toward the distant towering launch complexes that held the remaining two viable ships.

The launch blockhouse for pad 20 was some five miles away. En route he passed pad 18 and stopped for a moment to check the Orbiter assembly there. This was the key to their return, the great cluster of boosters looming over his head. The gantry was still in place, he saw. This would present some difficulties. He wondered if he could rig some sort of automatic sequencer to handle the launch, once they were aboard. If he didn't, then he would be marooned. It was a challenging task for one lone man.

He started the car again. Some ten minutes later he passed the silent assembly on pad 20. The upper stage carried a sheet of ice and frost. He could see wisps of boiling vapor coming from the vent. A good part of the liquid FLOX should still be in the storage tank. The metal-Teflon top-off hose was in place, its long catenary stiff with ice, which suggested that the reservoir still carried oxidizer. Luck was riding with him, he saw as he covered the last distance to the control blockhouse.

He dismounted from the car and looked back the long distance to the pad. Already mists were blowing in from the sea, hazing the outlines of the great beast so that its bright red markings became a faded pink to his eyes. He walked down the ramp, turned past the concrete blast shield, and walked the covered corridor, his feet echoing hollowly against the overhanging concrete ceilings. The place looked dank and lonely, with scrubby walls. A litter of cigarette butts and paper filled one corner before the metal doors that led to the control room.

At the end of the corridor, deep in shadow, he saw the red metal double door to the launch room. One door was partly ajar, framing the bright blue of fluorescent lighting within. Steinbrunner breathed a sigh of relief. He knew that the station pile was still operating or they would not have had use of the computers that Karen attended, but he was worried that power to the launch complexes might have been interrupted.

He pushed through the door and blinked his eyes at the sudden brilliance of the room. Rank on rank of monitoring boards filled the room, their jewel lights still glowing as though the five-man crew had just walked away from them and would return any moment. As he surveyed the room, a high-resolution tape deck near his left chattered and the spool rotated a quarter turn. It was still monitoring and recording data on the birds outside, he thought. Man's mindless servants still faithful after man had passed. A lot more constant than the mind that had created it.

He moved across the room toward the automatic sequencers that he knew lay behind the ranks of monitoring consoles. As he turned past the first bank, he very nearly stumbled on a body lying on the floor. The man was dressed in orange dungarees and sprawled with one hand still clutching a revolver. There was no sign yet of corruption on the body. Steinbrunner decided after examining him that he could not have been dead more than three days. There was no sign of a bullet wound, no clue as to what had killed him. His eyes were wide and staring, his skin white with patches of blue mottling under the surface.

At the rear of the room he found the bank of automatic sequences. Another body, also in orange coveralls, was slumped in a plastic shell chair before the main sequencer. Steinbrunner felt a faint nausea when he saw that the man had been shot in the back of the head at close range. It was a messy wound. The slug had exited from the right cheekbone just below the eye, carrying flesh and bone fragments which had spattered the console in front of the body. A heavy pit in the metal of the panel was the only sign of the slug that had ended the man's life.

Steinbrunner carefully pulled the body off the chair, wondering at the terrible drama that had led to this man's death and that of the other man among the monitoring consoles. Had the first man killed the second and then himself succumbed to some obscure cause? Radiation, or possibly the rickettsial agent that the Russians had released? More likely the second, Steinbrunner decided. He would have to radio back and make sure that all proper decontamination steps were taken. They had thought that the agent might not have penetrated to this continent yet, but it now appeared possible that it had.

He seated himself and checked the circuit layout on the console. He had been drilled in the sequencer two years before, but it took some minutes for the memories to return. There had been some modifications, he saw. He identified the patchboards that served the two pads that still carried live birds. He switched in the one on pad 20 and moved over to the monitoring board. Upper-stage skin temperature was quite low, he saw, but internal circuits still gave a Go signal. The lower stages were at full standby arming, needing only the red firing key for the primary ignition sequence to be triggered.

The FLOX tanks in the upper stage showed better than 60 percent full, which he found surprising.

He checked the monitors on the top-off umbilical. There appeared to be some blockage in the umbilical. He considered that this might be a fallacious signal, but decided at last against any attempt to top off the tank. Better 60 percent full than risk the chance of a leaking umbilical and the complete loss of the bird. He considered severing the top-off connection but decided against it. Better to move the gantry back and launch with the umbilical in place. It was safer that way.

He returned to the sequencer and set it up for launch, trying to ignore the bright orange form on the floor. The launch key was missing from its bright red slot. He knelt beside the man on the floor and searched his pockets. He found the key attached to a heavy metal tag in the man's breast pocket. He rose, flipped back the red protecting mask on the console, and inserted the key. Then he turned it to the right, and checked the arming light. It was still unlighted. He turned the key to neutral and began a step-by-step check of the board. Finally on the side of the console in the box behind the black panel he found a bank of fuses. One of them showed a clear separation in the wire.

He debated hunting for a fuse. It would be ironic if there were a short or an overload somewhere within the console. Finally, he decided that there was little to be gained in either case. He detached the fuse, and feeling inside the box with his heavily gloved fingers, he twisted the fuse contacts away from their plastic mount and joined them, bypassing the absent fuse. Then he returned to the console and tried the arming key again. This time he was rewarded with the red glow of the arming light.

He checked to make sure that the proper patchboard was still in place and then touched the switch that started the sequencing tape. From this point, the launch would be on complete automatic, with automatic holds if any one of the subsystems signaled a malfunction. He moved back from the console, stepping over the huddled orange figure, and made his way to the monitoring console. He keyed the launch pad pickup and watched as the cathode tube in the console flickered, then cleared. The long view of the bird was sharp, with the crispness that came from the fineness of the scanning.

He watched as the gantry moved back smoothly. The FLOX bearing top-off umbilicus became taut. Its surface glistened in the dim afternoon light. Frost and ice fell from it in a miniature snowfall. He prayed silently, hoping that the umbilicus would not cast loose before the launch. It held and he waited as the deluge system started, flooding the foot of the blast basin. After five seconds he saw the first wisp of smoke drifting from one nozzle closure. The pyrogens had ignited. A second later both closures blasted free of the booster nozzles. The bright metallic flames of the exhaust scored the pad, turning the coolant water into boiling steam. The steam rose to mingle with the boiling clouds of white aluminum oxide.

The bird balanced on a pad of flame and boiling vapor. Then it reached full thrust. The heavy restrainers retracted, and the bird began to mount slowly. It seemed to take forever to leave the pad. He saw brown fumes spilling from the thrust-vectoring manifold as the nozzle flames flicked back and forth, correcting for the wind shipping against the side of the bird. It mounted faster and faster, filling the screen with boiling oxide smoke. Then all vision was obscured by the boiling clouds. Only the bright flame was visible mounting into the sky and then this too was lost.

In the midst of the boiling smoke a new flame grew. It was a flame much brighter than the exhaust. The FLOX, he realized. It was spouting from the ruptured reservoir, igniting the steel of the gantry and the plastic and rubber fittings. He watched as the flame grew and suddenly it blossomed into an overwhelming brilliance before the pickup went dead. The blast reached him several seconds later. It sounded like low thunder from an approaching storm.

Afterwards he searched through the equipment lockers at the other end of the room. Finally he found what he was looking for, a variable timer with a relay. It could be set to close the relay at various delays up to one hour. He carried it back to the sequencer, cut the arming key, and closed down the tape system. He wired the relay into the bypassed fuse bracket, cursing at the clumsiness of his gloves. He armed the board and tripped the relay. The sequence began and he ended it immediately by turning the arming key. Then he reset the tape and switched to the patchboard for pad 18, where the other bird waited silently. He set the timer for one hour. It now remained only for him to turn the arming key and sixty minutes later, the launch sequence would begin.

On the way out, he stopped briefly by the second man and rescued the revolver. He checked it carefully, found that only one round had been discharged, and placed it in the utility pocket on his leg. He wondered what had prompted the man to kill his co-worker. Delirium or some unknown conflict? It was a mystery that would never be solved.

Outside, he mounted the electric car and turned the tiller to carry him down the asphalt road leading toward the distant blockhouse where the main computer section was housed. He checked his sleeve chronometer and saw that he had been occupied well over an hour. Rudenko should certainly have managed to activate the auxiliary cores by now. There remained only the rescue of the girl, and one final task. He tapped the bulge in his utility pocket and wondered how it would feel.

He reached behind him with one hand to check that the bundled space suit was still aboard. The package rested firmly in its niche in the rear seat of the electric car. It would probably be too large for Karen, but they had no information on her size and had decided that she could bear the inconvenience of a larger suit.

A heavier wind was whipping in from the sea now, driving the puddled moisture of the tarmack in ragged lace across his path. He looked overhead and saw that the clouds had lowered threateningly. The winds were likely to continue rising. That could mean a problem in launching, since the thrust-vectoring equipment of the solid boosters had a limited response. He had heard of the birds being launched in winds up to forty miles an hour, but no man-rated system had ever been committed to such turbulence.

He approached the massive blockhouse that housed the main computer banks with a sense of foreboding. The blacktop curved widely around the blockhouse, approaching it from the rear. As he directed the electric car into the approach drive, he saw that a single red car stood beside a concrete barricade. It was, he saw from the number, the car that Rudenko had taken. For an instant he felt a sense of regret and then a quickly overpowering anger. No, there was no time left for regrets. He had promised what he would do and there was every indication that all would be lost in the coming flight if he did not end it here.

He pulled his car up abreast of Rudenko's and dismounted. He removed and checked the revolver. The cold touch of the deadly steel seemed to invade his arms and he felt a tight nausea in the pit of his stomach. Did he hate the man that much? Truthfully, he did not know. There were warring emotions, something he had not found in his life for many years. Vasile had meant something to the man. That was a factor he could not dismiss from his mind. Was it simply an ego function, this need to destroy Rudenko? Or did he truly believe that this was the only way of diverting the station from the Mars project in which he did not believe? His sense of loss, he realized, had softened through the years and he did not hate Rudenko anymore. If he killed him, the motivation would be purely pragmatic.

He walked over to Rudenko's car and saw that the switch was still on. As he checked the charge, the radio crackled in his ear. Rudenko's voice said, "Steinbrunner, I need help."

"Where are you?" he asked, triggering the transceiver.

"Computer bunker," the man said. He sounded breathless.

"I'm outside," Steinbrunner said.

"Hurry," Rudenko's voice said. "Bring the extra suit."

Steinbrunner bundled up the mass of fabric and metal and moved rapidly around the concrete barricade. He didn't have far to go. At the end of the passage before the open metal door, he saw two figures, one of them suited. Rudenko was bending over a silent shape.

He hurried up. "Here, help me get her into the suit," Rudenko said.

"What happened?"

"She was foolish. She opened the door as I approached. She's very weak and God knows what she has breathed in the last few minutes. She didn't even wear a white suit.

It was true, Steinbrunner saw. She was clad only in red coveralls. The idiot girl. To have lasted so long and now to endanger herself so completely. "I don't like this," Steinbrunner said. "She's exposed herself needlessly and I think we're endangering the station by taking her back."

Rudenko looked at him with large sorrowful eyes. "Are we both to be left behind then?"

"What do you mean?" Steinbrunner demanded.

"I am not such a fool, my friend," Rudenko said. "I knew what dangers I faced when I came."

"I see you were thoroughly briefed," Steinbrunner sneered, bending down over the girl and inspecting her face.

"No," Rudenko said sadly. "It is just that I know the depth of your hate. I have lived with that thought for many years, hoping we might meet and I could explain— convince you."

"It's much too late for that," Steinbrunner said. In spite of his resolve, he could feel himself weakening.

"Yes," Rudenko said. "Yes, I suppose it is. Still, she is a brave girl and we must at least try. Let them make the decision."

Steinbrunner looked down at the silent figure. She was tall, at least five nine, and lean with fair skin and jet-black hair. Probably in her early thirties. Not a pretty girl, he saw. Rather plain, in fact, but even in her repose her face held a kind of strength and purpose that would have animated it with a striking attraction were she conscious.

"All right," he said. "Help me get her into the suit."

He threw his burden to the ground and Rudenko helped him unfold the suit and open the zippers with their plastic double seals. Her body was quite limp and unmanageable, her abdomen swollen with its burden, but they managed to position her finally and insert her arms and legs into the suit. Steinbrunner zipped the main seams closed while Rudenko handled her arms and legs.

"She must stay inside until she is in a sealed enclosure," Rudenko said.

"What if she starts to deliver?" Steinbrunner asked. "She looks very close."

Rudenko shook his massive head, his helmeted body moving with the effort. "Just pray that it will not be so," he said.

Pray? Steinbrunner thought. Do you still do that after all these years? He said nothing, however. They carried her to Rudenko's car and positioned her in the rear, using a wide webbing that had been intended to restrain cargo.

"I've set up the launch on automatic," Steinbrunner said.

"Will it be soon enough?" Rudenko asked, pointing at the clouds which seemed lower and more threatening. The wind whipped raggedly across the plain and Steinbrunner realized that unconsciously he was already leaning into it. God, this wasn't the season for hurricanes, he thought. Yet the wind held all the promise of hurricane force.

Rudenko sensed his thought. "Who knows what strange things we have done to this sad world," he said.

"We'd better get to the bird," Steinbrunner said. Rudenko mounted his car and Steinbrunner hurried to his. He touched the switch and heard the silent whirr of the electric motor. He engaged the clutch and turned the vehicle to the asphalt road. Once he looked behind and saw that Rudenko was following with his silent burden.

They made it to the edge of the launch pad in twenty minutes, fighting the wind all the way. Steinbrunner jumped from the car and hurried over to Rudenko. He helped him free the girl from the webbing. They carried her across the slick black end concrete to the elevator in the gantry.

"How soon can we launch?" Rudenko said as they positioned her silently in the elevator.

"An hour," Steinbrunner said. "I set it up for an hour."

Rudenko inspected the lowering clouds. The wind by now had reached a punishing whipping velocity. "It is not soon enough. Can you change it?"

"It will take time," Steinbrunner said. "Better load aboard and we'll take our chances. It's ten minutes to the blockhouse to trip the timer and ten minutes back."

"Which gives us perhaps a half hour of delay."

Rudenko looked at him, his eyes wide and waiting, their expression obscured by a stray reflection from his helmet. Steinbrunner touched his utility pocket.

"Is it now then?"

"Yes, it's now," Steinbrunner said fiercely.

"I was expecting it," Rudenko said. "It really doesn't matter, my friend. Not at all. I suppose I have been expecting to find you around every corner of my life."

"Damn it!" Steinbrunner groaned. "Why, why?"

"Why? It's a question we ask of chance all of our lives. But it is only chance."

"Why did you do it?"

"But I didn't do it," Rudenko said quietly. "I would have willingly seen him go with you if it would make him happy. He was young and very foolish but if it had been what he wanted—" He shrugged, not bothering to finish the sentence.

"You expect me to believe that?" Steinbrunner asked furiously. All at once he was seized with a rage that left him quivering. He fumbled with the utility pocket and produced the revolver.

"So it is now?" Rudenko said tiredly. "Then get it over with so you both can escape." A sudden blast of wind whipped driving rain across his faceplate.

"You—you bastards, you're insidious. I know the way you think. You'd convince me that he simply walked into their hands."

"He did, you know," Rudenko said. "You do not understand how closely we were watched. They knew that he had made his friendship with you and they followed him. They discovered finally that there was nothing politically dangerous in the relationship but that there was something much worse. You see, we were and still are what your Americans would call very puritanical in our outlook. They could not allow such a thing to go on."

"Damn it," Steinbrunner said, feeling his reserve begin to break. "What was the harm in it, and so much good?"

"How can I argue? He was dear to me since our early childhood. There was nothing I would not have done but I could do nothing to save him. They took him away and he killed himself that night in the prison. He took a steel slat from his bed and sharpened it on the concrete and opened his veins so that his life bled away the way my life has bled away until now."

Is it true? Steinbrunner thought. After all these years of hating, is it true?

And he knew, somehow he knew that it was.

"There's little time left," Rudenko said. "The wind will soon be too high."

"Get her into the capsule," Steinbrunner said. "I'll set up the timer."

"Can you advance the time?" Rudenko said, calmly accepting the change in his mood.

"I think so. It will be close," Steinbrunner said.

"Take great care," Rudenko said. He reached out a thick gloved hand and Steinbrunner automatically grasped it. For a long moment they held onto each other's hands and they looked through barriers of plastic at each other.

"Take care," Rudenko repeated softly.

It was like an echo from the far past and for the first time in years Steinbrunner felt his barriers dissolving. "Hurry," he managed, and turned to go.

The last thing he heard before Rudenko turned to the elevator was, "He told me much about you on those lonely nights. I thought you must have been a most unusual young man."

He mounted the electric car and turned it onto the concrete strip and then onto the macadam at some distance, thinking how anticlimactic his life was. But, in spite of the high points of a life, those high points loaded with potential drama, a man's life was not structured like a play. There was no order, only the endless ironies of the chance meeting, the lost moment, the endless pile on pile of mis-understandings and lost words.

He sped across the wide plain. Once he turned and saw that the elevator had ascended with the pair. When he next looked he saw it again descending, its bright yellow cab a splotch of color against the lowering drabness of the clouds. Some five hundred yards from the launch block-house, the electric car simply stopped. He looked at the charge dial, activated the emergency source, and saw that it too was depleted. He had taken the one with the lesser charge. It seemed, he thought ironically, that fate was still deciding too much for him.

No matter, he wasn't sure at all that he would have been happy in that new and violent world they wanted to build. Well, let them, with his blessings and his last thoughts. No regrets. He had lived well enough and he had done something of worth, if only by refusal to act.

He entered the blockhouse and walked to the sequen-cer. He cut out the timer and called Rudenko. "I can't make it back," he said. "The charge in the car is exhaust-ed."

"Isn't there another?" the man's voice asked, con-cerned, already impossibly distant.

"I'll give you five minutes," Steinbrunner said.

"You can make it back."

Steinbrunner checked the wind velocity on the bank of instruments mounted on an adjacent console. "No time," he said. "We're getting quite a blow."

"I am truly sorry," Rudenko said slowly.

"I know," Steinbrunner said. "I really know that you are. No matter." Then he added, "Ten minutes."

He threw the bypass on the timer and the ten-minute sequence began. He listened on the intercom and heard Rudenko's harsh breathing but the man said nothing. The only sound was a deep, almost wracking series of breaths. There was a special communication in that, Steinbrunner thought, as the time sequence approached the final ten seconds.

He counted down silently to himself until the red launch light glared from the board. He did not bother to turn on the pad monitor. He heard the vibrations from the boosters as they built strength and finally hurled the two from the pad into that lost, not-to-be imagined future that he had dreaded and would not know. He found the capsule Janice had given him resting in its lucite box. He considered it, thinking that perhaps this offered a solution. No, that way was not a man's way, he thought. He threw the box behind the console and sat down to consider what awaited him.

He sat for a long time and looked at the wall before him, seeing—not into the future—but into the dead and lost and terrible past.

Fifteen ▶━━━━━━━━━━━━━━━━━━━━━➤

The major administrative functions of the combined forces had been transferred to the new personnel capsules aboard the ship. In the last week before the flight, final dismantling of the two stations had begun. Janice Svoboda, her equipment, and her patient Karen had been transferred the week before. Now the final discussions on the flight would be held aboard a new expanded wardroom in the depths of the spidery ship.

"It is very close," Rodrigues said. "Without the extra oxidizer and the engines from the Cape, we would not make it."

"I don't understand," said Janice. "Surely we can reach escape velocity."

"It is the rendezvous," Longo told her. "We have to be at a precise point in the Martian orbit when the planet is there. A matter of a few hundred miles an hour at the time we leave Earth orbit could make the difference."

"I'm sure that we have a safety factor of perhaps ten per cent," Rodrigues said.

"That's not too encouraging," remarked Farrington.

"We could reduce mass appreciably," Rothgate declared darkly.

"We don't dare discard more from the B list," said Longo. "We need everything."

"The final components from the Russian station could be discarded," Rothgate said.

"That's enough!" Farrington said.

"You know they killed Steinbrunner," Rothgate said. "That bastard left him back there to die. They've made the transfer of their women. Why transfer the holding crew from the station? That will mean a lower mass since we won't need their life-support system."

"Colonel," Longo said slowly. "Maybe we're making a

mistake politically as you believe, but the only assurance we have of racial survival is in numbers. There comes a time when even you have to face that."

"Oh," sneered Rothgate, "have they done such a good job of winning you over, Captain?"

Longo sat, visibly controlling himself.

"I said that's enough," Farrington said tiredly. "We settled this question long ago. There will be no further discussion of it. We're committed completely to the mission and you're not helping with your persistence, Jeb."

"Steinbrunner——" Rothgate began.

"We know what happened to Steinbrunner," Farrington said firmly. "Now, that's all. That's an order and that's one order you will obey."

Rothgate lapsed into silence. After a moment, he rose and walked from the wardroom.

"I am afraid that we may face a problem there," said Lieberman. "It might be very wise to place a man with the colonel."

"Do you think he has reached that point?" asked Farrington.

"I would not mention it in front of the others if I did not believe so," Lieberman answered. "He is a man consumed with hatred past reason. I am sure that even Colonel Voroshilov is aware of this by now."

"He has mentioned it," Farrington admitted. "Still, he is a senior officer and I hesitate——"

"Perhaps after the meeting, I should give you more information," Lieberman said.

Farrington shifted uncomfortably. "I'm sorry that we have to air our dirty linen in a meeting like this, but perhaps it's best."

"He's been in a bad state for the past week," Janice observed. "Ever since Rudenko returned without Steinbrunner."

"How's your patient?" asked Farrington.

"It's too early to tell. From the information the Soviets have given me, I'm sure that she is not carrying the rickettsial agent. There's the question of radioactive poisoning, mostly Strontium ninety. I'm trying to detoxify that."

"What's your opinion?" asked Longo.

"It's hardly likely that we'll succeed," Janice said reluctantly. "We've placed her in hypothermia and have been cycling her blood through an ion exchange column. Then there are the chelating agents that should promote a calcium-strontium exchange. I think there's too much internal ionization damage, however. If it weren't for the hypothermia she'd probably be dead. The best we can hope for is to save the child."

"Ironic," Farrington sighed. "To spend so much time and effort to save her, and then lose her. She was the difference between success and failure for us."

"She's never regained consciousness," Lieberman said. "The baby is sound, I think. We can hope it's not damaged by the internal radiation."

"It will be a long time before we know," Janice said. "Long after she delivers, if she does."

"Why not a Caesarean?" asked Longo. "I thought that was the sort of thing you normally did."

"There wasn't much point," Lieberman said. "The child's blood is equilibrated with the mother's and the detoxification works as well with the child in place as separately. Besides, Karen would not survive the shock. We thought this the best that we could do. Frankly, though, I doubt if she'll make it."

"Longo, can you give us a final report? I have a meeting with Colonel Voroshilov in fifteen minutes aboard the ship."

"Oxidizer transfer is almost complete," Longo said. "We have the final sections from ours and the Soviet station to salvage and the last personnel transfers. Most of the personnel from both stations are now aboard. Dr. Svoboda and Dr. Lieberman have assigned Mulhill and Blaisdell to process them for hypothermia. This leaves us with an operating staff of thirty."

"When will the final oxidizer transfer take place?" Farrington asked.

"We have to bring the capsule into a higher orbit. It orbited near the Soviet station, as you know. I'll need five men for the transfer. The remainder of the crew will transfer the final components of the Soviet station. They're mostly power cells and the stand-by life-support system."

"We must be ready in forty-eight hours," Rodrigues said. "After that we will lose some velocity from Toro's approach."

"Can we make it?" asked Farrington.

"Yes, I think so," Longo answered.

The meeting broke up and Farrington gathered up the papers before him. Lieberman remained behind.

"What shall we do about Colonel Rothgate?" he asked.

"I think it's best that we schedule him for hypothermia," Farrington said.

"That won't solve your problem," Lieberman said. "We will still have to contend with him at a later date."

"My God, Doctor," Farrington demanded, "what do you want me to do? I have a second in command who is nearly useless, probably strongly paranoid. I can't have him wandering around, but I can't dispose of him."

"I'll schedule him for hypothermia, then," said Lieberman. "He'll probably object."

"He'll obey orders," Farrington said grimly.

"At this point, I wonder," said Lieberman.

Longo had followed Janice from the meeting with a certain feeling of trepidation. For the past week she had seemed to be avoiding him, and he felt that he had failed her in some crucial fashion. He reviewed in his mind the last time they had sex together, analyzing and worrying each statement, each whisper of passion, for some clue to her sudden depression and withdrawal. He was, he realized, beginning to act like every lovesick swain in the history of his race. It was a silly and frustrating feeling, but he could not rid himself of it.

He decided that he could no longer hold off. After passing on some last-minute loading instructions to Georgeoff, he made his way through the personnel passages toward the large hold anchored in the center of the ship. His path was devious—all of the personnel passages were not yet pressurized and he had to make several lateral transfers, either that or suit up, which was inconvenient within the confines of the ship.

The central hold was given over entirely to Janice's operation with its precious living cargo, shielded as much as possible from external radiation by the metal of the ship structure and by the radiation shield from the station. The huge heavy metal shadow had been transferred in the last day from the station after they had carefully assured themselves that there was no immediate prospect of a lethal solar flare during the operation.

He found her in the instrumentation adjunct, hovering over Blaisdell's shoulder as he monitored the body temperatures and vital signs of the personnel who had already entered hypothermia. In the larger laboratory, Lieberman and Mulhill were deeply engrossed in conversation. Longo looked at the two men and wondered how he might get her aside. She glanced up as he rounded the bulkhead and entered the instrumentation section.

"It's working out pretty well," she said. "We've had to settle on a temperature about five degrees higher than I like, but the oxygen and glucose intake is still very low."

"Let me buy you a cup of coffee."

"I'm very busy now," she replied, not meeting his eyes.

He moved in behind her and folded his big fingers about her wrist. "Look," he said. "You've been avoiding me for a week. What have I done?"

"Not here," she said, coloring. "Not now."

"Now," he insisted fiercely. Unconsciously he tightened his grip and she winced, drawing away from him. "Now," he said. "Here, if you won't have it anyplace else."

She bit her lip in confusion and looked at him with shadowed eyes in which pain and indecision warred for a moment. Finally she turned and spoke quickly with Blaisdell. He looked at Longo as she spoke and a faint trace of a smile crossed his lips. Longo felt a surge of anger at the man's obvious amusement. Well, he told himself, he had asked for it, barging in here like a bull. Still, he would have preferred to confront her more quietly.

"Come along," she said. "I've got to pick up some data in my cabin."

He followed her through the laboratory, nodding to Lieberman, who looked up questioningly. They passed into the passage and at the door to her cabin, she paused and said, "If you want to talk, come in, but that's all."

"Look," he said, "I deserve better than that from you. I thought we had reached a point where we could be open and honest with each other."

"Come in," she repeated and as he crossed the threshold, she keyed the hatch closed. She walked over to the cabinet on the far wall and busied herself sorting out papers from a metal file. She was pointedly avoiding his glance and this angered him still more.

"Why are you behaving this way?" he demanded. "This isn't like you at all."

"Isn't it?" she asked, turning. "Perhaps it's just the plain Jane reverting to type."

"I've never said that sort of thing to you. I've never thought that sort of thing."

"Never thought that you were carrying on with someone a little less than a complete woman?" she asked wryly. "I suppose it was all right when I was the only woman here. I knew that was the reason and for the first time I was the belle of the ball. I admit it. It pleased me. But there are others now."

"The Russian girls?" he asked. "What makes you think that can make any difference?"

"I know it will," she said. "That's very clear to me even if it isn't yet to you."

He felt a sudden frustration. How could he make her understand that in the past weeks he had grown in his view of her from a simple outlet of lust to something deeper and more moving?

"Can't you understand that someone can love you?" he demanded. "Is that so hard to accept?"

"Yes," she said. "Yes, it is when you analyze the whole situation. I suppose I thought it was very good to be involved with a virile man. I've never been a sex target before. For a while it felt good to imagine myself a giddy witless little girl who lives just to get screwed, but even that fades. It was a pretty little fantasy, I guess."

He walked to her and attempted to put his arms around her but she pushed him off. "What's wrong with that? What's wrong with being a good lay?" he demanded.

"Was I really?" she asked. "Or just the only one around?"

"Initially, yes," he admitted. "But not now."

"I wish I could convince myself of that," she said. "But I've reconciled myself to fading back into that drab creature I was before all this."

He swore violently, the rage boiling up in him. "Damn it, get that out of your mind. I slept with you because I wanted to. I could just as easily have gone into the john and masturbated but I wanted you and I want you now. We've got the whole new world to people once we land and I want to fill it with our kids."

He was quite unprepared for her reaction. Her eyes widened and filled with tears and in the next instant she had collapsed to the bunk and was sobbing uncontrollably. He tried to touch her and she pushed him away. "Get out," she sobbed. "Get out and let me alone. Let me alone."

He felt lost and ineffectual. There was nothing he could say that he had not said. It seemed not to matter at all. Finally in defeat he turned and left. The closing door cut off her sobs but they echoed in his ears as he returned to the lab. Lieberman was waiting for him.

"I thought it would come to a head," Lieberman said softly.

"You're as perceptive as hell," Longo growled.

"More perceptive than you are sometimes."

"What's wrong with her, Doc?" asked Longo. "I can't understand what's wrong."

"I can well believe that," Lieberman said. "What happened?"

Longo told him.

"Whether you realize it or not, you crazy Italian, you just touched the magic button, a uniquely Italian button," Lieberman said.

"What's being Italian got to do with all this?" Longo demanded.

"You and your fixation on kids."

"It seems to me that's a pretty desirable fixation now. I *want* kids. I want to fill the whole world with them. Is there anything particularly wrong in wanting to do it with her?"

"No," Lieberman said slowly. "Not if she could hold up her end of the bargain."

"I don't understand you."

"No, of course you don't," Lieberman said angrily. "You're a bullheaded highly emotional type who is so obsessed with the need for immortality of your own germ plasm that you elevate it to a mystique. Well, that's fine for this brave new world of ours, but it's not fine for Janice. She's never been a woman who had a great deal of confidence in her own femininity and desirability and when she had to have a hysterectomy——"

"What the hell are you saying?" Longo interrupted. "Why didn't she tell me that?"

"Tell that to you, you lumphead? God knows, men can't ever seem to understand the psychic trauma of this sort of thing to a woman. We talk glibly about castration complexes and we all know what it means to a man to lose his balls, but we never seem to understand that a woman reacts emotionally in the same way.

"She's less of a woman because she can't have children, even though she is not changed in emotion or endocrine makeup. That's Janice, a shy girl who worries about being a whole woman and then we make sure surgically that she is less than a whole woman. To add to that her first major sexual affair is with a guy like you who is obsessed with having children. She feels she's cheated you and in so doing she feels cheated herself. So she withdraws, rejects the very thing she's come to value and wants most."

Lieberman stopped and bit his lip. "I'm sorry. I didn't mean to make a speech. It's just that I'm damned concerned about two people I like very much."

Longo shook his head sadly. Of course, kids were important, but not that important, he realized. Yes, she had

been a substitute for Martha, little more than a convenient
lay at first. Only, he realized, you cannot continue to share
sex with anyone without growing to care for her—to love
her. It was a thing he had not really admitted to himself
until that moment. He had looked on her as a breeding
engine to satisfy his own bounding ego and the long-ago
conditioning of his father's family. Now he realized that
her pain was his pain and that there was much more to
having a woman than impregnating her. God, he thought,
if only he could make up for it.

The thought of what he had almost thrown away was
terrifying. If he could get back to her, find a way into that
wounded spirit, convince her that he cared and that it really didn't matter. "Thanks, Doc," he told Lieberman. "God
knows, I've been stupid enough, but thanks."

"Well, what am I to do?" Lieberman asked. "Stand
around and let two good people fall blindly apart? She's a
sweet girl and she'll give you a lot no one else could."

"I know that," Longo said. "I know that very well."

At this moment the page system crackled and said,
"Captain Longo, call Captain Georgeoff immediately at
extension twelve. Urgent. Call Captain Georgeoff immediately."

. He walked to the intercom and signaled station 12.
Georgeoff's voice crackled over the radio tie-in. "Longo?"

"Here?"

"Can you get over here? We've got troubles."

"What is it?"

"Rothgate has taken one of the bugs out, the one with
the armed rockets."

"Good God!" Longo exclaimed. "Where's Colonel Farrington?"

"He's en route over to the Russian station. You're senior here. Maybe you can stop him."

"What's he up to?"

"It looks like he's going to try to knock out the Russki
station," Georgeoff said breathlessly.

Sixteen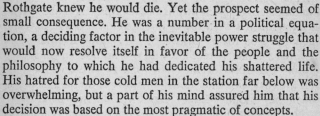

Rothgate knew he would die. Yet the prospect seemed of small consequence. He was a number in a political equation, a deciding factor in the inevitable power struggle that would now resolve itself in favor of the people and the philosophy to which he had dedicated his shattered life. His hatred for those cold men in the station far below was overwhelming, but a part of his mind assured him that his decision was based on the most pragmatic of concepts.

Now that the transfer of the female complement was complete and only the command personnel, including Voroshilov, remained aboard the station, a simple direct move would eliminate all future conflict. They would probably try to intercept him, he knew. Even his own people would turn their hands against him, but in the long view he was sure that he was right. Whether he returned to the station and the ship or simply expired out here was of no importance. The only important thing, the single driving purpose was to eliminate Voroshilov and his staff.

The bug maneuvered gracefully under his guiding hand. He had launched it easily from the station in spite of Georgeoff's crew. None of them had realized his intention until the last minute. He had appeared, apparently on one of his perennial inspection tours, and had entered the launch hatch before anyone thought anything of it. The bug with its complement of ten jury-rigged rockets, armed with Comp B warheads, was there, just where it had rested these past weeks when he had first set out to improvise a defense for the station.

By the time they realized what he was doing, he had suited up and triggered the cycling pumps. He saw their white faces at the port of the hatch, but the pressure had dropped too much for them to open it and stop him. When the shell doors opened to the star-specked blackness outside, he felt a thrill of triumph. He touched the release that ejected the bug into space and grasped the tiller, drawing faint steam from the after jets as he reoriented the craft.

He drifted across the expanse of black, rising above the station and moving past the slowly revolving Mars ship, his eyes fixed on the gleaming distant light that was the Russian station. Even at this distance he could see that it was fragmented from the cannibalization process that had been going on for a week, but in his mind's eye he imagined the command module with Voroshilov and his men waiting patiently for the final transfer. Waiting for that and the easy ascension to the authority and dominance for which they and their kind had plotted all these years.

The thought brought an angry reaction to his muscles and he felt a surge of acceleration as he overcorrected his course. He was rising above the great ballooning FLOX reservoir now. The reservoir had been emptied of nearly 80 percent of its contents, but because of the slight spin impressed on its long axis it was still fully inflated, as though it still carried the hundreds of tons of deadly chemical. He saw the points of light that were the transfer crew drifting away from the balloon shape with their transfer vessel in tow. They were heading for the ship and its nearly full oxidizer tanks.

The radio signal on the dash of the bug was flashing and he debated plugging into the circuit. They would try to reach him on his suit phone, of course, but he had turned that off. He knew that they would try to talk him out of it and he was in no mood to listen. There was no point in any conversation.

He was changing course with the FLOX tank behind him when he became aware of the distant point of light, another bug, approaching him fast. Of course, they would try to intercept him, but it would do little good. The bug was now less than five hundred yards away and he saw that a single figure occupied the pilot's seat. The gold helmet surprised him. Farrington? It must be. He had been on his way to a rendezvous with Voroshilov but they must have contacted him, and since he was the nearest craft, naturally he would turn and try to intercept Rothgate.

He increased his velocity, adding side thrust to rise above the intercepting bug. Farrington countered his move so that the two bugs appeared now on a collision course. He knew that he could maneuver in the last instant to avoid this, and that Farrington could not possibly cancel his velocity in time to overtake him. Then he saw the suited figure raise his hand and he realized that Farrington carried a sidearm. He saw the puff of smoke from the weapon and saw the man's hand recoil from the reaction.

Rothgate added a violent side thrust, turning in a half circle. He was being pursued now and he would have to lose Farrington before he could continue. He cursed silently. The Russians were undoubtedly warned, and that would mean that they might already be abandoning the station themselves. Farrington was coming closer, driving him back toward the FLOX tank. He realized that there was one strategem he might use if he could get close enough to the tank.

He maneuvered closer and then turned the bug and began to accelerate. Farrington again guided his bug on a collison course. He did not dare fire now, however, so close to the oxidizer tank. At the last moment his bug arrowed toward Rothgate's in imminent collision. Rothgate applied a sudden side thrust and felt his guts churn with the violent maneuver.

Farrington's bug shot past him and he turned, looking over his shoulder. It was as he had planned. The vehicle could not be brought to rest in time. Farrington was arrowing toward the complex of hoses and cables below the tank. He would enmesh himself in them like a fly in a web.

It was then that he realized to what lengths Farrington might go to save the station. He threw all side thrusters full on and Farrington's vehicle turned abruptly, mounting upward along a tangent to the great tank. It was too tight a maneuver, Rothgate saw. The bug wavered under the side thrusters and the impulse of the main thruster. It wavered and then touched and pierced the great plastic tank.

The effect was blinding. Farrington and his bug disappeared in a monstrous gush of brilliant flame. The tons of

FLOX under centrifugal force gushed from the tank, devouring the vehicle.

Only then did Rothgate see his own danger, as the expanding cloud engulfed his vehicle. He had time to think of those long-dead children, perishing in the flames of the Karachi Consulate, and that now he, too, joined them in the same manner.

Death by fire, he thought.

The cloud swept over him, turning the bug, his suit, the very flesh of his body to flame.

Without pain he vanished in a hot cloud of boiling vapor. All thinking ceased.

Seventeen

Gloom had invaded the ship like a tangible thing. The men who were still not in hypothermia went about their routine tasks without speaking, knowing that all of the effort of the past weeks was now to no avail. Longo found that even the normally ebullient Georgeoff had lapsed into a profound silence from which he would barely acknowledge the existence of the people around him. Bucholtz, the Russian chief engineer, became increasingly morose, lapsing into long silences during which he seemed to stare at some invisible spot in the air.

Voroshilov called a meeting to discuss the consequences of the loss of the fifty tons of oxidizer. "It seems useless to consider how we may best reorganize the joint effort now that your commander has perished," he said. "Still, in all conscience, we should consider this."

"I suppose," Longo said, "that the command of the American complement now falls to me. It's not exactly the way I would have chosen to get my first command."

"There is still the problem of the final command," Voroshilov said. "The thing that so obsessed your late Colonel Rothgate is very real. We must decide that."

"For practical purposes you outrank me," Longo pointed out.

"There is no authority that can change that ordering," Voroshilov said sadly, "other than the authority we have within our own confines. I suggest that we assume your promotion to colonel and that we start out on an even basis. The question now remains. Who will command?"

"It's a dubious honor, regardless," said Bucholtz. "Who would aspire to the command of a stricken ship?"

"I suggest that we continue with the original arrangement," said Longo. "We have no choice but to trust each other and I, for one, would consider it an honor for you to command the ship, Colonel."

"Thank you," Voroshilov said slowly. "But will your other people agree?"

"As the major remarked," Longo observed, "you take over an unenviable command. I don't think anyone will object at this point."

"Very well," said Voroshilov. "Lieutenant Rodrigues, we must now depend on you a great deal. Can we reorient our mission at this late date to the moon landing?"

"That's debatable," Rodrigues said. "I'll need at least four hours more before I can answer you. The loss of the oxidizer, of course, rules out the Mars landing. Off hand, I'd say that we've lost between four and eight hundred miles an hour in our terminal velocity."

"Is that so critical?" asked Bucholtz.

"Multiplied over the time of flight, allowing for gravitational loss, it means that we will miss our rendezvous point with the planet by tens of thousands of miles. It's a small velocity loss, but very critical to the flight.

"Very well," said Voroshilov. "Please make the necessary calculations and inform me as soon as possible. In the meantime, we shall continue with the final phases of the ship assembly."

"How about the personnel in hypothermia?" asked Longo. "Shall we begin their revival?"

"No," Voroshilov decided. "Let us hold to our plan for the moment. It may be a kindness to let them be if we find that the moon flight has now been jeopardized."

"Is that possible?" asked Georgeoff. "Surely we can still hold to that plan?"

"With such a change in ship design and so much time lost in computations, we'd have to discard a great deal of the needed material aboard the ship," Rodrigues said. "It may be too late. We may have compromised the original moon mission by too wide a margin."

They broke up on a subdued note of urgency and a deep feeling of regret. Longo had not seen the personnel of the station so filled with a black mood of pessimism since the first day following the Tel Aviv attack long ago.

He searched through the ship for Janice, going first to her quarters and then to the monitoring bridge, where Blaisdell kept watch over the scores of crewmen and women in deep, chilled sleep. She was nowhere to be seen.

Finally he found her in the capsule section where the sleeping Karen lived out her last days in the confines of a sealed enclosure. Janice was sitting nearby, contemplating the woman sadly. She had turned down all but the console and the interior lights and the shadows crouched menacingly in the corner of the room.

"Will she live?" he asked softly.

She looked up and silently acknowledged his presence. "No," she said at length. "Perhaps another three days or a week, Lieberman says, but I'm afraid she'll never come out of the coma. It might be just as well to cut off her life-support system. There seems little to be gained."

"And the baby?"

"Surviving. We've probably done a fairly good detoxifying job on it, but we can't know the extent of tissue or nervous damage simply from the radiation of its own mother's body. Fortunately most of the fetal calcium had already been laid down or was in a sufficiently unstable state that we could force the exchange and remove the strontium."

He peered into the depths of the enclosure, seeing the silent figure, her small breasts barely rising and falling. The hypothermia was not as deep as with the ship's crew, but he could see from the color of her skin that her body temperature was very depressed.

He reached out and placed his hand lightly on Janice's shoulder. Almost automatically she reached up and took it. The warmth of flesh against flesh seemed communication enough for long moments. Finally he leaned down and kissed her lightly, tenderly on the forehead, carefully avoiding any suggestion of sexual passion. She understood the need and smiled up at him.

"We'll make it," he said. "We'll still have a life together."

"Is that what you want?" she asked.

"Of course, it's what I want," he said fiercely. Then

more quietly, "No, it's not 'of course.' It's anything but a matter of course. It's a very clear and pressing need for you. It's something I've grown to know and nothing else much matters at this point."

She rose slowly with almost dreamlike grace and looked into his shadowed eyes. He could not read the expression in her face clearly because of the gloom, but he thought that she was smiling sadly. "You know I can't give you those sons you want so badly," she said.

"Lieberman told me," Longo said. "It was cruel of me, but I didn't know. It can't make a difference in any event. There will be children enough and we can spend our time caring for them. That is, if you can stand having me with you."

"I would want that more than anything," she said.

They kissed silently with a tenderness he had not known for a long time. "You know," she said, "there will be a need for children. There will be a need for good men to father them. I'd be very pleased if you would remember that."

"But you and me—?" he asked.

"If that is what you want, there will be you and me, but I want you to father children. It won't affect us. I'll be very proud of you."

He looked down at her wonderingly. She was making a remarkable concession and he felt that she meant it. It was, he realized at last, very much like her. He should have known. The little lost girl clinging, but wanting to give with every fiber.

He nodded without speaking and kissed her again.

"You're like a big bull," she whispered. "You charge blindly out without looking about and here I am, waiting."

He laughed and nudged her with his head.

"Here, toro," she teased softly. "Here, toro."

He reached for her, his lust aroused. A distant nagging refrain persisted above the head of physical need. He laughed, thinking Here, toro; and then he realized what it was that disturbed him.

"My God," he said. "Of course. Of course."

"What is it?" she asked.

He forgot the throbbing tumidity that had invaded him. "Please," he said, "I've got to check this out. It may be the answer after all."

Fifteen minutes later in Voroshilov's wardroom, Rodrigues said, "It may work. It's a wildly improbable chance but it may work. Give me fourteen hours and I'll let you know."

"It would be the greatest irony," Voroshilov said in wonder. "To ride, as you say, piggyback to the stars."

And so it was.

It was only a matter of slightly better than six hundred miles per hour that they needed, but it was this tiny increment that separated them from the fateful rendezvous with Mars. Only now they would have that increment and more, a satisfactory margin of safety if all went well.

The ship's crew, except for Janice, Lieberman, and the essential caretaking group, were in deep hypothermia now, their body functions muted to the most shallow of responses. It was the moment to break orbit and Voroshilov sat beside him as Longo activated the main engines. The response was ragged for a second and then all thrusts balanced. Somewhere in the depths of the ship he heard metal straining and creaking as the thrust transferred to the main structures of the ship. Acceleration pressed him into his chair with a weight close to that of his Earth weight. It built as he cut in new engines, shifting the flight of the ship slowly to a higher orbit.

Toro was approaching perigee with the Earth moon system and would pass near their position in ten minutes. They were better than fifty thousand miles out, very near escape velocity but still in a high Earth-centered orbit. There were some lunar disturbances but at this distance they were slight.

The problem was in matching path and velocity with Toro. Toro would pass them at a velocity of about nineteen thousand miles an hour, accelerating as it dropped to its perigee point. At this point its velocity would be near escape. Not enough, however, to completely escape the Earth moon system, so that it would eventually swing back

in a wide parabola. It was this final part of its progress to
perigee that was so important to them. In this final leg it
accelerated some three thousand miles an hour.

They could not depend on the slight gravitation of the
mile-wide chunk of metal to grasp their frail ship. The
ship's inertia was too great for such a weak interaction and
the moonlet would rush past without giving them the
needed component. He would have to navigate in such a
manner that he remained close on the heels of the rock,
balancing his thrust so that he would be constantly within
its small field, sharing its acceleration, gaining velocity
from the moonlet's downward plunge to perigee. It was
much like a matador working the bull with his cape.

"One minute," Sugiyama called from the radar post. He
hunched over the screen, checking the course corrections
and feeding them back to Longo. The great clumsy ship
responded slowly to his guidance, arcing down to the predicted orbit of Toro. The moonlet passed just under them
as the ship moved into its lately vacated path. He applied
acceleration slowly, building to the rock's velocity. At a
distance of barely a mile from the tumbling chunk of debris, he held.

The inertial navigation system frothed numbers across
the panels before him and erased them with tenth-second
rapidity. He cut motors, holding ignition at stand-by, and
waited. Yes, there it was—a definite increase in velocity,
and not from his engines. The distance to the moonlet widened slowly and he applied thrust gingerly, balancing the
inertia of the ship.

The long plunge to perigee continued. It would do so
for the next five hours, each moment of contact building
their velocity slowly. In the end they would fire their motors and break orbit like a stone leaving a vast sling, arrowing out to the stars.

The hours stretched out. They had acquired nearly a
thousand-mile-an-hour increment now. This meant they
would have nearly fifteen hundred miles an hour increment when they left. So much extra fuel and oxidizer they
could husband. The last-moment corrections could be
handled by remote control with the Cape.

They would make it, he exulted. This delicate capsule containing all the human life that existed in the universe would carry them out to the new world and the start of the most fantastic adventure the race had ever embarked upon.

He had a moment when Voroshilov took over and he signaled for the laboratory in the depths of the ship. Janice answered.

"It's good," he told her. "It's very good."

"Karen is dead," said Janice.

"I'm sorry," he said. "She, more than anyone, made it work. If she could have made it—"

"In a way she will have."

In the background, distorted by the tinniness of the tiny speaker, he heard the first keening cry of a child newly born.

Eighteen

It was a long and terrible nine months and at the end of it Longo and Janice stood on the deck, watching the first landing craft unfurl their plastic lifting surfaces and enter the tenuous upper Martian atmosphere. He felt a surging sense of triumph.

She tightened her arms around him and whispered in his ear, "I love you very much."

"It's a good feeling," he said.

"It will be a good world," she said. "I know it will."

"Filled with crazy kids and wonderful women and you," he said.

"Yes," she said, her face full and glowing. "Above all filled with all those crazy kids of ours. It's true, you know. They'll belong to both of us."

It *was* true, Longo thought. He felt as though he had fathered a race with her.